FAIR AND SQUARE

JUNO CHASE

ISBN: 978-1-947234-05-5

Print ISBN: 978-1-947234-22-2

They say you don't get over someone until you find someone or something better...That's why we run from distraction to distraction and from attachment to attachment.

Yasmin Mogahed

Chapter 1

*L*izbeth checked her watch as everyone filtered into the conference room at the ungodly hour of 6:30 a.m. It was way too early on a Monday morning for anything other than coffee or a good workout—which she was missing due to the cryptic instructions to assemble. She had another meeting across town at the Chinese Embassy right after this one. She hoped for light traffic, otherwise she'd be late.

She loved the congressman and everything he worked for and believed in. She often wondered at how he operated on his rumored four hours a night of sleep. Lincoln Ulysses Pierce, Link to anyone who'd worked for him for more than a few hours, was model good-looking. He had the easy charisma found in most successful politicians without any of the smarm. His main failing was being a single man who appeared to have a problem settling down.

Liz's dream job was to work in the U.S. Embassy in Beijing where she could use her Chinese on a daily basis and, eventually, maybe serve as the ambassador. Working for the congressman as his liaison to the Foreign Affairs and Intelligence committees had been the first in what she expected to be several stepping stones to that goal.

Lizbeth had a very brief crush on the congressman when she'd first started working for him. It lasted about a month, if that. When it was clear that Link was shooting up the political chain and would likely be President someday, she completely squelched any such thoughts. Having the press follow her around to ask for cookie recipes or to criticize every single outfit she wore would be its own particular kind of hell—one she wasn't willing to enter.

The congressman outlined his plans for a super-secret meeting in Las Vegas with three highly placed industry leaders. As he spoke, Lizbeth tried to fit her job into the scenario. Whenever she was given a new opportunity, she weighed its benefits to her personally and to her career. If there was nothing to be gained she'd move on to the next opportunity. As her Waipo, her grandmother, used to say, *A man who chases two rabbits catches neither.*

She wondered what her grandmother would say about her chosen career. Her mother's mother had been a mixture of old world and new—cooking and speaking only in Chinese while religiously watching American Idol. Waipo had escaped from China so she could be more Chinese than the communist regime allowed. And now, Lizbeth was working her ass off to go live and work in China. The irony of their lives wrapping around and coming full circle wasn't lost on her.

"Lizbeth will be working the Committee angles. Chloe will help her out as needed," Madeline said.

Lizbeth leaned forward to get another look at Chloe Cassell, the latest intern to join the crew. She wore a simple suit, understated and somewhat demure, sporting a bright-eyed freshness so many newbies had. Chloe carried herself like someone who could handle the heavy and fast-paced workload this office created.

Lizbeth found the shelf where this project would go in her work life and placed it where it belonged—up high and off to the side. She'd monitor the trade and intelligence angles as information came along and pull it down as necessary. If it became apparent that this deal would impact trade with other countries, or, perhaps, involve some new top-secret tech, then she might find something she'd need to tend to. As it was, this meeting in Vegas was a better opportunity for the legislative and legal policy aides than her.

Even if she didn't need to involve herself in this at the moment, she was required to stay for the entire meeting. Now that she had figured out her place in the scheme, she was free to let her mind wander. Instead of paying attention to the details, she concentrated on her schedule for the next five days.

She checked her watch again. The morning rush was starting. She would have to hurry to get to her meeting at the Chinese Embassy on time. Liz opened the calendar on her phone. Katherine, Lincoln's Senior Legislative Assistant, gave her a dirty look.

"I'm taking notes," whispered Liz.

Katherine shook her head and sighed, obviously not buying the excuse. Her gorgeous red hair bobbed like a model's in a shampoo commercial. Liz turned her attention back to Madeline.

When Eleanor started in on IT protocols for the meeting, Liz tuned her out. The woman knew what she was doing, and Lizbeth could trust Eleanor to follow up with her directly later. She was sort of type-A, and she was brilliant with the computer stuff.

Lizbeth navigated to the week view of her calendar. She'd spend Tuesday and Wednesday finishing up any last-minute changes to the schedule for the Chinese visit taking place Thursday through Sunday. She ran through the list of things she had to do, prioritizing each task in her head. Meeting at the Embassy, gala seating, Dragon Boat Festival security team, memorial tour follow-ups—she had a busy few days ahead.

As the meeting broke up, Carleen Bigalow, the head of the Congressman's staff, pulled Liz aside. "How're the plans for this weekend's visit?"

"I'm on my way to a meeting at the Embassy now. The team we've got on this has been awesome. Even the guy from State seems to have his act together."

"Will wonders never cease?" Carleen asked, her eyes going wide in mock astonishment.

Lizbeth excused herself and rushed out of the office so she wouldn't be late. Her map app told her it was going to take forty minutes to get from the Cannon building to the Embassy via transit and only thirty driving.

A taxi appeared as if out of nowhere, and she hailed it with ease. She could review some details about the upcoming weekend without the prying eyes of strangers in the privacy of the cab. Not that everything she dealt with was top secret, but there were a few sensitive items on her to-do list this morning. Her phone beeped her ten-minute pre-meeting alarm, knocking her out of her work focus.

The taxi had come to a near standstill. Why weren't they moving? The traffic blocking them in was not going anywhere anytime soon. DC traffic was normally unpredictable, but this was ridiculous, especially out in Embassy Land.

It didn't help that the driver was super relaxed about it all. He had the air of a Buddhist hanging around him. He sat in his seat with relaxed shoulders and his head bobbing to a sound track playing inside his head. His fingers barely gripped the wheel, and he paid no attention to the line of traffic blocking them in. She generally admired that ability, but, at the moment, she found it irritating. She wished he was making more of an effort to get around the traffic jam. Being late to the meeting at the Embassy would be embarrassing.

"I'll make it on my own faster than waiting through this. Stop here. I'm going to walk the rest of the way." The Embassy of the People's Republic of China was not far away, and she'd be lucky to make it as everyone was sitting down if she power-walked.

Once she got moving, she adjusted the cross-body messenger bag she'd chosen this morning over her hip for comfort. Lizbeth wished she had chosen her Tory Burch flats instead of her three-inch Manolo Blahnik pumps. They were comfortable as such things went but running in them was not an option.

By the time she flashed her ID at the gate, she was winded and sweaty. Fortunately, she was a regular at the Embassy and whizzed through their security. She was led to the conference room as if she hadn't been here three bazillion times already by a receptionist who insisted on holding the door open for her as she entered the room, using all the ceremony and manners one might for a formal visit.

She scanned the room looking for Michael Hong, her state department counterpart, but he was nowhere to be found. Liz considered taking her jacket off, but she didn't as it would hide any moons of sweat from her impromptu exercise. She hoped the Embassy's air conditioning was fixed.

Jiang Hu, the ambassadorial aide in charge of this particular visit, was pouring himself a cup of tea at the buffet in the back of the room. As usual, the Embassy had provided an array of Chinese delicacies. There was some amount of pride taken in their beautiful presentations as well. The rest of the attendees were busily seating themselves around the large lacquered table in the center of the room.

"Ah. Ms. Crandall. I saw the island of cars outside and wondered if you were caught up in it," said Jiang Hu.

"I abandoned my ride and walked the last couple of blocks." She checked her watch and grinned. "I still have thirty seconds before the meeting officially starts, sir."

"We value promptness, but we also value a sated appetite." Jiang Hu did the proper host thing by picking up a plate and piling it high with food. "Please help yourself to a plate before joining us."

The Chinese Embassy staff always put out the most glorious buffet. She wasn't shy about eating and piled her plate to match Jiang's. While she would have happily eaten six of the youtiao—the Chinese donuts that were basically like churros—she took only two. She wasn't going to skimp on the crispy golden fried sesame balls filled with red-bean paste. She took three of those as well as two pork buns to balance out all the sugar.

The chef at the Embassy was a Taiwanese man who specialized in dim sum, and the food here was better than any restaurant in town. It was better than anything she'd ever had back home in San Francisco, including anything her Waipo made. Her grandmother was a good cook, but she only cooked traditional Chinese foods; none of the fancy dim sum style dishes. Her mother was useless with a wok, and Lizbeth had learned everything she knew about cooking from Waipo.

She filled a large cup with hot tea and found her usual seat. She expected Michael Hong to be seated across from her. His salt and peppered hair always reminded her of her father and gave her a warm family feeling.

In his stead was a complete stranger. An amazingly handsome and hot stranger.

Holy hell. Who was he?

He wasn't looking at her, though. His attention was fully on Jiang Hu. He adjusted the pile of papers in front of him and placed his hands patiently in front of him waiting for the others to give them his full attention.

Lizbeth tried to focus on Jiang, but it was hard. She couldn't take her eyes off the gorgeous interloper. Divine intervention had replaced Michael with a perfect offering of manhood.

He looked like a young, happy Bruce Lee. His shiny black hair was cut super short, but he'd gelled it up into spikes as though he had to have short hair but no one was going to tell him how to wear it. His broad shoulders filled out a suit that was tailored to fit and without Michael's usual rumples.

Lizbeth tried to clear her head from the suddenness of this man's appearance and the reaction she was having to him. It wasn't like her to be gaga over a man at first sight. Even when she was a teenager, she had been slow to fangirl over boy-bands or matinee movie stars. Appearance always came in second to personality. Good relationships come from knowing a guy before deciding if there could be more. She was proud of herself for her exactitude. Impulsivity led to nowhere but heartache and pain.

When everyone was more or less paying attention to Jiang Hu, he made a small general bow to the center of the table before beginning. "Now that we are all here, I'd like to open with the itinerary details we didn't finish at our last session."

It would be rude to interrupt Jiang to ask who the new guy was or why Michael Hong wasn't there. Maybe she'd missed something by cutting it so close. It was possible there had been a more general introduction before the meeting. Handsome as this guy was, she didn't like that Hong wasn't there. They had worked together from day one on this project. He was comfortable to be around. He was much older than she was and there had never been anything but professional camaraderie between them. He was reliable, and they had built up a trust.

This new guy may be off-the-charts gorgeous, but his presence made Liz anxious. He might be the perfect person for the job, but she'd never met him before. She was good with faces. And names. Who was this guy? They'd long since stopped putting their name plates in front of them, but she wished they'd stayed with the more formal protocol.

She glanced around the table to make sure Michael wasn't sitting somewhere else, but he was nowhere to be found. She snuck a glance at her phone, and there was no missed message from Michael. No text. Nada. She hadn't missed anything. Why hadn't Jiang said anything to her when she entered?

State didn't like sending in replacements this late in the game. She narrowed her eyes on the handsome interloper. Something bad must have happened.

As if he had read her mind, he held up his hand politely to interrupt Jiang. "I'm sorry, sir, but since this is my first time being part of this group, perhaps we can have everyone introduce themselves."

He turned toward her as he finished speaking. His lip twitched upward for a second. Was he teasing her? Had he noticed her staring at him? It was impossible not to sneak peeks at him.

The attaché sat back, running both palms face down on the smooth table out to the side. "Ah, Mr. Wu. Of course. You are new to our team, so let us start with you."

Mr. Wu. Great. One of the most common Chinese last names on the planet. Any hopes of a quick and easy background check vanished.

He grinned broadly and bowed toward the table as a group. If he had been hot before, now he was stunning. His eyes twinkled. People talked about eyes twinkling all the time, but she had never experienced actual twinkling. Lizbeth couldn't quite believe the impact he was having on her. She'd never been blindsided by a guy at work like this.

Most of the men she worked with were older. Boring. Married. Liz straightened her back. She wasn't going to look at his ring finger. She shouldn't care if he was married. With a sidelong glance that was very subtle, she searched his left hand for a wedding ring. Nope. Then she checked for the tan line, showing where a ring might have been removed, and he had none.

"I'm Curt Wu, from State." He looked around the table slowly, meeting the eyes of all ten people, ending with Lizbeth. "Michael Hong's father was taken suddenly ill. Michael returned home to California be at his side, and I was called in yesterday as his replacement."

Curt Wu from State? Lizbeth narrowed her eyes at the interloper. She had worked closely with everyone at the State Department's Asian Affairs office for five years. There was no Curtis Wu in that office.

izbeth mulled over her response as others introduced themselves to this Curt Wu. It was possible she didn't know everyone at the Foreign Affairs office. She'd have to look him up when she got back to the office.

When it was her turn to introduce herself, Lizbeth's legs tingled from her upper thighs down to her toes. His intense attention was beyond anything she could have imagined—hyper-focused, critical. It was difficult to resist the urge to smell herself to make sure the sweat she'd worked up on her quick walk wasn't lingering.

"I'm Lizbeth Crandall. I'm here from Congressman Pierce's office, representing his efforts on the House Foreign Affairs Committee. I worked closely with Michael. Can you tell us more about what happened? When he'll be back?"

"I'm afraid I don't know any details. Our conversation concentrated on transitioning me into this position. I believe he will be gone for at least a week. He handed his entire workload over to me."

"That's unfortunate. And... when did you join the office?"

Wu smiled amiably again, nodding slowly. "Ah... yes, I should have added that I moved over from Trafficking a couple weeks ago."

Well, that would certainly explain her lack of knowing his name. She relaxed a little and let out the breath she hadn't even realized she'd been holding.

Lizbeth grimaced and hid her phone under the table. Why hadn't Michael texted her with a heads up? She'd thought they were close enough that he would have at least texted her.

L: Sorry to hear about your dad. Let me know if I can do anything to help.

While she'd never met his father, Michael had spoken of him often and fondly described him as spending time outdoors in his garden and playing the guzheng. Michael had given her a CD of his father's performance during the last Cherry Blossom festival, and her mom had raved about his technique.

They had bonded over being half-Chinese and

half-white. While her father was some Scottish-British-Italian blend, her mom was one hundred percent Chinese. Michael's family was the reverse of hers. He had a Chinese dad and a white mom. They'd both grown up with grandmothers in their homes and spoke Chinese until they went to school. They had never known each other back home in San Francisco, but they figured out a lot of connections after a few weeks of working together.

Being ambushed by a new person this close to the event made her stomach flip. She clenched her hands under the table. Handsome or not, she hoped he knew how to do the job. As each person introduced themselves and their role in the planning process, Curt paid them close attention, but Lizbeth caught him glancing at her almost as much as she was looking at him.

Magnetic attraction. Now, that was silly. She was a perfectly rational person. Magnetic attraction happened with magnets, not people.

As the meeting progressed, Lizbeth found her thoughts wandering off topic and constantly onto Curt Wu. At one point, she realized she was staring at him, memorizing the clean line of his jaw, the deeply intelligent dark brown eyes, the fine cut of his suit, the broad width of his shoulders—rather unusual in a Chinese man. He must work out—a lot.

The meeting was a fluid movement between the

two languages, each person speaking in their native tongue most of the time, changing into English for clarification on various points. Especially anything to do with logistics. Chinese could be vague when it came to timing.

His voice was soft spoken, but clear and without an accent. Michael's accents were strong in both Mandarin and English, but Curt was fluid and sounded authentic in each. Most State Department employees at this level were American, but it was impossible to tell by listening to him; his Chinese accent was perfect. He could be like her, raised with a Chinese grandmother in the house and speaking only Chinese.

Sitting across from her was the perfect definition of her ideal man—handsome, intelligent, multi-lingual, professional. Something must be wrong with him. He was probably an asshole. She needed to keep cool so they could maintain a working relationship. Getting all hot and bothered would cause problems.

Too late for that.

A bit of ink on his neck peeked out over the edge of his Brooks Brothers shirt. She pictured him removing his jacket, loosening his perfectly knotted tie. She wanted more than to look at his tattoo. She wanted to rip his shirt off to reveal what was hiding underneath.

She wanted to trace her finger between the edge of his collar and along his golden skin.

Lizbeth took a sip of tea to center herself.

Jiang cleared his throat and shuffled his papers to indicate moving on to the next agenda item. "Let's discuss the final seating assignments for the closing gala on Saturday evening."

They had decided months before that the event would follow Chinese customs. During the last meeting, they had discussed which direction the tables would be facing to ensure the best luck and where to hang the lucky lanterns. Lizbeth was in charge of the official seating arrangements for the gala, but she always found the discussions about seating arrangements and decorations amusing. Feng shui was neatly in the same category as astrology and magnetic attraction.

"Well, I'll be frank here," Lizbeth said. "I have done my best to keep certain senators and congressman away from each other—that and making sure wives and mistresses won't be seated at the same table."

There were no secrets in this town; everyone had a dossier. Most of them played like grown-ups at events like this, no matter their politics. It would be an interesting set of power-plays. If certain people had to be in the same room, then putting them in opposite corners was the best that could be done.

The Chinese had their own list of who played well together. When they insisted Lizbeth ensure that the seating chart was constantly updated, she found herself in the middle of a logistical mess.

"I'm constantly updating things as your protocol officer sends me new information. Eleanor, the chief technology guru in my office, has put together a program to help me manage the seating arrangement. It's been extremely helpful. My only concern, really, is the dance floor."

Jiang nodded along as she spoke. "We have no control over who might accidentally dance next to each other. Please assume people will behave appropriately."

Lizbeth hoped there wouldn't be a repeat of the gala at the Smithsonian two years before. A now disgraced and unemployed senator had a drink thrown in his face by a reporter, outing their affair in front of rolling cameras. She would need to double check the list of media that would be allowed entrance to the event.

The best part of the gala for Lizbeth was that she would be able to deduct the two-thousand dollar vintage Dior ball gown and six-hundred dollar red-bottomed Louboutins she'd purchased as a work expense. And, the banquet was going to be beyond stellar. Sixteen courses of Chinese food? Even the wine would be imported in from the Mainland. China had been working on a deal to get their wine into the U.S. and they were hoping to showcase some of their award-winning Bordeaux. Oh, yeah. She hoped her skin-tight dress had a little bit of give.

"Ms. Crandall?"

Lizbeth flushed as she realized Curt had asked her a question. She hadn't heard a word anyone had said in the last few minutes. Ugh. How professional was that? She gave Curt her most qualified stare.

Time to concentrate on the meeting, not Mr. Hottie.

"I was distracted. Could you repeat the question?"

Something shy of a shit-eating grin spread across his face. "I asked if you had finalized the security plans and itinerary with BDS, the Bureau of Diplomatic Security, for the memorial tour on Friday morning."

She took a sip of tea and returned his shit-eating grin. He certainly didn't have to spell out what BDS stood for; not for her sake, anyway. "BDS sent it a few days ago. I verified the last memorial on the list. In fact, I verified Minister Zhou wanted to visit the Franklin Roosevelt memorial, not the Theodore Roosevelt memorial."

Curt looked down at his notes. "Minister Zhou is the interior secretary?"

"Yes. It made sense that he might actually want to visit the Theodore Roosevelt memorial given that he is in charge of China's national parks. However, the secretary confirmed his request for the Franklin Roosevelt memorial."

"Good. I can see here on my notes we'll be at the Tidal Basin instead of Roosevelt Island. It's much easier to include it in the tour with the other monuments."

"Exactly. Besides resolving transportation issues, security on Roosevelt Island would be a nightmare. The trails are all spread out. With the limited access and general size of it, there isn't any way to control a group like this with ease."

Lizbeth sat back and bit into a sesame ball.

Curt spent a few moments reviewing the map in front of him. "You're right. Nice work. If we think a visit to the Island is a problem, how are we approaching the security for the Dragon Boat Festival? Michael's notes on this are minimal and say you were working on the details."

She had a sticky bite of sesame ball in her mouth as all eyes focused on her. She swallowed and followed it up with a swig of hot tea, hoping it would melt the red bean paste goo off her teeth. She tapped at her tablet and her PowerPoint presentation popped onto the screen.

"Here's a map. The event sprawls along the river. Here's where we'll have our tent and the various vendor trucks. The races start at the Thompson Boat Center." Lizbeth had arranged to have the pavilion and viewing stand set up for the best view of the races. She scrolled through the slides as she spoke, each one highlighting the areas she was talking about. "The Embassy contingent will have its own viewing platform and hospitality tent, here. After extensive negotiations, we have a twenty-foot floating barrier set up for added protection."

Local law enforcement was less than pleased about the official Chinese State visit because it took the event to a higher security level than in previous years.

She was already missing her time leisurely sampling all the food vendors and combing through the art stalls. She'd be working in an official capacity that day and tending to their guests instead of her own fun.

"All the vendors had to submit background checks for their employees. It's not feasible to force the public attendees through a background check, but we're set up for bag-check security points and metal detectors at each entry." Each entry-point lit up with the next slide.

Park planning and management was about as exciting as a re-run of a sixties television show. Lizbeth thought the level of detail for this was above and beyond what was warranted, but she was proud of her work anyway. She was sure that no one would care enough about this particular Chinese entourage. The highest-level official was China's Secretary of the Interior, Zhou Fengshan. If the Chinese President were coming, that would be another story.

"Do you have a background in security management, Ms. Crandall?" asked Curt.

"No. But I wanted to make sure this event went smoothly. The last thing I want is something to happen on American soil and we aren't properly prepared."

"You're a natural at logistics."

Was he being smarmy or real? She liked to think he was paying her a genuine compliment. One she absolutely deserved.

She couldn't explain it, but she wanted to be physically close to him. She predicted she'd be sleeping with him by the end of the week, if not sooner. There was something more than the physical attraction sucking her in. She didn't generally believe in woo-woo stuff, but she was not imagining whatever was going on. Or was she?

Lizbeth tried to not be distracted by the incredibly handsome Curt Wu.

Jiang rapped the table with his fingers three times, bringing everyone's attention back toward him much like a school teacher clapping hands. "All right. I would like to thank everyone present for making the coordination of this visit such a pleasant experience. I am looking forward to seeing it all play out as perfectly as it has been planned."

She tried to not look at Wu. She wasn't in the habit of succumbing to such an immediate attraction to a man. There would be plenty of time with him over the next few days for her to figure things out. Relax. Enjoy the week. If anything happens, let it go someplace natural and fun.

He caught her looking at him again as she gathered her belongings. She hoped he had no idea what was going on inside her head. It was as though there a tether between them, pulling her toward him like a fish caught on an invisible line. She rushed to the elevator hoping to escape the Embassy, not quite ready to face him directly outside of the meeting. Instead of escaping, she had only managed to make it so she arrived at the elevator at the same time as Curt. Their fingers hit the down button at the same time, side by side so they barely grazed each other. She jumped back, surprised by the unexpected jolt.

"Are you okay?" he asked.

Thankfully, the doors swished open before she had

to answer. He held it with one hand as he waved her inside ahead of him. He looked around the hallway and stepped into the car. She punched the ground floor button and relished the lingering feeling of his touch on her hand.

"I hope my being here hasn't been too problematic for you. I assure you, Michael gave me a very thorough briefing."

If only he would be thorough with her.

She swallowed hard, shaking her head to clear away the unexpected lust she was experiencing. "Oh, no. Not problematic. I was... surprised, is all. I'm a little disappointed that he didn't call or text me about the change."

Curt tilted his head, and his eye bored into her with an intensity that made her feel like she was under a microscope. "Are you particularly close to him?"

She widened her eyes as she understood the implication. "Oh. No. Not anything more than colleagues. He's a nice man, but no. Nothing like that."

His face relaxed.

Was he jealous?

As the elevator opened into the main lobby, he waited for her to get out first. Smart. Handsome. Gentlemanly.

Oh, her lucky stars.

Not that she believed in anything that had to do with stars like her Waipo.

As they left the building, the spring air was a welcome cool relief to the heat of the Embassy and the proximity of one Curt Wu. She turned her face into it, savoring the freshness. "That breeze feels good. It was pretty hot in there," she said.

"Only after you arrived."

He was flirting with her. She handed him her phone. "Why don't you add your number. I'm sure we'll be working closely together over the next few days."

He sent himself a text and handed her phone back. "That's my private number. I don't always answer the work phone right away."

She didn't have anything more to say to him. They stood in the Embassy's entrance. What would happen if she reached out to touch the ink on his neck? She brushed away the thought, blushing. Entirely inappropriate and not professional at all.

"Can I walk you to your car?"

"I don't have one," she said. "I walk to work. I ride the metro or take a cab when I need to." Why was she embarrassed admitting this to him? It wasn't that big a deal. In high school, she lived in downtown San Francisco, where everything was accessible. In college, she lived on campus so never needed to drive. Admitting that she'd never learned to drive was always an awkward thing for her, as if she had failed as an American.

"I'd offer to give you a lift," he said, "but I'm on my bike and I only have the one helmet."

That's weird. Would she sit on the handlebars? Besides, he was dressed awful nice for getting on a bike. She was surprised he hadn't changed into biking gear. She pictured him in black biking shorts, his legs tight and muscular, pedaling away. Standing against the pedals with his very charming ass up in the air as he worked at going uphill. Now, that would be awesome to see.

"Thanks for offering," she said. "I'm a public transit kind of girl."

He bowed in the Chinese fashion. "It was very nice meeting you, Ms. Lizbeth Crandall."

As he turned away, she stopped him. "I'll be going over the final security plans tomorrow afternoon. Why don't I come over to your office and you can help me verify the last few details?"

Curt nodded absently then shook his head. "Wait. No can do. I don't have the space—you have access to a conference room?"

Lizbeth had been to Michael's office dozens of times. There was plenty of room over there. Had Curt not been assigned an office yet? She shrugged, trying to be amenable. "Yes. Come at three? I'll be finished with all my prep."

A late meeting would be a natural segue into the evening and maybe drinks and dinner—and probably more. She was already planning to wear her new creamy silk matching bra and panties under her maroon pencil skirt that would show off her long and toned legs.

"Tomorrow at three. It's a date," he said with that shit-eating grin again.

With a professional, hands-off goodbye, she left the Embassy grounds with her insides all jumbled up. Would she really sleep with him? She centered herself with a brisk walk headed to the closest metro.

It would take her about half an hour to get back to the office. As she was waiting at a light, a man on a motorcycle slowed as he rounded the corner. The rider saluted as he passed. It took her a minute to recognize Curt Wu.

He wasn't on a bike. He was on a motorcycle. She almost hit her forehead when she realized her mistake. He zipped away down the street as apprehension flooded through her. Her stomach muscles contracted. Motorcycles were dangerous. And, worse, the guys who rode them were usually controlling jerks.

Chapter 3

----

izbeth breezed through the Cannon Building security and was in her office by mid-afternoon. She'd stopped by the shoe store and picked up her custom-fit Louboutins that went with her ball gown instead of eating lunch. She'd had enough Chinese pastries at the meeting to fill out her calorie card for the entire day, but it had been worth it. Once the Chinese visit was over at the end of the week, she'd be back to prowling the office's small coffee room for pastries and muffins soon enough.

Not that those were ever bad. Her coworker, Cheyenne, moonlighted as a pastry chef at a local cooking school on the weekends and brought in some pretty amazing things to share. But she'd been spoiled by the weekly visits to the Chinese Embassy and their specialty dumplings. She loved Chinese food and when this assignment was over, would probably miss the food more than the people.

Lizbeth tucked the shoes in the drawer where she kept a spare change of clothes and other personal items. She liked being prepared for whatever might happen, and sometimes going home to change for an unexpected post-work event was not always convenient. She unlocked her computer and wrote up a report for the Congressman. He had meetings with two of the visiting ministers on Friday morning, and the gala on Saturday evening. She sent him the schedule and asked him to confirm his date for the gala, reminding him that the event was at the Chinese Embassy and they required a basic background on all guests.

The program Eleanor had created helped Liz keep track of the data on the seating as well as the guests' background checks. There were only three people coming that were yet to be cleared: the Congressman's date and those of two Senators. She removed Michael Hong from the list and replaced his name with Curt's. *Well, well, well. Would you look at that?* His name sure did look good right next to hers.

After checking her to-do list, she called the senator's offices and spoke to their aides about their dates, reminding them they only had another forty-eight hours to get back to her or else they wouldn't be allowed into the gala. The Chinese Embassy had been very clear with them on security clearances.

Lizbeth had a calendar on her phone, but she liked to draw things out on paper when she had something big going on. She used an oversized sheet of paper, a ruler, and fine-point colored pens. She made five neat columns, one for each day, then added rows for the hours of the day from six a.m. to midnight. If she didn't plan out her sleep, she might forget and work herself into exhaustion.

She reviewed the week ahead, filling out the chart one day at a time. Was it really only Monday still? That super-early meeting Link had called for the top-secret meeting in Vegas had messed with her sense of time. She yawned and stretched.

Liz would check in with Carleen later. The other woman already knew Liz's eventual career goals would take her from the Congressman's office someday. It wouldn't be a surprise to anyone she wanted to graduate from Link's office to pursue diplomatic work.

She'd finalize the security plan with Curt for the following afternoon. She sent him a confirmation text and blocked out three p.m. onward on her calendar. If the meeting naturally went to dinner and drinks, how would they get from her office to wherever they were going? He had said he would offer her a ride, but he had been on a motorcycle.

Just because Curt rode one didn't mean he was a bad-boy or that he would judge her harshly for not wanting to ride one. Maybe he had practical reasons for owning it. Maybe he didn't want to pay for parking or other car-related expenses. Who was she to judge? She had never even ridden a motorcycle before; all she had to go on was the obvious stereotype and the high rate of fatalities she read about on the net. *Later*. She'd deal with it later. Maybe he'd show up with a car this afternoon.

And why had she never heard of him before? Lizbeth googled Curt Wu. She tried Curtis Wu next. Nothing. He wasn't on any social media as far as she could tell, not even LinkedIn. He'd said he'd moved from Trafficking, so he was not going to be in any regular database. Foreign Service employee information was kept strictly confidential. There were ways around that, though. Lizbeth dialed Randy Roberts, a guy she'd dated a year before who worked in Asian Affairs.

"Lizbeeeeeeeth, whatcha needin'?" Randy's cheerful California surfer-dude voice always cracked her up. But his voice was a complete contrast to the quality of work he did.

"Randy, what makes you think I need something?"

"Ha! It's not hockey season. I can't imagine any other reason for you to call me."

They had dated for a couple of months, but the only thing they had in common was their enthusiasm for the Capitals, the DC hockey team. They had met at a Capitals game when Katherine was dating a player on the team and had dragged Lizbeth along for company. The first game was all it took to get her hooked. Lizbeth continued going long after Kat had broken up with her boyfriend.

"I'm so predictable. Sorry. Yeah, you got me. There's this new guy over there. Ran into him at a meeting at the Embassy today. Curt Wu. Got any info on him?"

"Curt Wu? Let's take a looksee... Wu, Wu, Wu, Wu... Hmmm..."

Lizbeth waited as he clicked away at his keyboard.

Randy let out a slow whistle. "You're gonna owe me on this one, girlie-girl. I had to enter a passcode I don't keep memorized."

"I'll buy you a hotdog and a beer at the next game, good enough?"

"Deal. Found him. Not much I can tell you. He's legit, though."

"He said he came over to AA from Trafficking."

"That'd totally explain it, then. His history is blocked with a security clearance I can't get around. But, next best thing—I can find his rank through payroll. Hold on a sec..."

Curt must have some interesting stories to tell from working in trafficking, probably mostly heart-breaking.

"Here ya go. He's a three-nine."

"Did you say three-nine?" Lizbeth's arms broke out into goosebumps. Waipo's frail voice from a childhood memory washed over her. *"Three and nine are your lucky numbers. You must pay close attention when these numbers appear in your life."*

"You owe me two hot-dogs, Liz."

"You got it." Lizbeth leaned back against her seat and dropped her phone in her lap. What the fuck? Liz didn't have the Foreign Service pay-scale memorized, but she knew it well enough to know Curt was definitely way above her pay grade. He must have some pretty good connections and would be a good resource for her eventual move into Foreign Service.

She got a text back from Curt confirming the Tuesday afternoon meeting. She colored Tuesday evening in with parallel purple lines with the word "private" in neat block letters. Maybe it wasn't such a great idea to chase after a man who might be better suited to helping her with her career instead. Did it have to be one or the other, though? They were adults, weren't they? She'd managed to keep Randy as a friend after they stopped dating. He was a great guy, but he was certainly no Curt Wu.

Wednesday was going to be final prep and documentation day. She had a few unrelated meetings in the office and planned to use the day for catch-up. It would be low-key, she might even be able to work from home. She sketched in her usual morning tai chi class, which she'd missed this morning thanks to the early meeting.

The Chinese delegation arrived on Thursday, and she'd be on duty 24/7 all the way until they left Sunday afternoon. She used a different color to block out each event to help her remember the details. Thursday morning, she had a coffee date with Madeline Asher, the Communications director to discuss the press releases. Then she'd head over to the hotel where she planned to stay with the delegation. She was free from any particular duties Thursday night, but needed to be on site in case anyone needed assistance.

On Friday morning, the delegation broke into two groups. The working group would head off to meetings and official visits. The rest would be on the tour she'd organized. Friday afternoon, they would be free to go shopping or do other private exploration around the city under Embassy guidelines. Each guest was assigned their own BDS agent for the afternoon. The group would be recombined in the evening. Half were going to a Nationals game while the other half were going to the opera. Liz had ensured she was assigned to the opera detail.

Saturday morning was the Dragon Boat Festival, followed by an afternoon reception at the Embassy for a joint Taiwanese-Chinese celebration. That was followed by the gala on Saturday evening. Their plane would depart on Sunday morning at ten a.m. She held up her chart, admiring the neat lines and pretty colors.

The act of creation had cemented the details of the event in her head. Instead of tossing it, she pinned it on the wall above her computer. She had spent fifteen minutes drawing it up, she might as well enjoy her handiwork for a bit.

The prep work they'd all done assured a smooth visit. Unless something unexpected happened, and, in her line of work, she had seen pretty much everything. The actual visit should be a lot of fun.

She checked her watch. It was only four-thirty. She was ready to crash for the night. Maybe she'd duck out early and head home to snuggle with her cats before the rest of the week crashed in on her.

Madeline Asher, the Communications Director, sidled up to her desk. "Are you joining us tonight?"

Lizbeth jumped in surprise, a little disconcerted Madeline had been able to get so close to her unnoticed. "Tonight? What's tonight?" Lizbeth searched her artwork. "I don't have anything…"

"You wouldn't. After you left this morning, or should I say left the doors spinning behind you, Kat and I decided we'd all get together at the Capitol Hill Bar. The Vegas meeting is important and we need to decide who is going."

Lizbeth breathed in. "I don't have time. Besides, I'm not interested in going to Vegas."

Madeline's eyes widened and narrowed quickly on her in disbelief. "What? Why not?"

The theatrics. The drama. Lizbeth was tired of living in DC. She loved it in many ways, but she wanted to travel. Usually, she had one trip a year, to visit her parents in San Francisco. Normally she didn't long for a boyfriend, but being able to travel with someone to explore the ruins of Rome or hike up Mount Fiji was a big reason she wanted a companion in her life.

The job working for Congressman Pierce was a perfect stepping stone for her, but she wanted to be part of something bigger. Working with the Chinese in an official capacity was the first step. Lizbeth had busted her ass to get her masters in Public Policy for a reason.

This gig with the Embassy had been her first opportunity to use her languishing Mandarin in three years. She'd taken to going out to Chinese restaurants a couple times a week to practice the language with the waiter, the host, and anyone else who would engage with her. She was naturally shy, but when faced with a purpose, her uneasiness fell away. There was a noodle shop where she was greeted like family.

"I can't. I'm in the midst of this huge Chinese thing."

"You are always busy, all the time," Madeline said with a sly wink. "Come out with us. Free drinks, Lizbeth...come on. I'm putting the tab onto work expenses."

Lizbeth was a light-weight when it came to booze, but she didn't turn down free drinks. There were too many other things for her to throw her money at, especially since she rarely finished a drink. Booze money was at the very bottom of her list. Besides, whenever this group got together for drinks, a lot of gossip was dished out and she didn't want to miss any of it. Gossip, as much as she didn't like it, was its own currency in DC. The trick was to know when to dish it out and when to shut the hell up.

"Well, when you put it like that. I'll come."

"That's my girl."

"Only for the free drinks, though. If you are up to anything, my answer is already no."

"But Liz..."

"No."

"That's what you say now, anyway. See you at happy hour, but *only for the free drinks."*

THE CAPITOL BAR was like almost any bar on the hill. The smell of food warming on the chafing dishes and the underlying odor of stale beer was not Lizbeth's favorite combo, but she knew it would move into the background. As they settled in and ordered, Lizbeth found herself with Cheyenne LaFleur, pastry chef extraordinaire and Madeline's assistant on one side and Katherine O'Malley, Senior Legislative Assistant, on the other. They both seemed content with their jobs, as if they've found what they wanted to do forever.

Why couldn't she be happy with her job and settle down with what she was doing? Was there something wrong with her for wanting more? It wasn't as though her job was bad. Congressman Pierce did good work, and the gig had opened new doors for her. Even though it was a lot of work, she found herself having fun. Still, she envied Cheyenne's and Kat's ability to be complete Pierce-heads. They'd probably both move with him to the Oval Office someday. At the very least, their career trajectories were both headed toward being top level aides to men high in government.

Public Policy 101—get the stakeholders involved in their own solutions. She knocked on the table three times, like Jiang had done earlier. It was an effective way to get everyone's attention. "You all need to decide which one of you are going."

With a quiet chuckle, she retreated from the discussion to let the people who really cared about the solution be involved in the discussion. She didn't want to go to Vegas, but her contribution was to help the team arrive at an answer that did not include her. When they started talking about Yukika Matthews though, the Chinese entrepreneur—a woman in tech with a skyrocketing career, Liz wavered a little bit on her decision to dismiss the Vegas meeting so lightly.

As the others delved into deciding which one of them would go, Carleen Bigalow slid into a seat at the bar, ignoring their entire group. As chief of the Congressman's staff, Carleen was in every real way her go-to boss. Technically, she reported directly to the Congressman, but their encounters were brief and all about their committee work. The older woman was aging gracefully and probably looked ten years younger than she actually was. Lizbeth guessed she was fifty or older, but it was hard to tell.

Carleen wore a simple camel-brown boat-neck sheath dress. The outfit was strikingly softer compared to her usual starched collar. It was still conservative, and she looked great in it. The dress was tight enough to reveal she still had it, but not so tight as to be tacky. Carleen had recently divorced, but it wasn't a secret around the office.

A young man joined Carleen at the bar. He was smoking hot—built without being bulky, curly dark hair, and dimples when he smiled. Carleen put her hand on his shoulder and leaned in to kiss him on the cheek. He glanced around before patting her bottom with a familiarity that told Lizbeth this was not a first date.

"Is that the intern from Congressman Bingham's office?"

Cheyenne glanced over to where Lizbeth was looking. Her eyes widened. "With Carleen? Wow. Yeah. That's him. She's really flaunting her cougar status, isn't she?" Cheyenne shook her head and sipped at her drink. "I hope I'm half as spunky as she is when I'm her age."

"She's not that old."

"She's old. She's gotta be in her fifties. Damn, that dress looks good on her." Cheyenne straightened her shoulders. Cheyenne had no trouble landing men. The woman had a different man on her arm at every event, and she was never shy about why she was late some days.

"She looks younger than fifty."

"Yeah. I sure hope my game is as hot as hers is when I hit that age. Whatever it may be." Cheyenne was one of the most beautiful people in the office. She would, undoubtedly, look fabulous at fifty, sixty, or ninety.

"You think we should invite her over?" asked Cheyenne.

Katherine leaned in close to them and shook her head. "Nope. She won't want to interfere with how we go about doing this. It's probably no big deal." Katherine was the resident expert on Carleen since she was a family friend. Kat's dad had worked with Lincoln Pierce early in Pierce's career, and Carleen had run their office.

Katherine was watching Carleen as closely as she was. "Hey Cheyenne, could you go grab us another stool? We forgot one for Opal."

When Cheyenne was out of earshot, she whispered to Liz, "Did you see that kiss? What is she thinking, bringing him here like that?"

Liz replied quietly, not wanting anyone else to hear, "It's a statement. A declaration. But, that guy is older, he's not a baby-intern. Not like, you know, Chloe."

The waitress was actually carding Chloe. Lizbeth hadn't had much interaction with her, but she was definitely young. She had a very wholesome, Midwest aura about her. She was cute, and smart as a whip from what others had told her.

"It's poor taste to date an intern, and in public, even if he is an ex-marine and thirty," said Liz. "How many people are going to notice? She's lucky that Gretchen Hughes hasn't shown up yet."

Katherine shuddered. "Please. Don't mention that woman's name. She's been prowling around at every event I've been to in the last six months."

"You think she's got it in for the Congressman?"

"Not in a bad way, necessarily. I'm pretty sure she wants a scoop."

"You think his being listed as one of the most eligible bachelors in the country has something to do with that?" Lizbeth asked.

Katherine tilted her head back and shuddered. "Oh, I so wish that hadn't happened. But yeah. I am betting that when he does get serious with someone, Gretchen will be right there. Telling the whole planet."

Lizbeth had no patience for the annoying reporter. "Do you think Madeline's noticed Carleen and her date?"

"No. She's too involved with her phone right now. And Carleen will do what Carleen will do. She wouldn't bring him here if she didn't want people to see them." The tone in Katherine's voice made it clear that the subject was over. "Now, let's get this Vegas ball rolling."

Katherine did a perfunctory official hello to Chloe and jumped into the heart of why they were really there. "Not that you aren't important Chloe, but we need to figure out who is going to Vegas."

"Why couldn't he pick by seniority? This is ridiculous," said Lizbeth. She straightened her suit jacket. *Why was she even talking? She didn't want to go.* She'd barely had half a drink and her mouth was working ahead of reason.

"That would put you in first place with seniority then, right, Lizbeth?" teased Katherine with a smile.

Lizbeth hadn't thought of that, but she might as well have a little fun with this and go with some fake bravado. "I *have* earned it."

"Link is not playing any game," said Eleanor. "He trusts us enough to come up with the best candidate. Madeline, what are you doing? Get off your phone. We need you!"

"I'm almost done. Hold on." Madeline was obsessed with being connected. She had her phone out all the time. Lizbeth wondered if there was an addiction there.

"I say we pick straws then. We are all pretty much the same caliber, right?" asked Opal.

Lizbeth loved Opal. "Straws?" she asked, loving

the simple elegance of Opal's suggestion. Straws would be quick and simple. An easy solution that made them all even players on the field.

Opal's cheeks flushed, and Lizbeth winced. Her question had sounded derogatory in a way she had not meant it at all.

"It's just an idea," said Opal.

Lizbeth would have to find a time to apologize to Opal. No one gave Opal as much credit as she deserved, and Lizbeth's outburst came out more snarky than she had meant.

"Opal is right," said Madeline. But she was glued to her phone and hadn't heard what Opal had said. "Send! Okay. Apologies, I'm with you now." Madeline made eye contact and smiled at Opal.

"I have the perfect idea," said Madeline. "And, it'll be fun, too. We are all single, right? Chloe, do you have a significant other?"

Chloe looked up from her white wine, a little doe caught in the headlights. "No, I don't have a boyfriend. I'm in law school, what time do I have for a man?"

"Great. Okay. We are all single. With that, I propose that we play a BINGO game of sorts. First, you meet a man, perhaps like a lobbyist or a fundraiser, and then... you kiss him. The first girl to spell BINGO wins."

Lizbeth mouthed the word bingo, repeating it to

herself a couple of times as if she had to convince herself she'd actually heard it right.

"Come on, Madeline, very funny. Let's have a random drawing like Opal suggested. I'll get the straws," said Eleanor.

"Oh no, ladies. We are going to have fun with this game. Vegas is high stakes. The individual who goes? This will change her career, change her life path even," she said, her gaze leveling on Cheyenne and Chloe.

Leave it to Madeline to bring out the theatrics. "So dramatic," said Lizbeth. "Don't be ridiculous. It's a meeting in Vegas. We don't need one of your crazy ideas."

"Come on Liz. Don't downplay this. And besides, you always end up loving my crazy ideas."

Lizbeth wasn't going to get into it with Madeline. They had worked together at a PR firm when she first moved to DC, and she knew exactly how stubborn she could be. While some of her ideas had been a lot of fun, this one struck Lizbeth as crude, even for her. She snorted in dismissal, hoping Madeline would move on to the next option.

"It's true, Liz, and you know it. You always end up loving my ideas."

Madeline raised her hand, waving someone over. It

was a courier. He handed Madeline a manila envelope and she signed off on his electronic clipboard.

"Here are the BINGO cards I made up. That's the beauty of having a Send To Printer app on my phone. Now. The point. The BINGO game is to kiss five different men at five different monuments."

So that was what had Madeline buried in her phone. Busy bee, that woman. "You're crazy," said Lizbeth. "We can't have a kiss and tell contest." Even if she wasn't going to get involved, she didn't think it was a good idea for the other women to do it either.

"Yes. We can. Here are the cards." Madeline passed the cards out to everyone. "Don't lose these, I've deleted the info already. The kicker is that you have to kiss them at one of the monuments. The Jefferson Memorial, the Lincoln Memorial, etc. This game will be quite exciting. I promise you."

"No way," said Opal. "Whoever works the hardest should go."

"Let's stop being so selfish," said Madeline. "Chloe here is new to this side of town, and what better way is there for her to have a chance at this trip? And also get to know the locals?"

"I'm in," said Cheyenne. "It's sort of fun and flirty. God knows I need some of that." Cheyenne nudged Lizbeth with her elbow and grinned at her over her glass.

It figured that Cheyenne would love the game idea.

"Are you kidding? A kissing game?" asked Eleanor. "I can't believe this."

"I am partial to the idea," said Katherine. "I don't know why, though. It is crazy."

"It's *just* a kiss, it's not sex. I'm not asking you to prostitute yourselves. It's just, you know, something... different. Something fun."

Liz didn't like this one bit. She looked at the card. Most of the memorials listed were part of her tour on Friday morning. Too bad it wasn't one guy at all the memorials. She could totally see finding a couple free seconds at each to lay a smack on the handsome Curt Wu. *Right. Get a grip Liz. You know that's not gonna happen.* "If we get caught, the Congressman will have our asses."

"I never get caught," said Eleanor. "I'm in."

Lizbeth's jaw dropped a little. Even Eleanor was going to do this?

"So far, that's me, Katherine, Cheyenne, and Eleanor. What about the rest of you?" asked Madeline.

"We'll need proof though, of some sort," said Katherine. "A selfie on Instagram with an image of the monument. Fancy it up if you want."

"Tag each other. Make sure you're friends with everyone before the night is over," said Cheyenne.

"Helps keep the game honest. Chloe, let's do it. It'll be a lot of fun, and honestly, a different way to meet guys."

"Okay. I'm in. But I don't know, do I even have a chance?" Chloe asked, looking down at her BINGO sheet. "I wouldn't know how to find a lobbyist or a fundraiser, or any of these people."

"Stick with me, I'll help you. Is this your Instagram?" Cheyenne held her smartphone up to Chloe, who nodded.

Madeline lifted up her BINGO card and a Cheshire grin appeared. "Check, check, and check!"

Liz rubbed her temples. There was no way to stop this insanity, but she wouldn't be part of it. "Honestly? You guys, I'm way too busy for this," she said. "I've got a hundred Chinese people coming in on Thursday and the guy I was working with at State ended up on emergency family leave. I have no idea how well-prepped his replacement is and…"

She paused, took a deep breath and held her hands out in a gesture to indicate she gave up. "Look, it doesn't matter. You guys go for it. As much as Vegas sounds like fun, I don't have time for these kinds of games."

She tipped her wine glass towards Madeline and eyed the other women around the table. "You all should keep your eyes on Madeline. Even if I'm not playing, I think every single letter must be earned from this day forward. No back-dated kisses."

"We are looking at you, dear," said Kat, tipping her wine glass toward Madeline. "En garde!"

"And lose out on an opportunity to meet new men? Never!" Madeline's elbow swung back into a fencing defense pose. "I would never squander such an opportunity. If we are going to play this game, all of us have to play and all of us have to swear to secrecy."

"Oh all right. I'll play," replied Opal. "And, of course, I'll swear to secrecy." Opal held up her pinky finger in the middle of the group. Madeline, Katherine, Lizbeth, Eleanor, Cheyenne, and Chloe all held up their glasses. Opal blushed and brought down her pinky before raising her glass.

"I'm not playing," said Lizbeth, holding her ground. "But I will swear to keep your dirty little secrets." She stuffed her bingo card into her purse, shoving it to the bottom.

"To secrecy!" said Madeline.

"To secrecy!" repeated the women in unison. They clinked their glasses in a toast as they eyed each other warily, sizing up their competition.

Chapter 4

*E*very day was the same routine. Lizbeth opened the can of wet food and her three kitties tore into her tiny kitchen. Cinnamon, Ginger, and Pepper swished around her ankles, rubbing against her like land-sharks surrounding a bleeding animal.

"One of these days, you're going to trip me. And where would you be then? Circling my dead body and still hungry."

How she'd managed to take half a litter home was still a mystery to her. She'd gone to the shelter to look at the offerings, but, by the end, she'd come home with three kitties because they were so closely bonded and needed a home that could handle all of them. She couldn't split them up, and she needed the companionship.

She divided the food into three ceramic dishes and placed them on the floor. Pepper always got his food first, then his two sisters. From the backside, the kitties all looked alike hunched over their food bowls; they were nearly identical triplets. Body shape helped her identify each one. Pepper was bigger. Ginger was a smidge fluffier. Cinnamon was more delicate-looking from the front.

Casual visitors could not tell them apart unless they were side-by-side. The last couple of boyfriends she'd had never managed to get it straight. Not that you could really call them boyfriends. Dates? Short-term boyfriends? She'd seen a few guys over the last few years, but none of them stuck around for more than a month or two. If she could find a man who could differentiate her cats in the first month of a relationship, she'd probably propose.

"Love me, love my cats." She hummed a few bars from the musical as she finished getting ready for her day.

With a cup of coffee and her smart phone in front of her, she planned out the day. The morning would be filled with other duties at the Congressman's office. Lunch. Then, she'd spend the afternoon double-checking various details and reconfirming the contractors she'd hired to help with the visit—translators, tour guides, and security.

And then, there was the meeting with Curt. A so-called *business meeting* she had made up on the fly. The timing was perfect for a natural leeway into happy hour. Maybe something beyond that. Maybe all night. She moved aside the concern that he rode a motorcycle. It was unfair to categorize him as a jerk based on a single data-point. He had been a complete gentleman at the meeting and in the elevator. He hadn't talked to her like an over-adrenalized creep. He'd been sweet when he flirted.

Liz stood in front of her mirror as she put on her clothing, one layer at a time. Over the matching cream silk panties and lacy bra, she chose a goldenrod silk blouse and her maroon skirt. The jacket was a stylish tweed with a base that matched the skirt and little nubby flecks of gold that matched her blouse. The outfit was perfectly accented with stud earrings and a layered necklace that looked like it was three different pieces of jewelry. One landed like a choker around her neck, the second curved under the first button on her blouse, and the third draped nicely around the outside of her collar with a dangly metal triangle that landed an inch above her waistband. She loved dramatic jewelry, even if she wasn't a fan of drama.

Her skirt zipper wasn't lined up right. She sucked in her tummy and adjusted it, twisting the blouse. After a few more unladylike machinations, she was finally dressed with all the seams lining up where they should be.

Could she be wrong about Curt's interest in her? She might have misread all the vibes coursing through her during the meeting. Curt might be all business, but she wasn't very often wrong about a man's interest in her. Curt had been broadcasting clearly as she had the entire meeting. And then he'd outright flirted with her outside the Embassy.

When she'd said it had been hot inside, he'd said, *Not until you'd arrived.*

She tamped down any long-term expectations. They would work together this week, and she would end up falling for him. He would do something douchey, and they'd stop seeing each other. That was pretty much how things worked out for her. She'd have to ensure they had a good time while they were together.

Stop lying to yourself. You want to be with someone.

Lizbeth wanted someone for life, but maybe her love for Darius had been the one chance she'd had. Did it matter that they had been high-school sweethearts with a bone fide star-crossed love affair? Nothing had worked out for them the way they had hoped or planned: not for Darius, or her, or their baby. Did people get that kind of love twice in their lives? That had all been so long ago. Liz glanced back in the mirror. This was who she was. Her career was huge, and some guys couldn't handle her dedicating so many hours to work instead of them.

She picked up Pepper as soon as he was done eating and gave the cat some love scratches under his chin. He had a special kitty-sense and always knew when she was upset. If she was crying, he would practically launch himself into her arms and purr madly. She nuzzled her cheek against his soft fur and dropped him next to his sisters who were still eating. It was time to get to on with her day.

Her favorite project by far had been this latest gig with the upcoming Chinese visit. After all these years of slogging through domestic politics, it was thrilling to move into foreign relations in such a visible way. She was sure the success of the event would get her noticed. Having Curt Wu see her potential as a future Foreign Service officer couldn't hurt, either. Someone at his level acting as a reference would practically guarantee her making it in.

Her parents had helped her buy a brownstone in an older neighborhood close to work. As she locked her front door behind her, she stopped. *Wait.* Maybe she shouldn't meet up with Curt tonight. If one thing did lead to another, would he still be professional enough to recommend her for a job?

She extended her walk to work by stopping for a

waffle at a little shop that sold hot Belgian waffles encrusted in sugar pearls. She stopped by at least twice a week to indulge herself. While waiting in line, she realized she hadn't updated her LinkedIn profile for a long time.

When she got to the office, she'd spend a few minutes to update her online resume with the Chinese visit. She reconsidered the possible connections that going to the Vegas meeting would bring her and dismissed them again. Her rationale from the day before was still sound. SUNFLOWER was in the very baby stages in a long process. It would be months before the project would find teeth. Lizbeth would be out of here in six months, tops. She would keep doing the good work she had always done and focus on her goal. She'd started her application process into the Foreign Service office and was waiting for the next step.

As she sat down, a text came from Michael Wong telling her he was busy with his dad and would update her later. She texted that she was relieved to hear from him and offered to help if she could. Her family lived in San Francisco too, and she offered their help. Her mom wouldn't turn down a plea for taking over comfort foods if needed.

Wanting to be free of pinging text and meeting reminders, Liz turned off her phone. There was another reason she had to come by this place often, and it wasn't the waffles. Directly across the street from the waffle shop, the playground of the elementary school was crowded with kids, and her heart thumped in her chest. She scanned the crowd and found Bella.

She watched her daughter from a distance. It was sort of stalker-like, this behavior, but she always kept a distance so she wouldn't be seen. When she'd given up Bella for adoption, she hadn't expected this yearning to see her every day to become so strong.

Bella tilted her head back and laughed, outlining the jaw that was identical to her father's. Darius had been Liz's high school sweetheart. He was in the class ahead of her in school and had joined the Army right after graduation. They'd had sex only three times, all during the week of his first leave, before he was shipped off to Afghanistan. They'd taken precautions, but apparently not enough.

He'd never even learned she was pregnant. The love they'd promised each other, the babies they'd promised each other, the life they had promised each other had been blown to pieces when Darius's transport was hit by a bomb.

Her intense grief over his death had over-ridden all the signals pregnancy might have made for her—that and the fact she'd always had irregular cycles. The doctors were sure her grief and stress had ended her periods. Why they hadn't insisted on a pregnancy test when she had gone two months without one, she'd never understand. Either way, she was five months pregnant and still three months from high school graduation when she figured out what she was pregnant. She couldn't possibly choose abortion. She had to choose—adopt the baby out or raise it herself.

Adoption. Without Darius, Lizbeth couldn't raise a child on her own. She'd spent five months not knowing she was pregnant. Her periods were always flaky. She had been busy thinking about the next step in her life after high school, planning her career, mapping out what that looked like and how she could get there. She hadn't even noticed she'd missed one period after another. She had been accepted at Berkeley—her dream school.

She hadn't been ready to raise a baby. Maybe it was a little selfish in some ways, but giving up her baby was the ultimate grown-up decision. It would have been a different kind of selfish to have kept her. The baby would be better off with a family who could give her the attention she deserved, with parents who had their life worked out and were ready to give this baby all their love.

She'd had counseling right after Darius' death. Her therapist had helped her understand that the love she'd had for Darius would have probably diminished and they would have broken up over the years of separation and school.

Determined to do this her way, she had put on bigger clothes and pretended to eat a lot at school. Her classmates knew about Darius' death, so she let them assume she was stuffing her grief. *Girls laughing in the hallway seems so juvenile now.*

Lizbeth's parents, on the other hand, had responded in their typical fashion—her father with stoic support and her mother with passive-aggressiveness. She had chosen to tell them over dinner on a Saturday night. Her mother had ordered in Italian which meant she had been in a good mood.

"I'm pregnant. It's Darius' baby."

Her father had put down his fork and reached his hand out for hers. "Oh, honey…"

"I thought you were getting fat. Is it too late for an abortion?"

And, a small part of her had always wondered if she'd waited to tell her parents precisely because of this. Had she subconsciously waited to tell them until adoption was the only real option?

"We will help you find a good family to take it in." Her mother picked up her knife and fork and continued eating, case closed.

Her father had liked Darius, and loved him with

puppy dog eyes, but her mother had always spoken of him in terms of 'first boyfriend.'

"I've already contracted with an adoption agency." Her father squeezed her hand for her to continue. Her mother stared at her plate, waiting for Liz to finish. "There's a couple in Washington, DC who've been trying for a baby for ten years. The adoptive dad is black. Like Darius. He's a scientist of some sort. And the mom is American born Chinese, like me. She's a pediatrician."

"You've made up your mind about this?"

"Yes, Mama, I have."

"Good. Will it interfere with you going to Berkeley this fall?"

Her mother was so pragmatic. There were no emotions, no begging. And that was that. Her parents supported her the rest of the way through her pregnancy and never spoke of it afterward. Things might have been different if Waipo had still been alive.

Bella was six years old when Lizbeth moved from Berkeley to DC. DeMarco and Angela had granted Lizbeth monthly visitation while expressly forbidding any interaction with Bella if they were not present. They didn't have to do any of that. They could have insisted they stay with the original agreement, which was a yearly picture and letter. Liz had found herself seeking Bella out more and more often like this in spite of the fact Bella's parents would be livid if they found out.

Bella twirled around, scanning the area behind her as if she knew she were being watched. Could she see Lizbeth through the plate glass of the coffee shop window? Lizbeth stepped back into the shadows.

"Hey watch it, lady!"

She narrowly missing a collision with a man carrying a tray filled with coffee drinks.

"I'm sorry!" she said. He scowled at her and left without further comment. Liz returned her attention to the playground. A circle of friends gathered around Bella and their heads bent toward each other, temples touching in a tight ring. When the bell rang, calling them inside, Lizbeth crumpled up her napkin into her paper coffee cup and tossed it in the trash. She knew she shouldn't be there. When Bella's back was to her, she continued on her way to work, picking up the pace in the hopes that her extra effort would burn off a few of those sweet calories.

izbeth filled her morning by answering the emails she'd let linger for the last couple days. Someone had rerouted all the incoming email with anything related to the Congressman's work on the House Intelligence Committee to her and now she was swamped. Being the go-to girl had its downside.

"Lizbeth, can you take a break?"

Cheyenne never asked her to join her for a break without wanting something. She took a deep breath and signed off her computer. Coffee would be welcome after the literal four-hundredth email.

They found a private corner table in the small coffee shop in the lower floor of the Cannon building. This late in the morning it was mostly empty, but it was still a good idea to be as far away from other people as possible. Gossiping was the number one activity in DC, next to listening in on others' conversations.

"So," Cheyenne started, "about this game."

Lizbeth blinked at her, momentarily confused. "Game?"

Cheyenne leaned forward and dropped her voice. "You know, the B-I-N-G-O game? The one we planned last night?"

"Oh. What about it?" Lizbeth asked, trying to remember the details. She didn't have a hangover which was a minor miracle in itself, but she didn't quite remember the details of the game either. She wasn't going to play. Instead, she had been sneaking glances at Carleen and the intern all night.

"What about it?" Cheyenne sat back in her chair, mouth dropping open for a second. "Seriously, are you not even interested?"

"Why should I be? That meeting..." she paused and looked around before continuing in a near whisper. "That meeting would do nothing for my career. And that game? I don't play games—especially sex games."

Cheyenne's eyes narrowed on her, considering her for a long, uncomfortable moment. She must have decided to take Lizbeth at face value. "It's only kissing. It's not a sex game. Fine. You're not playing, but that doesn't mean you can't help those of us who are."

There it was. Cheyenne was going to pump her for information. Contacts, probably. She didn't answer but took a long drink of her coffee.

"Look, Liz, I've already got two dates lined up over the next five days. To fill out this row, I need someone at State, the CIA, and someone at the Smithsonian. Hook me up?"

"You want me to set you up on a date with someone from the CIA?"

"And, *or* State. You know lots of people at both... it'd be easy, right?"

Lizbeth wasn't about to drag herself down by hooking anyone up with Cheyenne, let alone people she had to work with. "No way. You're on your own."

Cheyenne crossed her arms and pouted. "Oh, come on, Liz. It's not like you have to tell them that we're playing a game. Can't you think of someone who would be happy going out on a date and getting an amazing kiss from me?"

"CIA like to date their own kind. And it's tasteless. And it's wrong. So, no."

The few people in the shop turned their heads to look at them.

Cheyenne held her hands up in a defensive gesture. "Okay. Okay. You can't be upset that I asked."

"Be careful, Cheyenne. You're going to be in a shit-heap of trouble if you get caught." She stood up.

Cheyenne sat back in her seat, pointing at her half-finished drink. "I'll be up when I'm done."

Lizbeth shrugged. "Suit yourself. Thanks for the invite, but I've got to run. Emails don't answer themselves."

Her phone buzzed with a text before she got back to the office. It was from Curt.

C: Confirming meeting today. 3:00 your place

Lizbeth wanted to respond appropriately but a little cheeky.

L: Check. Looking forward to seeing you again.

C: Seeing you is going to be best part of the day.

Little flutters of excitement danced around inside her. The heat building from a slow burn ignited when he first touched her at the elevator. It had been way too long since she'd had any passion in her life. Thoughts of Curt consumed her with a desire she hadn't expected. For now, ending up in bed with him was her priority, but she'd take more if it came. She slipped into the bathroom. It was empty, so she took the last stall and leaned her back against the wall, praying no one would notice her if they came in.

She lifted her skirt and slid her hand into her panties and conjured up Curt's face. She imagined unbuttoning his shirt and tracing his tattoo. Then she imagined her hand running along his firm abs, across his taut stomach. She found the magic spot on her clit and went to town while picturing Curt's head between her legs and pretending her finger was his tongue. It only took a minute, possibly two, before she came hard and almost slid down the wall of the bathroom.

There was no doubt in her mind. She was going to sleep with him.

Lizbeth straightened her clothes out and flushed the toilet to make it seem like nothing was out of the ordinary. As she washed her hands, she examined her facial expression. She was glowing. And she was about to go back to her office. She tried to look serious and patted down a few wild hairs. *Shit*. How does one put on a proper business expression after a powerful orgasm? From masturbating... in the bathroom.

Back in the office, Liz glanced around taking mental stock of who was in their offices and cubicles. Fortunately, no one looked closely at her or noticed her glazed eyes and goofy expression. She knew she was smiling, and she couldn't stop.

Liz didn't really have an office, but her cubicle was roomy enough to house a low bookshelf next to her desk and a few photos on the wall above her desk. She wished she could put one of Bella up there, but only Carleen and Katherine knew this particular secret and she didn't want to explain her past to everyone who came to her desk. She coveted Carleen's office. Actually, she coveted the door. And the privacy. Hell, even Katherine's tiny one would be a step up from this.

Lizbeth had gotten into the habit of putting in earbuds and listening to white noise so she could concentrate. The loud crashing water of Niagara Falls was blocking out office noise when a hand grasped her shoulder. Her hands flew out in surprise, one hitting a water bottle causing it to spray water all over her wall. At least this time she had her earbuds in and had an excuse to be surprised.

She spun around and found herself looking up into a grinning Curt Wu. She'd forgotten to set an alarm, and it was twelve minutes into their scheduled meeting time.

"Sorry about that. I did try to get your attention."

Opal was watching them from her own cubicle. Liz nodded at her, then grabbed a tissue and blotted the water on her wall and desk. The heat rising in her cheeks made her feel like she was back in middle school. Dabbing water spots was so incredibly sexy—*not*.

Curt picked up the bottle from the floor and set it on her desk. Pointing to the diplomas hanging over the book shelf he said, "Hey, you went to UC Berkeley? *And* Kennedy?"

This was surprising. "Undergrad. And no one calls it Kennedy unless they went there. What year?"

"Yeah, well, I'm sure I would have remembered if you were there at the same time. It's interesting that we went to the same schools."

She gave him a questioning glance at first. Schools. With an "s." Liz crossed her arms and looked at him like he was making things up. "Seriously?"

He held up two fingers. "Scouts honor. Berkeley with a degree in forensic economics and Kennedy for ID."

"You mastered in International Development? At Kennedy?" How likely would it be that the man she had the sudden hots for had been on her near-exact path? Their majors were different but in the same departments. *Holy hell.* They couldn't be that far apart in age, but still.

"I'm older than I look." He smiled again like he knew it would knock her into a different train of thought. The slight lines at his eyes had her guessing he was at least five years older than she was, maybe more. A couple years would be all it would take to ensure they never crossed paths at school, though. At least she knew some topics of conversation. "Let's go to the conference room. We can spread everything out on the table."

As she said it, she blushed. An image of her spread out on the table with him hovering over her filled her head. *Damn.* This was going to be a tricky meeting. Especially if they worked together well. He could be the defining connection to get her into the State Department—personally working with someone on a project like this? He could vouch for her if things went well. Or, he could be good in bed and they'd hit it off. Would it work out so she could get both? If not, it was possible he'd become another Randy—ex-lover and friend.

As they wound their way through the office, a few of her workmates gave them the once over and raised an eyebrow. Cheyenne smiled at her with a Cheshire Cat grin and gave her a knowing look before popping up out of her seat and thrusting a hand toward Curt.

"Are you the Michael Wong we've been hearing so much about?" Cheyenne asked, her voice all low and husky.

Not only had Cheyenne got the wrong person, she made it sound like Lizbeth had been talking about Michael to her office mates. In fact, she had intentionally kept any information about Michael on the down-low because frankly, there was nothing to talk about. Which of course, now, she realized, had made

Cheyenne think the opposite. Well, she'd already told Curt the day before that Michael was a friend and nothing else. A much older, family-oriented, not interested kind of friend.

Before Curt could respond, Lizbeth said, "Cheyenne LeFleur, this is Curt Wu. He's taking Michael's place for the remainder of the project. He's here for a briefing since he's new."

"Pleasure to meet you, Ms. LeFleur."

Cheyenne practically purred as their hands met. "So, you're from State, then?"

"Yes, I am."

Lizbeth needed to put a stop to Cheyenne's ludicrous behavior. If she let this go on, Cheyenne would be licking her lips, wondering how to get him to a monument. "Cheyenne, Katherine is trying to get your attention."

Cheyenne dropped Curt's hand and turned towards Katherine's office. Katherine happened to look up at that moment and waved Cheyenne in.

"Bye you two. Have fun in the conference room," Cheyenne said as she disappeared inside without looking back at them.

Lizbeth forced herself to resist that magnetic attraction again; she wanted to reach out to him, to touch him. As they settled into the conference room, Curt pulled papers from his briefcase and laid them out perfectly in nice organized piles. They started with the security requirements for the gala.

Wu had already finished the required list, a lot quicker than she had expected. That was odd. It became apparent that Curt was already caught up on all the security protocols. Was he showing off or did he accept this meeting because he wanted to see her as much as she did him?

"How are you so up on the event? It's as if you've been with the working group since day one."

"I'm a quick study. Michael and I discussed it over the phone at length."

Liz couldn't quite believe a phone call would convey every detail of the plan.

Before she could question him further, he said, "What he didn't tell me about was *you*."

Lizbeth flushed. They were definitely veering into teasing territory. She could shut it down now. She didn't want to fall for this guy, not when he could help her get what she really wanted—a career boost. She could get sex with anyone. Resisting her base urges would be the wise thing to do. *Focus on work, girl!* Lizbeth drew in a steadying breath.

"I was worried about getting the final qualifications from the BDS. They are very thorough and super slow, you know. I wasn't sure how new you were. I was prepared to carry it on my own through the week."

"I assure you, Lizbeth, I will be very much carrying my own weight."

"Well, it looks like we're pretty well set for the weekend." She checked her watch. She shouldn't go out for drinks with him.

Ugh. Who was she kidding? He's irresistible...

It was as if she had an angel on one shoulder and a devil on the other, both talking to her at once. She wasn't sure which was leading her in the right direction.

"Michael filled me in, yes, but I'd like to hear the details from you. Let's pull out the maps again, I want to check the route around the memorials."

"Double checking is an admirable trait. I like it."

"No one wants to be caught with an unplanned event. Especially me." He traced his finger around the planned route. His fingers were well manicured and neat. She couldn't help but imagine them tracing them between her breasts and around her nipples, then moving downward... With a surprised gasp, she swallowed hard.

He looked up at her with a funny expression. "Are you okay? Did something get stuck?"

"No. I'm fine." She blushed again. So not sexy.

"Ok, I don't think there'll be any real security threat. Honestly, the big guns will be in meetings, except for their Secretary of the Interior, Zhou Fengshan. He specifically wanted to do the walking tour. The Chinese want to update their own monuments with a balance between honoring communism without bringing up the devastation of the culture revolution."

"Knowing Zhou he probably wants to be outside instead of cooped up in boring meetings."

"How do you know so much about him?" Curt asked.

"I pay attention. It's pretty obvious, if you ask me." She leaned her elbows on the table and cradled her chin in clasped fingers. "To tell you the truth, I think there's something off about him."

Curt narrowed his eyes. "Off? In what way?"

"I have this feeling. It's like he's coming for business, but not doing any. His staff communications have been the least of any of the delegates. It's like he's coming because his wife wants to. She's the one who spear-headed the opera excursion on Friday."

"Interesting. I don't know how that plays into anything that we are working on, though."

"It doesn't. Like I said, it's a feeling, and not one I can justify with anything tangible. Are you going to the opera with the group? Michael was slated to go…"

"Il Trovatore is one of my favorite operas."

Lizbeth looked at him over the top of her glasses. "Did you say what I think you said?" Opera wasn't exactly an obsession so much as a deep romance. If she could do the Wagner Ring Cycle once a year she would. She also loved the more lyrical Italian operas. The lilting tenors sent her into as much ecstasy as the chest-pounding German choruses.

"That Il Trovatore is one of my favorite operas? I take it you're a big fan?"

"I love opera. Ever since I was a little girl, I've loved it. I went to the Ring Cycle last year at Washington National Opera. It was phenomenal."

His smile flattened out. "Sorry, I actually have no idea what you're talking about. I've never been to the opera, I was trying for a joke."

She was disappointed, but not stymied. "Do you remember the Bugs Bunny cartoon? The one with 'Kill the Wabbit'?"

Curt's brow furrowed, but then he started to sing it, perfectly in tune with a decent tenor voice. "Kill the wabbit... kill the wabbit... duh de duh?"

"Yes, that's the one. That whole cartoon is based on Wagner's work. It's complicated, but people who are into Opera call it the Ring Cycle. It's actually four long operas, and they are performed over a month." She waved away the details with the flick of her wrist. "It's about fifteen hours long, but you don't watch it all at once. And, you know the whole Lord of the Rings?"

"The movies? With the elves and Frodo?"

"Yeah, them. They're based on Wagner's opera.

Well, very loosely. But, trust me, it's *the thing* Opera lovers want to do at least once in their lives."

"And you've already done it?"

"Yeah, but I'd totally go again."

He nodded slowly, not very convincingly. "Maybe I'll check out a beginner's guide or something. Is Il Trovatore fifteen hours long?"

"Oh, no. It's about two-and-a-half hours."

"Like a long movie, then."

"And it has an intermission around halfway in. The musicians need a break. It is a live performance."

Only one of the guys she'd dated in the last five years had shown interest in opera. She had season tickets and had to work to find a date for any of them. Her latest boyfriend, one who had actually stuck for three whole months, went with her once. He had fallen asleep after complaining about the music. They had agreed that the opera was better suited for a girl's night out and he would be free to stay home and play video games. No wonder she dumped him. She didn't want a skateboarding video game playing boy, she wanted a man.

He laughed. "Okay, I have no idea. I've never been to an opera. It sounds interesting."

"Oh." *Did he like video games along with motorcycles? Two strikes.*

"Oh, hey. You really like opera, don't you?"

"I do. And, I also happen to think Il Trovatore is awesome. Some of the most famous music ever."

His delicious looking lips twisted for a second, and his suddenly serious eyes met hers. "I am sorry if I offended you. I didn't know anyone under sixty genuinely enjoyed opera."

Her heart thumped loudly in her chest. Good lord. What eyes... "I... I accept your apology. When we go on Friday, give it an honest chance. There's something amazing about an opera performance. There are people on the stage acting, singing, dancing. Live musicians. Take any one of them and it might be interesting. But... when you put it all together? There's this amazing synergistic thing that happens. Live. Right there. No two performances are identical." She stopped herself before going into crazy-opera-lady territory.

"Seeing how you're so into it, I'll have to give it a chance. Besides, I'm an open-minded guy. Just because I haven't experienced something doesn't mean I won't love it."

Lizbeth resisted the urge to beam at him like an idiot. It was so refreshing to find a man who would give opera a chance. Collecting herself and trying to remain calm was almost impossible. "Good. Okay. Um. Anyway... I got an updated list from BDS a little while ago."

The Bureau of Diplomatic Security had been surprisingly easy to work with on this visit. They didn't like the Dragon Boat event because the venue proved to be very challenging. Not only were there multiple entry-points for people attending the event, but the races took place on the river. The BDS would concentrate on the delegation and their assigned pavilion to minimize the potential threat to the guests.

Curt flipped it around so he could read it. "Six people from the original roster are out with the flu?"

"I know. It's kind of late in the season for it, but that's not entirely unusual."

"So, we've got six replacements coming in for security on Friday. And," he flipped through the pages, "the same six will be here on Saturday, too. I prefer having the same security on detail the whole event. Fewer faces to get to know."

Lizbeth thought that was an interesting observation. She tended to look at the guys in the BDS as the same as the guys in the SS. They all wore black suits and had coiled communication cords hanging out of their ears. They did what they were told, like bouncers at a bar. That might be the strength in their uniformity. They blended in and made you forget they were there.

"You know," she said, drawing out the last word to give her a moment to think. "I've visited every memorial on the list except for the Roosevelt. I'd like to make sure I've got my head wrapped around the flow of movements. Want to join me in a walkthrough?"

"Right now?"

Lizbeth's heart sunk. He suddenly looked like a guy with plans that she wasn't part of. She glanced at her watch. "It's four o'clock. We'll be at the memorial earlier in the day on Friday, but I feel like seeing it in person will help me understand why they want to put extra agents where they are suggesting. Rush hour traffic is kind of low today. There are no big conferences in town and Boy Scout season hasn't started yet."

Curt tilted his head and examined her, his brown eyes sliding from her ankles up to her face. "It is a beautiful day, did you notice?"

She'd asked him out, and he's talking about the weather?

"How comfortable are you on a motorcycle? In a pencil skirt?"

Lizbeth had hoped he wouldn't offer her a ride on his motorcycle. She should have mentioned taking a cab first. There was no way she was going to tell him she'd never been on one, or that she didn't even want to get on one. Liz looked down at her legs and pictured how the skirt she was wearing would ride up all the way to her hips if she climbed up behind him on a bike and how that would feel to be pinioned behind him, pressing her bare thighs against him. Would he feel the wet heat of her sudden desire?

Now, where had all that come from? How had she gone from never wanting to ride a motorcycle to practically quivering with anticipation?

"Do you mind wearing a helmet?"

She swallowed, hoping her flush of embarrassing excitement and complete fear didn't show on her face. "A what? A helmet? Of course I can wear a helmet."

"You aren't afraid of helmet hair?"

"Nooo?" *Helmet hair is a thing? What am I getting myself into?* "And well, I... I... have a change of clothes in my desk that would be a bit... more... suitable for... erm... riding."

"You keep spare clothes in the office?"

"You never know how the day is going to end."

"Oh, then, let's go for it."

Lizbeth started gathering up the pages they'd scattered across the table, but he shooed her away before she got very far. "I'll get this organized. You go get changed. I'll meet you in the parking lot."

She left him in the conference room. In the office, she grabbed her bag. Opal was giving her the side eye, but she ignored her and escaped to the bathroom. Cheyenne was coming out as she was going in. She followed Lizbeth back inside.

Lizbeth rolled her eyes as she shut the stall door.

"Man, that guy is hot."

Lizbeth peeled off the skirt she was wearing and shimmied into her jeans. "Yep. Totally hot."

"You're not playing the game because of Curt?"

Lizbeth opened the stall.

"Sweetheart, I am not playing the game because I am not willing to risk my career."

"Interesting mode of dress. Where are you going?" Cheyenne said, ignoring her question and assessing her new outfit.

She shoved her skirt into her bag then brushed past Cheyenne who was leaning against the stall divider, a wolfish grin on her face. "None of your business."

Chapter 6

There was only one motorcycle in the lot, and there was a helmet attached to each seat. He had come prepared. She wasn't sure whether to be flattered or angry. She went for somewhere in between—amused.

"Was I that easy to read?"

Curt unhooked the helmets from the bike and handed her one as he smiled broadly. "When you set our meeting for so late in the day, it seemed obvious you were inviting me for something more. Was I mistaken?"

When was the last time she'd met someone who was so blindingly open and forthright? No games with this guy. She tilted her head back so her hair fell away from her face as she put the helmet on, pretending like it was no big deal. Like she was a pro. She didn't want him to know she was scared out of her mind; she wanted him to think she could handle him and his bike.

"Let me make sure it's on right," he said as he adjusted the straps. He gently cupped her cheeks in his hands as he ran a finger along under the straps. "We want it tight enough it won't fly off, but loose enough to not choke you."

He might be thinking only about the helmet and her safety, but the warmth of his fingers and lightness of his touch against her face was mesmerizing. Intoxicating.

"Have you ever ridden on a motorcycle before?" He patted his machine like it was a giant tiger. And maybe it was.

It was a sturdy looking bike with a single seat with the back a little higher than the front. It didn't look that much bigger or scarier than a regular bike. The seat was actually closer to the ground than that of her bicycle, the one that leaned up against the back wall of her house collecting dust and cobwebs.

She shook her head.

"I'll get on first. This is the tailpipe." He touched it and withdrew his hand quickly, shaking his fingers. "It's still pretty hot. You'll want to be careful of that, okay? When you get on, don't let your leg get too close. Swing your leg over and place it on the passenger peg, here." He leaned over the bike and popped it down. "Then hop on behind me."

Hot tailpipe? Yikes.

She took a deep breath, telling herself lots of women did this every day and lived to talk about it. Cheyenne had gone on at length one night about her ex who was in a motorcycle club. She'd loved it. Lizbeth wracked her brain trying to remember any specifics about it, but she came up with nothing helpful. For Cheyenne, it was all about the sexy fun of the ride and nothing about safety tips.

Lizbeth was glad Curt explained the whole thing to her. Even so, with her luck, she'd klutz right over the side. He climbed on and waited for her to settle in behind him. There wasn't anything to hold onto besides him, so she grasped his shoulder, knowing that was all that was between her and flailing onto the ground.

She carefully put her foot on the peg, silently congratulating herself for changing shoes as well as her skirt. She put the ball of her foot on the peg and did a mini-step, testing it for balance before putting her full weight on it and swinging her other leg around him. Unaccustomed to the motions, her body fell forward onto him and she grabbed around his head, helmet and all. He held his hand up to help her find balance.

"Sorry. Sorry. Oh my god."

She found the other peg and slid into the seat behind him, releasing her accidental strangle. There weren't many options once she was balanced on the seat. It was instinctual to close her legs against his body, to lean up against his back and hold onto him for dear life. And he hadn't even turned the bike on yet.

He craned his neck around so she could hear him talk. "Go ahead and grab on wherever you can when we get going. Well... maybe not around my neck, but you can grab my shoulders or wrap your arms around my body. Whatever you're comfortable with."

Curt adjusted himself on the bike and patted her thigh with his hand. "You'll be fine."

His hand on her thigh was both comforting and thrilling, and they hadn't even moved yet.

Was his confidence in her misplaced? Was she actually about to do this? He hadn't even cranked the engine and she could feel her heart rate zip into cardio mode.

She leaned in close like she'd seen others do it to feel safer. He had a clean and spicy scent. Sandalwood and lemongrass, maybe? She couldn't quite place it. Breathing deeply had usually worked to calm her before; breathing in his fragrance only exacerbated the adrenaline coursing through her.

He patted her thigh one more time and revved the engine into life. The smell of exhaust bloomed around them. The rumble of the engine surprised her. It was almost like... well... a gigantic vibrator.

He kicked the stand back and Liz grabbed onto his waist, unused to the sudden momentum. He hit the gas, and she grabbed his waist tighter and yelped. Her breasts jiggled and she leaned in against him, wondering what they felt like against his muscular back. She couldn't hear him, but she could feel his chest as he chuckled.

And then, they were moving. Fast. She had to work to not dig her nails into him as he zoomed into traffic. She pressed her inner thighs against his waist, not because it was sexy, but out of sheer survival instinct. He reached back and rubbed her leg again, patting it reassuringly.

Her body melted into his, leaning with him around corners. He zipped between slower moving cars, passing them with mere inches to spare. Liz reminded herself to breathe. At a stoplight, he let his hand rest against her the entire time. It was the most natural thing in the world to be leaning against him like that, waiting to get moving again. She caught the eye of a woman in a car a lane over. The smile that spread over her face as their eyes met told Liz she'd joined some sort of club—the woman knew exactly what it was like to ride on a motorcycle behind her man. The woman winked at her. And Liz finally understood what it was all about.

As Curt took off out of the intersection, a completely new sensation overcame her. Fun. She. Was. Having. *Fun.* The exhilaration of the ride increased as he sped up. She relaxed a little bit at a time the rest of the ride, but she continued to cling to Curt. The rumble between her legs and the warmth of his back against her was the most intensely sensual thing she'd ever experience while fully dressed. She glanced down to make sure a dark wet spot wasn't spreading through her jeans. She *had* dressed for sex this morning, but she hadn't expected to find herself on a motorcycle, dripping with desire and horny beyond belief.

Curt slid the bike in between two poorly parked cars and cut the engine. "Reverse the moves you used to get on. And be careful as the pipe is going to be really hot now."

The memorial entrance was only a few yards away. A couple of tour buses idled as a crowd of elderly people made their way from the memorial to the buses. Fallen cherry blossoms dotted the ground.

He put the kickstand down and turned to her. "You're a pro."

She beamed in response.

"Let me help you off," he said. Lizbeth legs were

wobbly, but she managed to stand upright without stumbling. She unstrapped the helmet and handed it to him once he was off the bike. One good thing about her long, straight hair was it wasn't ruined by a few minutes under a helmet. She shook out her hair and combed through it with her fingers.

Curt was trying very hard to look like he was busy putting his helmet away, but he was watching her. She tried to ignore the continued throbbing between her legs. Was this what guys called blue-balls? What did women call it when they get excited without the happy ending?

"So, was it as good as you thought it would be?" His smile created deep dimples in his cheek. His eyes shone brightly.

"That was way better than I thought it would be." She barely managed to get the words out. Talking through her latent fear combined with overwhelming excitement was difficult.

"It doesn't have the best shocks. The seat rumbles quite a bit."

"Tell me about it." *Rumble... vibrate... same-same.* She turned slowly to get her bearings, and it gave her a chance to cross her legs to quell the throbbing between them. It helped a little bit to calm her hungry pussy, but barely. She swallowed heavily and told herself it was time to focus back on work.

"This is the sixth stop on the walking tour. We'll be coming from over... there." She pointed to the walkway leading toward the Martin Luther King Jr. Memorial.

"The layout of this one is problematic. We won't be able to keep the group together very easily," Curt said.

"Fortunately, BDS has that mostly figured out. They'll have people circulating around the area making sure no one gets too far from the group. I need to make sure I give the guide the right directions."

"But this is the most difficult to manage. It's, what, seven acres? And it is broken up into a bunch of smaller spaces."

There was no single large physical structure like the Lincoln Memorial or the Jefferson. Instead, the Franklin Delano Roosevelt Memorial was a series of four outdoor rooms, each representing one of the president's terms. She'd read about it when she first moved to DC and had always meant to visit.

"Are you leading the tour?"

"Me?" she laughed. "Hell no. We have a native Chinese guy doing that part. Plus, he's been tasked to learn the history about these specific monuments. I'll be directing things behind the scenes."

"Show me what you got."

"I'm really glad it's *this* Roosevelt. Not the other one," she said.

"Why's that?"

"Well, mainly because it wouldn't be easy to walk to as part of this tour. Logistics. No bathrooms. No water." Theodore Roosevelt Island was a refuge in the midst of the city that a lot of hikers and runners frequented to get away from the hubbub. Teddy Roosevelt was all about the outdoors while Franklin Roosevelt governed from a wheelchair, not a horse.

"I've never been over there. I hear it's a nice place to jog," he said.

"We'll start here," she said and led the way into the monument, past the official entrance and the first fountain. Each section of the monument had a different fountain related to Roosevelt's administration. The Chinese speaking tour guide planned a whole spiel about the monument, and to note any points of interest it may have to their culture. The signage was all in English, but she'd provided Chinese translations for everyone.

"I want to give the tour guide specific instructions about the path they should take through the monument. If they follow him, we should be able to get BDS to wrangle any stragglers."

They meandered through the monument, reading some plaques, ignoring others. She wondered what it would be like to travel with him. Would he be the kind of man who buzzed around the Italian hills on a motorcycle or would he be the kind of man who took his time examining masterpieces in the Louvre? Maybe he'd be both.

The sun was close to setting, and the evening chill made her shiver. The whole monument glowed a pinky-gold. In spite of trying to keep her mind on her work, her body still buzzed from the motorcycle ride. She glanced towards the parking lot and found the bike where they'd left it. It had a whole new meaning for her now. She had enough pent-up throbbing going on, another ride might tip her over the edge. Into what? Could it be more than a week long party?

They came across an alcove depicting a man listening to one of the president's famous radio addresses. Curt pulled her into the recess with him, his arms warm around her waist. "Can anyone see us in here?"

Lizbeth flushed and leaned her head outside. There wasn't anyone around. She swiveled back toward him. "Are you asking me for security purposes?"

"Absolutely. I need to make sure we know about any hidden corners that could hide someone dangerous."

"So who's the dangerous one?"

His eyes were dark, but they reflected the rich sunset even in the dim surroundings of the recess. He swept a stray lock of hair away from her face, and ran his thumb along her lips. "So soft," he said. "I've been wanting to kiss you since the sesame balls."

"You are such a romantic." He *had* been watching her the moment she entered the room.

"So willing to eat."

She laughed. There was no denying what she was feeling. It was more than a simple attraction, and it terrified her. It made no logical sense, and yet, here she was. Amped up from a motorcycle ride with a man she hardly knew, a man who could be a valuable asset to her career, and all she wanted was for him to kiss her. No, she wanted way more than a kiss.

"Oh, wow. That's a first. Are you flirting with me?"

Their eyes met. His warm and brown, dark as her own, mirrored velvety pools she could slide right into.

"I am."

"Are you going to kiss me?"

"In a moment." His face grew serious as he examined her, taking in every bit of her.

"Do your kisses require a biometric scan? Maybe you want to run my fingerprints, too?" She tilted her head to one side, amused and confused. He was looking for something, but she had no idea what.

A ray of sun hit them, illuminating them in a rich

golden glow. He leaned forward to kiss her, pulling her tightly against him. She parted her lips, and her breath caught as his lips touched hers for the first time.

Curt's smooth lips brushed hers with a gentle questioning touch. Her tongue darted eagerly into his mouth to dance with his, pushing back for more. The built-up excitement during the motorcycle ride roared back into life—from zero to sixty in no time.

His hands slid from her waist to cup her bottom, pulling her into him. His erection pressed against her stomach. She ran her hands along his firm back and up into his thick dark hair. She moaned, and it came out as a near-whimper of a cry. He broke the kiss and ran a finger from her brow to the tip of her nose. "Getting what you need from this little field trip?"

She caught her breath before answering. "I'm not quite sure that this corner is safe. What is your expert opinion?"

"At first, it might seem dangerous, but we will have enough security. It's safe, I promise." His lips twitched into a teasing smile. "What should we do now?"

She knew what she wanted to do. She wanted to get back on the motorcycle and hold him close against her as he zoomed back through town to her house. Or his house. She didn't really care. He'd been so forthright earlier, she would try the same with him.

"Take me back to my place."

His eyes narrowed on her. Had she jumped the gun? Had she been unclear in her intentions in any way?

"Before... drinks and dinner?"

"We can go out after."

Chapter 7

When Lizbeth approached the motorcycle the second time, it was with a completely different attitude. She could get addicted to this. Curt made sure her helmet was on right, like he had before. This time, though, he held her cheeks gently in his palms and kissed her while he snapped the straps in place.

She knew what to expect, and when she mounted the bike, she laid one hand on his shoulder for balance but didn't fall into choking him. She leaned into him right away, fully prepared for the vibrating, exhilarating ride back to her place.

He weaved through the rush hour traffic, buzzing between stopped cars. There were a couple of heart-pounding moments on the way. The sensations were slightly overwhelming. *The way the bike rattled under her... The way her breasts jiggled against his back, even when she pulled herself against him as tightly as she could... The way her inner thighs pressed up against his hips...* The space between her throbbing pussy and his back was only a few inches; she wanted to press that against him too, but she could wait the twenty or so minutes it would take to get to her little brownstone.

They lucked out with a spot right in front, a rare thing indeed, and she practically jumped off the bike like she'd been doing so for years. The ride had reignited all the nerves in her body. She was so wet, she was sure her jeans had soaked through. They stopped to kiss every few steps, half-staggering to her house.

She opened the door, the keys having magically appeared in her hands, and they crashed into the wall opposite, the door swinging wide as they kissed again. She kicked out with her leg to shut it behind them.

Lizbeth had planned ahead. The living room was tidy, and her three cats were on the sofa. All three of them sat up, their ears perked up, awoken by Lizbeth and Curt's fracas.

"Cute cats," he said, breathing hard between kisses.

"You can meet them later." She pushed Curt toward the set of stairs straight ahead. "Bedroom is upstairs."

He rotated around at the base of the stairs and surprised her by sweeping her off her feet.

She tilted her head back and giggled as she linked her arms around his neck and leaned into him, breathing in his rich spicy scent. He carried her as if she weighed nothing. The stairs opened directly into her bedroom. She nuzzled him behind his ear and grasped his earlobe between her teeth, letting it slide out slowly.

He let out a long, low moan in response, and deposited her on her feet next to the bed.

He placed his hands on her shoulders, searching her eyes. "You're sure you want this? You think we'll be able to maintain a professional relationship after?"

That question could encompass so much. *Want what, exactly?* Was he talking about more than sex? And now he had to bring up their work relationship? Right when they were getting hot and heavy? What an amazing man. She wanted him even more because he'd asked.

"Good Lord, yes. I want you here, and on the bed, and everywhere." She wrapped her arms around his neck again, catching his lower lip between her teeth and drawing it out in a gentle tug.

His hands roamed across her back and along her sides, tugging at her blouse, freeing it from her jeans. Slipping his hand underneath, he cupped her breast through her bra. His thumb and forefinger found her nipple and coaxed it into a hard nub.

Lizbeth broke the kiss, leaning away from him and breathing hard. He looked at her curiously, his hands falling to his sides, waiting for her lead. She traced her finger along the inside rim of his collar between the fabric and his neck, the ink she'd seen the day before hidden beneath. She met his eyes and pulled out his shirt and unbuttoned it without looking away until she had pushed the shirt off his shoulders, exposing his flesh. His chest muscles twitched, and he dropped it off his wrists.

The head of a glowing emerald green dragon draped over his shoulder. Demon-eyes glared at her from below his collarbone. The long whiskers twisted around each other and curled up toward his neck. It had been one of these that she'd seen the day before. She traced the path of one of the longer whiskers around his shoulder and to his back. Curt turned under her finger so she could continue. Gold scales shimmered as if they were metal. She outlined the dragon's belly. The talons of one wing dug into Curt's upper left arm while the other stretched across his shoulders toward the opposite arm, as if balancing itself while riding his back.

She stepped back to admire the artistry. He basically had a dragon draped over his shoulder—as masterful as any tromp l'oiel she'd ever seen in a museum. And yet, it was only ink on skin. He moved his arm, and the dragon undulated as if it were about to take flight. It must have taken days to complete. The pain he must have withstood, for six or seven hours at a time, probably for three or four sessions over a month or two.

"You know, this is like a bad-boy tat." She said it half as a joke, half as a question, "and you ride a bike."

The dragon was similar to tats Chinese mob people wore. Her mother had warned her about that kind of man—motorcycle riding, inked-up men. And yet, here Lizbeth was, riding a motorcycle and about to have sex with a man wearing a tattoo that covered most of his upper back. There was a cool threat about it that sent a wave of anxious excitement through her. In spite of those signals, Curt radiated safety and calm, not danger.

Curt looked at her over his shoulder, a bemused grin on his face. "Are you done inspecting Malachi?"

"You call him Malachi? You have a *Jewish dragon* on your shoulder?"

Lizbeth's knowledge of Jewish names was limited, but she'd dated a guy named Malachi for a couple of months when she first moved to DC and knew the meaning. "*My angel*," she murmured as she traced a whisker that trailed up his neck. The dragon perched on his shoulder, like a guardian angel. Interesting.

He laughed. "The name... is complicated. I'll tell you about it later. Over dinner."

There were so many questions, but she sensed his reticence was there for a reason. She traced her way back around his body to face him and circled a freckle on his chest. Curt's back muscles flexed involuntarily under her touch, and the hardness under her fingers excited her. Inexplicably, a sudden and deep connection with Curt threatened to overcome her. She'd been in love before, but it had never overwhelmed her like this. This was primal. Instinctual. Absolute. Was this *real* with Curt? She didn't care. She'd figure that out later, too.

His lips were on hers again, his tongue spreading her mouth open with a demanding hunger. He worked his free hand between their bodies, unbuttoning her blouse by touch and let the shirt fall apart. He released one breast from her bra, tugging it over the top of the cup. The strap cut into her shoulder with the weight of it, sending an unfamiliar jolt of excitement along her spine. He unleashed her second breast.

He pinched her left nipple between his thumb and finger and drew it away from her until she gasped. He grinned as he released his grip, his eyes on her breast as it bounced back into shape. Her nipple stood out fully erect. He repeated the trick on the right breast. He kissed her lips gently, eyes meeting hers for a second, checking in.

"I'm good," she said, her voice crackling with impatience and desire.

He tapped his nose against hers and returned his full attention to her breasts. He alternated between cupping them and teasing her nipples with his thumb and pulling them taut by the nipple and letting them bounce back into shape. She thought she was going to come from this alone.

Curt's deliberate attentions were wholly new to her. They were focused. Intentional. Lizbeth's legs trembled with the effort to remain standing. His eyes met hers briefly again. Her lips parted, but she didn't say anything. She knew he would stop the second she told him to. He pressed his body against her side, one hand on her back supporting her as he unzipped her jeans and slipped his hand past her soaking panties and entered her with two fingers.

"Did you like riding on my bike today?"

His warm breath tickling gently at her neck contrasted with the strength of his fingers in her. The smell of him when she first leaned against him, the initial fear of being on the bike mingled with her bravery, set her off. She groaned as he slid his fingers out and up either side of her clit before delving back inside her. Lizbeth sucked in her breath, wanting more.

"You were terrified to get on, admit it."

"I was."

"But you were turned on, too. Weren't you? Your legs enclosing mine. Your breasts against my back… the vibrating of the engine." His voice was low and sensual as his fingers slid in and out of her slowly. "And then the ride back. You are all super-charged from being on the bike, aren't you?"

"I didn't know." It wasn't only the bike. It was him. It was his muscular warmth against her body combined with the ride. Her mouth couldn't form the words to explain all that though. She thrust against his hand, seeking even more force from his hand, hungry for the orgasm that was building and building. "I, oh my god, I can't. P-p-lease d-d-don't st-st…"

"Are you ready for another kind of ride?" He stopped short of letting her come, withdrawing his hand from her right as she reached the precipice. He held her until she could stand without support, kissing her along her neck and across her collarbone.

"Finish undressing for me." He dropped to the bed, leaning back casually onto his palms, his erection a sharp tent in his pants.

She caught her breath. Her blouse was hanging open, and her jeans were already half-way off. And, there was actually a man in her bedroom ordering her to get naked. If anyone had suggested she'd be taking orders from a man about getting naked, she would have slapped them. In any other circumstance, apparently. Right now, it was all she could do to not jump on him. Her face was warm with excited embarrassment. She wasn't a lights-out kind of woman, but she had never performed for a man like this.

She glanced down at her unbuttoned blouse and jeans around her thighs. She wanted to make this as sexy as possible, but she was pretty much half-naked already. His eyes were on her body, watching her every motion. This wasn't the exact scenario she'd planned for when she dressed this morning but it was pretty close. She had on a matching bra and panty set designed for romance. She shook her blouse off and let it slide from her arms down to the floor. It billowed around her ankles like a cloud.

She turned around and looked over her shoulder at him, smiled her best teasing smile as she shimmied her jeans over her hips. She bent over so he'd have an excellent view of her rounded ass as she peeled the jeans off the rest of her legs, stepping out of them one at a time. She stood up slowly, reaching up overhead, her long dark hair cascading down her back. She turned back to him in her creamy bra and underwear, it glowed against her tawny skin.

"Beautiful," he said.

She unhooked her bra and dropped it to the ground in front of her. The only thing left was her soaked panties. She slid her hands into the lacy rim and pushed them off in one fell swoop.

He watched her every move with an intensity Lizbeth was not used to. After her panties were on the floor, he sat upright and held out his hands to her. She hesitated as she approached him.

"Your turn to get naked," she said.

He unbuttoned and unzipped his pants in one frenzied movement, peeling the rest of his clothing off, kicking everything out of the way. His smooth golden chest and stomach free of hair. He offered her his hands again.

Taking them both for support, she straddled his thighs. His cock pressing between their bellies. She ran a finger along his ink, pausing to admire the tiny details of the magnificent dragon. Many of the scales had been left blank, but she saw now that most of them had been filled in with miniature images—plants, animals, tiny buildings. She kept going back to the little rabbit on his chest over his heart.

"You noticed my charms?"

"It's incredible. I think I get it now," Lizbeth said. She traced around the edges of the Eiffel tower, then the Taj Mahal. "Whenever you go someplace you get a tat as a charm? To commemorate it, right?'

"Yes. I had the artist leave 64 scales blank, to fill in. I don't want to cover my whole body in ink, so the blanks still give me spaces to put in special events."

Lizbeth leaned over to look at his back. Indeed, there were still about forty scales left untouched. It was going to take a while to look at each scale's tiny image. She hoped she would get to know him well enough to make a full study of it. She circled the rabbit again and did some calculations in her head. She was born in the year of the goat. That would make him five years older than she was, if she was right. "Soooooo, you are a rabbit?"

He chuckled. "Since I'm not a dragon, I decided to put the rabbit right at my heart."

She touched the empty space next to the rabbit but didn't say anything.

"And you are…?" he asked.

"I'm a goat," she said laughing and looking away.

He tilted his head thoughtfully, a slow smile spreading across his face. "You know, rabbits and goats are supposed to get along really well."

He kissed her between her breasts, up and around the outside of one, back to the center and around the other. Lizbeth giggled as his lips tickled her. He retraced his kisses in the same pattern. The giant heart shaped pattern he'd made was the same as a ram's horn.

Chinese astrology stuff was Waipo's arena. She had always told her that Lizbeth was stubborn and would need to chase after a rabbit to balance out her life.

"You don't believe all that woo-woo stuff, do you, Mr. Wu?" she said, giggling at the pun.

"I pick and choose."

Lizbeth slid her hands up his chest and over his shoulders, shifting so she hovered over him. She took her time licking and kissing him, nibbling her way down the length of his body. Lowering herself to the floor so that she could kneel between his legs, she ran her tongue along his inner thigh from his knee up to his groin. She hovered over his cock, breathing on it without touching it with her lips before continuing her journey out to his other knee.

He moaned as she teased him, propping himself up on his elbows so they could maintain eye contact.

Cupping his balls in her hand, she met his eyes. They were looking at her, but he was clearly losing focus and blissing out. She sucked his balls into her mouth one at a time, rolling them around gently. Placing her tongue flat against the base of his cock she licked it all the way to the tip like a lollipop. She paused at the tip, caught his eye and repeated the motion without looking away.

She wrapped her fingers around the base of his cock and stroked him firmly as her lips circled his tip and first four inches. She bobbed her head up and down along with her hand, her tongue swirling around the tip of his cock and pressing against the hole. Her other hand gently cupped his balls. He tensed and she stopped abruptly, breaking the flow and releasing him before he could come.

"What the...?" His eyes flashed and narrowed and widened. And then he laughed.

She looked up at him from her kneeling position on the floor. "Tit for tat, baby."

He fell back on the bed laughing, his cock rigid, red and ready.

Lizbeth opened the drawer on her bedside table and dipped her fingers in the box of condoms she kept there. *Empty.* "Damn." Lizbeth dug into Curt's pants and handed him his wallet. "Please have a condom in here..."

"Ever prepared," he said. He pulled out a trio of condoms and let them dangle between two fingertips.

She ripped one off and gave it a quick inspection, tossing the other two on the bedside table.

"Can you come during intercourse?" he asked.

Another surprise—Curt was a man who didn't

assume sticking his dick inside her would result in instant orgasm. Liz had never orgasmed with a man on top and usually came only during foreplay. The only time she could come with a man inside of her was if she were on top, controlling all the motion.

"I'm one of the lucky ones, but it's almost guaranteed if I'm on top." She rolled the condom down the length of his cock, it stretching tight, barely big enough. She guided him into her lowering herself onto him inch by inch. She adjusted to the fullness of him, resting with him inside her for a moment before finding a rhythm—steady but slow, so that her clit connected with him on every stroke.

Curt held her lightly at the hips, letting her take full control of the motion—his hands there for balance should she need it. The motorcycle rides, their hot kisses, and his teasing earlier had primed her for an easy orgasm, but she didn't want to come yet, she wanted this feeling to last as long as it could.

Curt clenched his jaw. She could tell he was holding back. Lizbeth increased the speed, wanting to make him come all the while wanting to make this last as long as possible. To tease him as much as he had teased her. She changed her pace when she got close to coming, forcing herself to wait a little longer, lifting herself as high as she could and lowering herself a quarter inch at a time until he was buried deep inside her.

Suddenly, she hit the point of no return, surprising herself. She came hard, her pussy clutching at his cock inside her. Every inch of her tingled.

She leaned into his arms, continuing to rock the orgasm as it hit her in several solid waves. They flooded through her from head to toe before receding into a pulsing pleasure. She buckled toward his chest as she lost control of her body, crying out in ecstasy. He caught her, holding her so he could see her face. She met his eyes and he locked onto hers.

He pulled her toward his chest and stroked her back as she continued to gyrate slowly around his cock, savoring the waning orgasm. It was as if she had gone somewhere else entirely, but was connected to him in a way she had never experienced.

"You're beautiful when you come," he said, holding her tight. She didn't want to let him leave her —to never lose this amazing connection between them.

After a few moments, she realized he was still hard inside her. "You didn't come."

"Not yet. I wanted to make sure you got what you needed first." He cupped her bottom, running a finger between her cleft. "You ready for me to take my turn?"

"Okay, I'm ready." She wanted to revel in feeling

him still inside her, to stay attached to him like this for hours.

Suddenly, she was on her back and he was on top of her. He'd managed flipping her over without pulling out. A devilish look came over him, and he withdrew from her, kissing her lips gently before licking his way down to her still throbbing pussy. She thought she might die if he went down on her, and pulled at his hair, urging him back up.

He laughed into her pussy, insistent on doing things his way now. His warm, wet tongue against her pulsing lips sent new shivers of desire through her. Was this a new orgasm? Or had the previous one even ended? She bucked her hips at his face as his tongue lashed at her clit.

The intensity of it was almost painful. She grabbed the pillow at the head of the bed and shoved it over her face and screamed.

Curt pulled the pillow away. "I want to hear you scream when you come." He spread her legs wide and rose up to his knees between them, his cock just an inch from her hungry, drenched pussy. "Ask me to fuck you."

All she wanted was to feel him inside her again. "Fuck me, Curt."

"How?"

Wasn't it obvious? She thrust her hips upward,

reaching for his hovering cock. "Hard. Hard and fast. Curt, fuck me like there is no tomorrow."

He thrust into her.

"Deeper. I won't break."

He took her at her word and rammed into her, his balls slapping against her ass.

"Harder. Curt. Faster."

The headboard hit the wall, wood against plaster, thumping, thumping, thumping.

She dug her nails into his skin. "I'm going to come again."

He shifted so that every time he moved, his cock grazed against her clit. He was thick and heavy with her juices, sliding in and out with ease.

And then, a new wave crashed down on her, sending her hips up against him as she cried out. "I'm coming. Oh my God. I'm coming again."

He bucked against her. "Me, too. Oh, Lizbeth."

After slowing to a stop, he stayed inside her, hovering over her with a deep look of concentration on his face. Finally, he pulled out and gazed down her body. He traced his fingers around a breast and then made a pattern on her stomach. He sighed with contentment, shuffling in close and turning her to the side, so he could spoon her from behind. He laughed against the back of her neck. The vibrations tickled and she shivered against him.

"Hey," she said, "don't you dare go to sleep. I'm hungry."

He had promised her drinks and dinner *after*. Besides, she wanted to know how a Chinese guy working for the State Department had ended up with a mob-style tattoo he called Malachi on his back.

"Up and at 'em, Mr. Wu."

Chapter 8

They dressed, keeping their eyes on each other with the intensity of new lovers. Every time she looked at his tattoo, some new detail popped out. It was almost like reading a personal journal all in code.

They'd get on a piece of clothing, kiss, add another layer, kiss again. Lizbeth sensed the beginning of something big with him—a deep familiarity and ease had settled over them in mere hours.

They walked arm in arm through her neighborhood, the cool evening air whisking away any traces of post-sex lethargy she might have had.

"The houses here remind me of home," he said.

The row-houses were built up close to each other making it hard to tell where one ended and the next began. If it weren't for the individual paint colors, they would all meld into one homogenous block. Most had knee high fences in front of a postage-size front yard that was not usually much more than the walkway to the front door surrounded by potted plants. None had room for grass, and their owners probably didn't have time to care for one.

"Mine too, a little bit anyway. We moved to Richmond when my dad got out of the Navy. It seemed so upscale compared to Chinatown. It was like moving to another country, in some ways, even though it's only a few miles away."

Curt let out a snort of delight. "No, way... We were in Inner Sunset."

"I used to jog in Golden Gate park all the time," she said.

"This is so cool. I can't believe we grew up within a couple miles of each other. I bet we jogged past each other."

"I'm pretty sure I would have noticed you, if I'd ever seen you."

Curt snorted. "I was a pretty scrawny little looking teenager. You'd have run right past me without a second glance."

The familiar place names made Lizbeth a little homesick and comforted her at the same time. New immigrants often started out in Chinatown before making enough money to move to the other San Francisco neighborhoods.

"My dad made the move when he was young, before he got married. But he kept his shop in Chinatown," Curt said. "That's how he met my mom. She'd arrived in the States a couple of years before she started working for him."

Lizbeth put the numbers together in her head. Curt was about her age, so his mom was probably born in the sixties. "Wait a second. That means your mom came over in... what, the eighties?"

"Yeah. She was orphaned at nine and given to a family in a small village somewhere in Guangdong province. She doesn't talk about it much, but there was some program when she was a teenager that allowed her to get into University. She managed to get a student visa to get to the U.S. She refused to go back."

Lizbeth's stomach flipped as she ran through all the dates, comparing them with the history. You couldn't become a policy specialist in China without knowing their history pretty damn well. She stopped in her tracks, placing a hand on Curt's forearm, her eyes wide. "Oh, my God. Curt, were your grandparents killed in the revolution?"

Placing his free hand over hers and squeezing it, his slow, sad smile made her want to hug him. He patted her hand, dismissing it as he turned them back into their walk. "So few people can put two and two together, Liz. They were both university professors. My mother never forgot them. She fed on her memories to get herself out of China."

Lizbeth wanted to know more. She hoped she'd get to hear the rest of Curt's mother's journey. If she had grown up during the cultural revolution in China, she must have an amazing story.

Before she could push Curt for more details, he asked, "So, where were you before Richmond? Chinatown proper?"

"Yep. We lived with Waipo in a third-floor walkup above a noodle shop. I loved it. Anytime I smell scallions, I feel like I'm at home again."

Lizbeth stopped abruptly, pulling Curt to a halt next to her. It was a little disappointing that they'd arrived at the hole-in-the-wall Italian place she'd chosen. She would have liked to continue this conversation, but their conversation had already shifted. *Later.*

The restaurant sign was hand-painted and weathered. The front of the was dilapidated and looked as if it might be closed for good. A small white scrap of cardboard leaned against the front window said *aperto* in faded black marker.

"You're sure about this place?" Curt asked, his left eyebrow arching in question.

"Trust me, this is *the* place for Italian."

She pushed the door open and led him through to the hostess podium. The furnishings were old, but the wood was buffed and the brass adornments gleamed. A soft background music played at a low level, enough to give diners their privacy.

She tilted her head toward a corner where a senator and a woman not his wife leaned in close over the table. "A lot of people come here because Georgio has a very low-profile establishment."

"So, what happens in Georgio's stays in Georgio's?" he asked.

The hostess beamed at Lizbeth. "It's so good to see you again, Ms. Crandall." She led them to a table near the back. The closest table was occupied by someone who was possibly a famous singer, but she wasn't sure.

She wanted to know more about Curt's past, specifically Malachi, but he'd pretty much shut her down on the details for now. She focused on the menu to get her bearings again. The gnocchi was hands-down her favorite. The waitress frowned when they said no to wine with their dinner order as if it was a personal affront.

Liz tried not to stare across the table at Curt and fiddled with the salt shaker. It was kind of backward asking a man you'd already had sex with about his history. She usually knew the most basic things about a man before she let him get that close.

"So," she said after the waitress had left them. "You, me... Berkeley? And Kennedy. Plus growing up within a mile of each other. I'm finding the similarities pretty cool. A little weird, but cool."

"It is interesting." Taking her hand in his and squeezing it. "I bet there are more things in common than that."

"Okay, let's see if we can find them."

They went through their list of common school acquaintances, and realized both had been mentored by the same professor through their senior projects, but five years apart.

"I loved Professor Wilkins," she said, still unable to refer to him by his first name even after all these years. "He was the one who pushed me toward graduate work at Kennedy. If it weren't for him, I'd probably have gone into a whole different career."

"What I liked most about him was his inability to lie," Curt said. "He was straight as an arrow and as principled as anyone I ever knew."

"I take it you don't like games."

Curt's jaw clenched, making it firm and more angular. "I don't have time for them."

Lizbeth smiled in appreciation, remembering the elaborate game her office mates came up. She opened her mouth, about to tell him, but decided not to. Even if she refused to play, she'd keep the secret as promised. "People in Washington love their games. Why are you here? You must hate it."

"I like doing what I'm doing. What's your long-term goal? It doesn't make sense that you would tie yourself to one person's coattails for a whole career."

"Congressman Pierce is one of the best," she said, defending her boss. After working closely with him for so long, she knew he had the integrity to make it all the way to the presidency.

"You're limiting yourself by staying."

"It's not forever. This assignment will open all sorts of doors for me," she said. She leaned forward and dropped her voice. "What I'd really like is to work at the Embassy in China."

"You want to be on the Embassy staff? That doesn't seem... hmmm... very ambitious."

"Did I say I wanted to be a staffer?"

"Ah. But it's not particularly humble to admit you'd like to hold a high-level Embassy position."

"Being humble isn't a job requirement. I'm getting the right experience and working my way there." Lizbeth paused, considering if she should say anything and decided to go ahead and broach the whole subject of the Foreign Service. Maybe he'd offer to give her a leg up. "I've already started the application process to the Foreign Service. Man, navigating that whole thing is tricky."

He didn't bite. "You know half the people at an Embassy are CIA, right?" he asked, narrowing his eyes. "You're not *already* CIA, are you?"

"No." There was a persistent rumor about a lot of the CIA jobs being clerical staff at embassies. It made sense, but it stung a little that he'd ignored what she thought was an obvious play for help on her part. "I'm not CIA."

"You should apply. Guaranteed to get you to China with your language skills, you know."

She laughed off the suggestion as images of cloak and dagger movie moments popped up in her mind. She had a hard time getting on his motorcycle without worrying about safety issues. There would be a whole lot more to being a CIA agent than being able to speak several Chinese dialects.

The waitress brought them their main entrees. They ate without talking for a few minutes, savoring the first few hot bites of their food. It was normally awkward when there was no conversation, but this was different. The silence with Curt was companionable. It was comfortable. *Contented.*

"So, you grew up in a household speaking Chinese, right?" she asked, wanting to get more from him.

He nodded. "My father was fourth generation, but

the first to move out of Chinatown. What about you? You speak like a native."

"Waipo basically raised me. My mother worked all the time I was growing up, and my dad was out to sea, on and off, until I was twelve. Career Navy." She sucked her lip in between her teeth, sighed and added, "My dad is white."

Curt's lips twitched at the corners, and he nodded as if he knew that already. White people thought she looked Chinese. Chinese people thought she looked white. Her comfort zone had been firmly Chinese for a long time, but she could pass for white when she wanted to.

"Your mom didn't want to move with your dad's postings?"

"No. She wanted us to live with Waipo, to give us some stability."

"Doesn't sound like..." he paused.

"Much of a marriage?" she finished. "They made it work, I guess. After Dad retired from the Navy, he got a job as a facilities manager at the park. They've been together ever since."

"Siblings?" he asked.

"Nope. I'm an only. I wanted one though. So bad. But my dad was never home long enough, I guess. You?"

"Three sisters. They all live close to home. Two

are married. My youngest sister and I are annoying my mom by not settling down."

What would his Chinese mama say about a half-white, half-Chinese girl going after her only son? Liz pushed the worry aside—this was America, anything was possible.

After sharing a helping of tiramisu heavily laden with cognac, they ambled their way through the neighborhood back to her brownstone, their fingers intertwined and arms swinging gently between them. They paused on the sidewalk in front of her house. He looked over at his motorcycle and then at her front door. Was he waiting for an official invitation?

"I don't want to go home," he said.

ithout hesitation, Lizbeth led Curt through her front door. The cats jumped from their lazy perches on the sofa to rub up against their legs. They sniffed at Curt's shoes with typical curiosity.

"How do you tell them apart? They look like triplets."

"It's easy once you get to know them," she said. She held them up one at a time for an introduction, pointing out the variations in the patterns of their striped coats.

Curt scratched each one's ears as they were introduced, repeating their names. "Pepper. Cinnamon. Ginger. I take it you like things spicy in your life."

"My cats *and* my men." She was thinking of Curt's

scent as she stumbled into him on the motorcycle earlier.

"Men?" He asked, teasing. "I'm not sure I like the plural in that."

"Keep doing what you're doing and it'll be singular," she said, surprising herself. What a promise to make after barely more than twenty-four hours. She dropped onto the sofa and patted the seat next to her. "I feel like this Dragon tattoo story is important. Out with it."

He looked around the room from where he stood, examining her walls and bookshelves, as if he was weighing her worthiness to continue, or perhaps looking for a way out. He ran his fingers along a row of books. She couldn't tell if he was reading the titles or checking for dust. Either way, she hoped he wasn't disappointed. After an excruciatingly long moment, he acquiesced and sat down next to her, then paused and shifted so he was lying sideways with his head in her lap.

She massaged his neck. Pepper jumped on top of Curt and spread himself along his upper leg and tummy. A rumbling purr filled the silence between them. The cat's ability to sense apprehension was uncanny. Suddenly, she wasn't sure if she wanted to know what Curt was about to tell her.

Curt buried a hand in Pepper's thick fur. The cat's

rumbling purr increased and seemed to spur Curt to speak.

"When I was ten, a new kid moved into the neighborhood."

Lizbeth could picture Curt's general neighborhood pretty well. Inner Sunset was a lot like Richmond and both areas were densely packed housing. Both areas were heavily Chinese, but loads of other nationalities had found their homes there as well. A Mexican taco shop adjacent to a Chinese dim sum joint with a Vietnamese pho restaurant was not at all unusual.

"His name was Malachi. He was this short half-Chinese, half-Jewish kid. His dad had died in the first Gulf war so his mom had moved in with his grandmother. Kinda like you."

Lizbeth could relate to this kid already. Not the Jewish part so much, but the half-Chinese half-white and the grandmother part.

"He didn't really fit in anywhere. Our neighborhood was very heavy Chinese. He spoke Yiddish and English, but no Chinese. Everyone on our block spoke Mandarin or Taishanese depending, but mostly Taishanese."

Like him and the majority of Chinese in San Francisco, she'd grown up with Taishanese spoken in the home. It was like the comfort-food of dialects. Curt switched between English, Mandarin, and Taishanese with a fluid ease. But when he spoke Taishanese, his voice was more relaxed, and he breathed easier.

"Malachi became the easiest of bully bait in school. I kind of ignored him at first, but it was pretty apparent the kid was super smart and really funny." Pepper curled around Curt's hand, his tail looping around over the top of his face, encouraging Curt to knead his belly."I had to punch a couple of bullies to get them off Malachi's back. After that, they basically left him alone. By the time we were getting ready to graduate from high school, we were inseparable. We were both heading to Berkeley. We were planning our future there together. Same frat. Similar majors."

The tone in Curt's voice changed, became tighter. There was no mistaking the change in tense. *We were...* Something had happened to change all their plans. Liz held her breath waiting for the real explanation for the tattoo. No one got that much ink for their best friend unless something terrible had happened.

"I'd always been getting pressure from the local gangs, but I'd managed to avoid them. They wanted me to run drugs up to school in the fall. They found my weak spot, but I refused to cave."

"Malachi?" Lizbeth whispered.

Curt nodded quickly and closed his eyes. "They caught him as he came out of his job, late at night. They grabbed me at the same time. They started by torturing him, but I swear, I thought they'd give up when I didn't give in to their demands. Malachi had gotten stronger over the years. He was fit. I figured he could take a lot... more than he could." Curt's voice was strained. He was speaking English again. "I was naïve, certain I could wrangle my way out, but they killed him. I was responsible for his death as much as anyone."

"So you got the tattoo? As a memorial of sorts?"

Curt breathed in deeply. "No. That came later."

Curt was dressed, but she knew the lines of the dragon without seeing them. She put her hand on his shoulder where the dragon rested and squeezed, telling him she was there, waiting, ready to listen.

"To the world, Malachi had disappeared. Poof. I knew where they had left his body, but they had told me my sisters were next. How they'd rape them and put it on video before torturing them like Malachi if I didn't comply. I did what they wanted. I became their connection at Berkeley to protect my sisters. I didn't know what else to do. I was powerless against them."

Lizbeth sucked in her breath. Curt had dealt drugs? Against his will, sure, but still. How the hell did he pass his background check for the Foreign Service? Maybe he never got caught?

"I spent three years dealing their drugs, but I never forgot Malachi. I never forgot their threats to my sisters. I pretended to buy into it all. I got the tattoo as part of my pledge to them. Everyone in that gang had to have a dragon on their body somewhere. Some went for tiny little things, something they could hide from the police. But, I went for this instead. I called him Malachi for my own personal sanity. Every day, I'd look at it in the mirror and pledge to make amends, somehow."

Lizbeth had plenty of questions, but she waited for him to finish.

"My last year in college, I went to the police. I told them everything I knew and got a promise of immunity for all the drugs if I helped take down the gang."

"You turned on them."

Curt shuddered. "I was never theirs in the first place. Even as Malachi bled out in front of me, I was planning my revenge. They handed me the opportunity by trusting me after three years. They got lax. They moved me up in the chain of things. It's like they thought Malachi meant nothing to me. They forgot him, but I never did."

"And now you have him... the angel dragon... riding with you forever," she said. "You found justice for your friend in the end, right? Did the gang go down?"

"Most of them," Curt said. "Some of them died

during a huge final confrontation. Some of them went to jail. A couple got away."

"Would they come after you? Are your sisters safe now?"

"I was one that 'escaped' the shoot-out. There were plenty of witnesses to verify the police were shooting at me. It was part of the deal. To help me get out and not have to worry about them tying up loose ends. I moved away for grad school. To Kennedy. Moved on with life."

"What about Malachi's body? Did you ever tell his mother what happened to him?"

"Yes. She would never speak to me again. I tried to tell her what had happened, but she blamed me for her son's death. She still refuses to have anything to do with me."

Lizbeth sensed a lurking darkness within Curt. "You learned to ride motorcycles with them, didn't you?"

Curt tilted his head, a smile playing at his lips. "Admit it, Liz. You like it. It's pretty fun, don't you think?"

Pepper sensed a change in emotion and jumped off Curt. He sat up and stretched, reaching a hand out to Lizbeth. "Time for some sleep?" He was worn out from telling his story. "Do you hate me now?"

How could she possibly hate him? "For being

forced to sell drugs? No. You did what you had to do. You found justice for your friend. That's more than a lot of people would do."

Curt grasped her hands and kissed them both. "I want to hold you in my arms all night long."

She led him back up the stairs and into her bedroom. This time, they undressed quietly. Almost shyly. Malachi was less formidable, less scary to her. It was a fierce, protective dragon now.

As they climbed into bed together, Curt wrapped his arms around her, bringing her in close against him.

"I need to feel your skin against mine tonight, feel your heart beating close to mine," he said, his breath a gentle whisper against her neck.

"I'm right here." She wrapped her arms around him, entwined her legs with his so that every part of her was touching some part of him, flesh against warm flesh as they fell into a cozy slumber together.

Chapter 10

*L*izbeth carefully raised herself on an elbow so she could look over Curt's sleeping frame and get a look at her alarm clock. She'd completely forgotten to set it as they climbed into bed the night before. It was six twenty-five. Her body was stiff from the adrenaline and excitement of the day before. She needed to stretch and move to loosen up. A group of cute old people met in the park across the street for tai chi. If she hurried, she could make it on time. She backed away from Curt, inching her way to the other side of the bed to keep from waking him. She wrote him a quick note, letting him know she'd be back in about an hour and placed it on her pillow. Part of her wanted to slip back into bed and wake him up with new kisses.

She was dressed and ready to slip out of the room

when he sat up, startling her. "Where are you going? You can't sneak out of your own place." He wiped at his eyes. "That's supposed to be my job."

"Sorry. I'm running to the park to get some exercise. I thought I'd let you sleep."

He leaned against the pillows and looked around the room. He had been wearing a suit the day before, even on his motorcycle. "I don't suppose you have some sweats that would work for me? I could join you."

She tilted her head to one side. She had a drawer of odds and ends left by previous boyfriends. Surely some of them would fit him. Did she want to explain where they had come from or why she had them, though? She'd see what he had to say.

"I was going to do tai chi."

"Hurry up. I'm guessing it starts in a few minutes?"

Lizbeth had never had a guy ask to join her. It would be interesting. Maybe even fun. She pulled a pair of sweats and a Caps jersey out of her bottom drawer. She tossed them at him, a dare. How much was he going to pry? Shoes might be an issue.

He slid the jersey on over his head and swung his feet off the opposite side of the bed. She got the barest glimpse of his sweet naked ass as he pulled the sweats up and over.

"Commando style?"

"I don't want to get my underwear sweaty, and I sure as hell am not going to borrow one of your many men's underwear." He was obviously kidding, but the truth stung a bit.

"Ohh. Was that supposed to hurt?" she smiled back, not willing to let him get her so early in the morning.

The jersey was a quarter sleeve and fit him well enough. He was stocky for his height, without an ounce of fat on him. Curt looked down at his legs. "Well, I take it your last boyfriend was taller than I am."

The sweats had an elastic band around the ankles, so they didn't slip down over his feet, but they did pool around his ankles, several inches too long. She thought they must have belonged to a guy named Mike she dated the previous fall. She wasn't entirely sure.

"What size shoe do you wear?"

He wiggled his toes. "Probably the same as yours."

Interesting. He wasn't a man afraid of little things like a wearing a pair of women's sandals. She fished through her closet and found a pair of tired-looking canvas slip-ons that would protect his feet on the way to the park. Tai chi was done barefoot, so they wouldn't have to do more than that. As it was, they were a little small for him and she gave him permission to squash the heel down.

They made their way to the park a few blocks from her home, early joggers passing them by. The tai chi group was small, but loyal. They weren't particularly talkative and a few of them spoke dialects she didn't recognize. She'd never said more than a quiet hello in Mandarin to those nearest her. Usually, people gathered and did their own quiet stretches until Sifu, the old man who led the class, showed up.

Curt grinned broadly and greeted Sifu in formal Mandarin. The old man's face little up and crinkled with animation. He glanced back and forth between them. Lizbeth had never brought anyone to class before.

Sifu called the class to order and they began their exercises. By the second form, Lizbeth was beginning to sweat. The morning was unseasonably warm for this time of day. She glanced over at Curt as he was ripping the jersey off over his head. With the next move, his muscles made the scales of his dragon undulate and shift like it was about to take off and fly. One of the older women raised her eyebrows a tiny bit as Curt stripped off his shirt, but Lizbeth couldn't tell if it was in disapproval or merriment.

He was the only guy there without a shirt on, and it was very distracting. His muscles were refined, compact in a way that came from plenty of exercise without the bulginess formed in weight lifting.

It was obvious that Curt was well versed in tai chi. He followed the moves with ease though he kept his eyes on other people. They were moving through a movement called *fan through the back* when Curt's hips snapped into place, rather than rotating smoothly and slowly.

She recognized that hippy snap for what it was—karate. Curt had said the night before he'd punched some kids to keep them away from his friend. He probably had done some form of martial art while in school. In San Francisco, all the kids took some form of martial art. It was almost a bad stereotype. At the end of practice Curt thanked Sifu for letting him join them, bowing formally.

Sifu bowed back, giving Lizbeth an approving grin and wink over Curt's bowed head. She'd begun to consider Sifu as extended family, and his approval made her feel warm all over.

Lizbeth took Curt the long way home to stop at the coffee shop. She was always hungry after tai chi and had no food in her fridge. At seven forty-five, there was no chance that Bella would be at the park across the school. Drop off was at eight thirty. At the counter, she talked him into a waffle along with his black coffee, and led him to her usual spot at the counter window.

Children were already being dropped off for school? She frantically scanned the playground across the street looking for Bella or her parents. When did they usually drop Bella off? The last thing she wanted was for them to see her here. They'd think she was looking for Bella when she actually wasn't. She relaxed a little when she didn't see them.

"What's the matter? You seem tense?" said Curt. He was half-way done with his waffle.

"I'm thinking of ways to burn off these extra calories," she said with a flirty smile and touched his hip. "What do you normally practice?"

"Me? Nothing, why?" Curt looked at her sideways.

"You caught on way too fast for someone who's never done tai chi before. Besides, you snapped your hips like an old karate-ka."

"Maybe I watch a lot of Jackie Chan movies," he said, shoving the last bite of his waffle into his mouth.

"Right," she said. What harm would there be to admitting he'd practiced karate before? And yet, here they were. Straight forward and then both of them—evading each other. She wanted an answer, but as she was about to ask him, she saw Bella swinging gaily between her father and mother. She instinctively pulled back from the window, afraid they might see her. They swooped their arms upward to help her get some air. All three of them laughing, a happy family.

"There's something wrong. What is it, Lizbeth?" his stance turned protective, as if he was about to kick some ass, ready to defend her.

This was not the place to tell Curt about Bella. It was too public. "I'm okay. There *is* something really important in my life that I want to share with you, but I... I can't. I'm not ready yet and this isn't the time or place."

He leaned forward and kissed her gently. "You know my story. I hope you'll tell me yours soon."

"Soon, but not now. I need to go home and get ready for work, okay?"

It was hard to miss the obvious hurt he was feeling at her lack of willingness to share. He wanted to know about her as much as she had wanted to know about him. As they left the waffle shop, she snuck a glance at the playground. Angela and Demarco were nowhere to be seen, but Bella was there, her hands linked with another little girl as they whirled around in circles, their faces turned upward into the bright spring sun and laughing.

She turned away from the playground and snuggled close against Curt. A shiver ran across her and the hair on her arms and neck prickled. She didn't dare turn back to look at Bella now, but she was sure *something* was wrong.

BACK AT HOME, Lizbeth closed her eyes and centered herself. It was too early in the day to feel so out of control. Half of her wanted him to stay and half of her wanted him to go so she could regain her sense of self. The cats zoomed out of the kitchen when she opened the door, mewing loudly at her for forgetting to feed them before going off to tai chi.

Curt dropped to his haunches, petting them gently. "Okay, kitties. Pepper... Ginger... Cinnamon... Looks like you need some food, eh." He named each of them as he touched them, and he got all three of their names right.

"I don't know what the ruckus is about," she said. "It's not like this is much later than when they usually get food." Lizbeth led him into the kitchen and opened a can of cat food. Usually she was alone during the cat feeding routine.

As soon as the bowls were on the floor, they were in each other's arms again. His lips were sweet from the waffle. His warm arms around her comforting and natural, as if they'd been holding each other for ever. Like they *belonged* around her. The dragon protecting his own.

He broke the kiss and leaned his forehead against hers. "I need to head home. Shower. Get a change of clothes. I have a busy day, but am hoping we can go out again tonight?"

"We have the whole weekend," she said.

"Oh. Okay. You probably had plans tonight anyway."

"That's *not* what I meant. It's your last free night before all the Chinese delegation events. You want to spend it *with me*?"

Curt sighed, and cupped her chin, so he could look into her eyes. "I want to spend every night with you, Miss Crandall."

If Lizbeth were prone to swooning, she would have. She had no idea how to respond to that kind of romantic statement with words so she kissed him again to avoid saying the wrong thing. After one date—one amazing, unbelievable, long date—she was terrified to believe what her heart was telling her.

He gathered up his suit into a roll under his arm. "I'll wash these sweats and get them back to you."

"Oh. Don't bother. I'm not even sure who they belonged to..." She immediately regretted how it came across. A brief shadow that crossed over his face. A little jealousy? Concern? Hard to tell. Ugh. If only she could take that last sentence back, make it disappear.

"Great. I'll put them in the charity bag."

He kissed her on the tip of her nose as he slid his helmet on. "Wear slacks, or bring another change of clothes," he said. "I'll pick you up at your office at five thirty."

Liz hurried back to her room and flipped through her closet only to realize she didn't own any slacks or pants that would work in the office—something else her mother had drilled into her about professional attire. She wore either dresses and skirts to work, never pants. She had considered mixing it up lately—after all, if a presidential candidate could rock a pantsuit, why couldn't she? If she was going to spend much time on Curt's motorcycle, she'd have to change her wardrobe. It wasn't as if other women in her position always wore dresses anymore.

Jeans and sweatpants were for play, and she had plenty of those. She tucked a pair of boot cut jeans and a seductive top into a bag along with a pair of really cute brown ankle boots. Maybe she'd buy a leather jacket if things worked out with Curt. Isn't that what people wore on motorcycles?

Everything her mother had taught her about motorcycles and the men who ride them warred with her new-found experience. Nothing was all good or all bad. She was seeing the good in this for the first time. They did get through traffic a lot faster than a car as he zipped between packed-in cars. *Who was she kidding?* Traffic was not the reason she was enjoying her rides with Curt. It was about pressing against his back, holding onto him, the tight connection.

Lizbeth had just enough time to run through the mail that was piling up on her desk. She normally did mail on Saturdays, but she'd be gone this weekend. A large, sturdy enveloped marked "Do Not Bend" from her mother made her grin. In this day and age when everything was digital, her mom still had prints made of photos. She slit the envelope open carefully and slid out several pictures.

They had been taken at Yosemite during a family reunion two months before. It had been a glorious bright day, but still brisk. The first photo was of the three of them. They were so dorky in a cute, loving way. Her mother had purchased them matching sweaters. Liz stood in the middle behind them, her arms over their shoulders. She had her father's round eyes and long nose. She thought maybe her few freckles must come from him, too. She had her mother's luxurious black hair, eyebrows, and cupid lips. She shuffled the photos of her to the back, ignoring them for the time being.

There was a large 8" x 10" of the whole Crandall family. Her father's parents were there with her three uncles, their wives, and her seven cousins. She was the oldest of the cousins, the youngest being eight—a year younger than Bella. She put the large group photo and the one of her with her parents back in the envelope and slipped it inside her bag to take to work.

She should call her mom to thank her, but she didn't feel like talking to her yet. The conversations always turned to her dating life. She hated lying to her mom, and there was no way she wanted to talk to her about Curt. The first thing her mother would do is look into his family in San Francisco. She'd be delighted that she was dating a Chinese man, a rare thing for Liz, but that entailed a level of connection Liz didn't want made quite yet. Could she technically call it dating? It'd only been a day. What if things didn't work out between them? Her mother would be even more disappointed in her than usual.

Once she got to work, Lizbeth put the photos her mom had sent up on her wall and ended up re-arranging everything on her cubicle. Instead of calling her mom, she snapped a photo of the new arrangement and sent that with a brief note via text. Her mom would text back telling her to call.

Focusing on anything work related was almost impossible. It was hard to care about social protocols when she could be thinking about Mr. Gorgeous. *Smart. Karate-man. Mysterious. Protective. Chinese.* And, he knew her cat's names after only one introduc-tion. Admonishing herself for going all romantic and gooey, Lizbeth forced herself into work mode.

She put on her noise canceling headphones, prioritized everything on her to-do list and delved into the most important task at hand. She had a thirty-minute meeting scheduled with Madeline to discuss the press release and then the rest of the morning to finish any remaining tasks. A clear desk before Thursday at noon would let her focus completely on the Chinese event without any niggling work bits being left undone.

She was finishing up a report unrelated to the Chinese gathering when a new IM from Curt dinged on her private browser. She looked over her shoulder to see who was around. The office was pretty quiet. The only person within sight was Opal, and she was leaning in close to her screen and very focused on what she was doing. Lizbeth clicked on the IM.

C: *Hey, huáli. How's your day so far?*

Lizbeth wasn't used to being called gorgeous in Chinese. It was sweet coming from him.

L: *Why didn't you text?*

C: *IM is faster*

L: *True. But, now your words are on a giant monitor anyone walking behind me can see. I can't hide this in the palm of my hand like my phone.*

C: *I like how you think.*

She had always been a detail-oriented person. It was odd that Curt picked up on it. Most men didn't.

L: *I'm practical.*

C: Miss Crandall, are you suggesting I would send you anything inappropriate at work?

L: I was hoping you would send me something entirely inappropriate. But to my phone, not to my big old monitor.

C: Be glad I'm not a creeper who sends random dick pics.

Lizbeth wanted to throw herself over the monitor to hide the mention of dick pics. She minimized the window until it was barely visible in the lower left-hand corner. No one was watching her, but she didn't want anyone to sneak up on her and see this conversation.

L: I definitely like my dicks better in person.

C: I'll make a note of that.

Lizbeth wondered if spyware was recording their silliness. She had her IM on a private browser, but still. It would be embarassing if anyone else ever saw this conversation—even if it was basically innocent. They weren't discussing state secrets or business. She'd delete the conversation and unisntall that browser. Would that be enough?

She lulled herself into a sense of happy contentment. She would get through this day and have another evening with Curt before the big event. If last night's sex was any indication...

L: Just delete this entire conversation when we're done, okay?

C: LOL. This never happened. BTW, I forgot to ask, but I am assuming you just switched my name out for Michael's on the reservation at the hotel?

L: You assume correctly.

C: Try to get us rooms with a connecting door between them? If that's okay with you.

She looked over her shoulder several times before they ended their little chat. Fortunately, no one was paying any attention to her.

L: It's more than okay with me, but I didn't want to make assumptions.

C: Please do. I meant what I said this morning.

L: I believe you.

C: Gotta go. See you in a few hours. XOXO

She closed down the screen and repeated his words from earlier in her head over and over. *I want to spend every night with you, Lizbeth Crandall.*

The certainty in his words made the whole world brighter. It was all moving so fast, could she trust him? She could trust him enough to tell him about Bella. That wouldn't scare him away. There was so much they had in common—things they could talk about— college, his job, his family, being Chinese. Maybe dating all those other guys over the last few years had given her clarity on what she wanted. An inner peace flooded her as she returned to work, able to focus on what she needed to finish before her date with Curt.

THE ALL-STAFF MEETING was short and sweet. Carleen kept those running smoothly. Liz checked in with the staffers who would take her work for the next couple of days. And then she had lunch with Katherine to review personnel backgrounds she'd ordered for the other important set of hearings.

As they entered the office, Kat nearly tripped over a tall guy dressed in a black overcoat coming out. His twin stood resolutely next to him, only glancing down at the women. They weren't twins, really; one had brown hair, the other black. But otherwise, they dressed alike and wore the same serious expressions. Lizbeth pegged them as secret service types and vaguely wondered what the congressman was up to. She was supposed to be looped into anything involving the intel committee.

At her desk, Lizbeth busied herself with some more paperwork, telling herself Link had always included her in things in a timely manner, and he would do so as needed. There was always plenty of paperwork to do, mind-numbing, boring, easy to do work that required little brain power.

In mid-afternoon, she needed a pick me up and wandered into the break room. She found a selection of half-moon pies Cheyenne had baked in the fridge. Someone had even put on a fresh-brewed pot of coffee. She returned to her desk with two of the treats and a fresh cup of coffee ready to tackle the last few items on her list.

The protocol director for the Chinese Embassy called with some new information about the delegates and their spouses. One of the delegates was having an affair with the wife of another official, and the four of them—the two ministers and their wives—were not getting along. Small wonder. They wanted to ensure that none of them sat at the same table.

Lizbeth assured him it wouldn't be a problem. As soon as she got off the phone, she opened up her seating chart application. The people he'd called about were seated right next to each other. Fortunately, Eleanor's seating program made this kind of problem go away with a few clicks.

Logistics work had its place. She sighed. It was interesting, for a while, but Lizbeth wanted policy work. Diplomacy. Something bigger. Wasn't that kind of what had brought her to DC in the first place? Hadn't she told herself it was merely a coincidence that Bella was in DC? Her internship with the NGO in China had taught her she wanted to be involved in higher level decision making. She'd been grateful for her time working on a small collective and learning about sustainable agriculture. She was also grateful for the opportunities at the Congressman's office, but they were stepping stones to the field she wanted to pursue.

Carleen's smooth-smoky voice cut into her thoughts. "Lizbeth, Congressman Pierce would like a moment with you. Alone."

Lizbeth's stomach did a quick somersault. The Congressman didn't usually call for individual meetings. She didn't know why, but she had a feeling she'd be finding out why the suits had been here. "Am I in trouble?"

Carleen cocked her head to one side, giving her a curious look. "Should you be?"

If the congressman had somehow learned about the BINGO game, she would certainly be in deep shit, even if she wasn't playing she *was* keeping mum about it. She was guilty of complicity at least. But no, she wouldn't be the first to go in for the chopping block if it were about the BINGO game. Others would already have been there and the office wouldn't be so calm.

This had to be something about something she was working on, probably something to do with intel. She hoped there wasn't anything unplanned going down with the Chinese visit. She had spent months in planning, and she didn't want any of her hard work wasted.

"No, I'm not sure why the Congressman would need to see me."

Carleen looked peeved. "I actually have no idea why he wants to see you, either."

Lizbeth got a couple of interested looks as she opened the congressman's door. He looked up from his desk and waved her in. "Close the door, will you? Take a seat while I finish up a couple of things here."

Lizbeth's hands went clammy. Lincoln Pierce's schedule was pretty strict, and he rarely had impromptu meetings. It was as if she was being called into the principal's office. She perched on the edge of the chair opposite his desk and watched him flit through the pile on his desk, scanning each page with intense focus before adding his signature "P" followed by an illegible couple of swooshes.

After a couple more pages, the congressman took off his glasses and rubbed at his eyes. He clasped his hands in front of his chest as he relaxed into his chair. "How's the Chinese visit coming along? I understand I have to put on my monkey suit Saturday night for this gala thing."

"Yes sir. You're welcome to attend the Friday night opera party as well."

"But that's not required, right?"

Something about the way he was looking at her

told her not to try talking him into it. "Of course not, sir."

"I have a date planned for the gala. She's an attorney at a criminal law firm. Basically, keeps her head down and doesn't have any known political leanings. You think that will be okay?"

Lizbeth was pretty sure he hadn't asked her in to vet his date for the gala. "Sure. Email me her name and birthdate. I'll have her info run through BDS. Has Carleen given you the go ahead?"

"She thinks this woman would make a good wife for me. I'm inclined to agree, on paper anyway."

Lizbeth did not like the way this conversation was heading. She was willing to talk about anything else, cheater seating charts, security detail, but she didn't want to discuss his future, very personal life of who he should marry. "Is there something else you wanted to talk to me about?"

Congressman Pierce nodded slowly as his face shifted into serious concern. "I had a lengthy interview with people from the CIA about you."

His eyes met hers with a harshness she'd never seen from him. Was that hurt or anger? Lizbeth didn't quite understand what he was saying. "Sir? The CIA contacted you about *me*?"

"That's what I said, Lizbeth. I had two agents here for an hour asking me about you. This wasn't their regular quickie follow up about anything you normally do here, either."

"Maybe it's about the Chinese visit. That's the only thing I can think of."

"But they were here today. Any security requirements for the Chinese visit were established months ago."

She shook her head. There was absolutely nothing to make the CIA interested in her.

The congressman tilted his head to the side. "Have you applied for a position there? Their questions were pretty focused. I'd like to know if you're making plans to leave."

"I haven't applied to any jobs anywhere. Sure, I have told people that I would like to eventually work on the Embassy staff, but that's general knowledge in terms of my career goals. You know that already. But, sir, I don't have any concrete plans for leaving you. And I certainly have not applied at the CIA."

He stood up and walked around to the front of his desk. He leaned against it, his hands in his pockets. "The CIA is interested in you. Did you do anything unusual lately? It could be you are connected to another person. Investigations sometimes work like that."

"Sir, you're on the intel committee, don't you think

you could find out why the CIA is investigating your staff?"

"This is a specific interest to you, nothing to do with national or international theater. You sure you have no idea why?"

Lizbeth ran through all the interactions she'd had with people from the Chinese delegation, wondering if that could have triggered something. She'd spent dozens of hours at the Chinese Embassy in the last month. But that was expected for this type of collaboration.

The only person new in her life was Curt Wu. She had a loyalty to Congressman Pierce that compelled her to speak frankly. "The only thing that's different is I started dating someone at State. But, that's new—as in the last couple of days new. I don't know how or why that would trigger any kind of investigation. Certainly nothing this soon."

"I would hate for someone to bring you down. I'll put some feelers out there. Maybe I can find out what is really going on."

"Thank you, I'd appreciate that. Is there anything else, sir?"

"Not at the moment. I am happy to hear you're not handing in your resignation. But be careful out there. I'm serious. I've got a strange feeling about this whole situation."

Chapter 11

She was in a daze as she walked back to her cubicle. Why in hell would the CIA be investigating *her*? It made no sense. People gave her questioning looks. Before she could sit down, Cheyenne linked her arm into hers and was pulling her toward the bathroom. Count on Cheyenne to try to get information from her.

"What is going on?"

Lizbeth shook her head. She looked under the stalls and didn't see any feet. "I can't say. But, it's nothing. Nothing that concerns you, anyway."

"Did he ask about the game?"

It took Lizbeth a few seconds to remember what she was talking about. This whole Monument BINGO thing kept blipping off her radar. "Are you worried about getting in trouble, Cheyenne?"

"Seriously, Lizbeth? It looked like you were about to be fired."

Lizbeth dropped her shoulders in exaggerated submission. "I'm not even playing that damn game. I'm barely able to get what I need to completed for this Chinese visit. I have about fifty people arriving in two hours, and a shit ton of work to finish before they get here."

Cheyenne held up her hands. "No need to get snippy. You do know that everyone saw you go in there without being on the schedule. It's not normal for him to call you in there like that. So what was that about if not the game?"

"I can't tell you. It's got to do with State Department. Classified."

Cheyenne pouted. "Come on, you can trust me. What's going on?"

Lizbeth pushed past Cheyenne and stalked out of the bathroom, shaking her head in annoyance. There was no way she was going to tell Cheyenne the CIA was investigating her. Before she could get back to her cubicle, Opal waylaid her. She asked her to come with her to the break room, but it wasn't a question. Lizbeth sighed as she closed the door. She'd managed to escape from Cheyenne's questioning only to find herself under Opal's scrutiny.

She had a great deal of respect for Opal. Maybe it

was because everyone seemed to treat her like the office dump but the woman kept her chin up and kept getting things done.

Opal stood in the doorway, blocking her exit. Liz wouldn't have been able to leave if she wanted to. "What did Link want with you?"

"Nothing to do with you, Opal," said Liz, with her fists clenched. She shifted her hips to a karate defense position. "I need to get back to work. If all you want is gossip, you should hang out with Cheyenne."

"You're in charge of the Chinese Gala at the Embassy on Saturday, aren't you?"

The subject took her off guard. Liz relaxed her breathing and unclenched her fists. "Yes?"

"What did Link tell you about his date? Did you get clearance for her?"

This line of questioning was not something she expected. She'd never seen Opal like this before and recognized in her the same stance that Curt had taken earlier at the waffle shop. The girl looked like she was about to kick ass. "Opal, what is this all about? Why don't you ask him or Carleen?"

Opal eased her position, crossed her arms and leaned against the counter. "Did you know that in the years since I've worked for the Congressman, he has been out with eighty-nine different women? He has only dated three of them more than once."

Lizbeth knew he had a reputation for being a ladies' man, but that was a lot of different women. "I'm not keeping track."

"Do you think anyone is going to vote for a man who can't keep a single woman attached to him?" she said, biting her lip.

Lizbeth hadn't thought about it quite like that before. He was charming. Handsome. Intelligent. But completely unattached. It was kind of unusual now that she thought about it. "He doesn't seem like a player to me, though. He's a busy man."

"People are beginning to call him a *confirmed bachelor*."

Lizbeth tilted her head to the side. The way Opal said it like that... "Wait. People think Link is gay?"

"That's one of the latest rumors."

Lizbeth thought about it for a second and anger welled up in her. "And would that really be a problem, in this day and age?"

Opal tilted her head back in exasperation. "Seriously, Liz, what planet do you live on? It looks like he's hiding something. Of course it's a problem for someone running for president. We can joke all we like about living in the modern era, but we can all agree on the fact that America is not ready for a gay president."

"You're wrong, Opal."

"That's not the point, Liz," she said, leveling her

gaze. "He's *not* gay. We're not trying to cover anything up. We have to get Link hooked up and married. What did you find out about his date for Saturday?"

She shook her head. "I can't even remember what Link said about her. Some attorney or other. Not affiliated with any major lobbying groups. You know. Safe. He's going to email the info later so I can clear her with BDS."

"Find out. I want to do some deep digging. Backgrounding. Just in case."

"BDS will do that for the gala, but I'm not privy to the results. This is probably their first date. Besides, it's not our job to find him a wife."

"Of course it is. Our job is to do everything in our power to keep his reputation clean. To make sure he represents well. To ensure he can become president."

Liz was about to disagree when she realized the conversation wouldn't go anywhere. Besides, she was done with this line of questioning. "Look, I'll tell you what. When I'm at the gala on Saturday, I'll check her out. I'll report back next week to let you know how well things go between them."

Opal's jaw tightened then relaxed. "Thanks. These rumors really get to me."

"Opal, I'm certain Link is not gay. He's picky, that's all."

Opal nodded absently, accepting Lizbeth's assertion. "You're not going to tell me why he had to talk to you off-book, are you?"

"Not this again? Look, it was a classified conversation. As his liaison to the intelligence committee, sometimes we need privacy. Drop it, please?"

Opal opened her mouth to argue but was interrupted by Liz's phone. Thankful for the interruption, she waved it in the air. "I've got to take this." Ninety percent sure it was her mom, she swiped to accept the call without looking at it, grateful for the easy escape from Opal's scrutiny.

"Lizbeth? We need to meet with you as soon as possible. It's important."

That wasn't her mom's voice. It was Angela, Bella's adoptive mom.

Her heart clenched with worry. Had they seen her at the waffle shop? She had known something was wrong. Sensed it somehow. Did they know she watched Bella every morning?

Chapter 12

"Hold on a minute, Angela," she said, leaving the break room. Opal seemed a little offended that she cut off the conversation, but Liz didn't care. She headed for an open conference room. "Is Bella okay? She's not hurt, is she?"

"No, she's fine, but you need to come over today. As soon as possible. Now."

Lizbeth checked the time. It was already three; she could leave early. "All right. But, Angela, what's this about?"

"We'll talk when you get here." Her voice cracked with a hard edge.

Demarco and Angela had never called her to a meeting in the middle of the week before. They were usually pretty chill about things. Lizbeth was confused. She calculated the time it would take to get there. If she left work now, she'd have to come back in the morning to finish a couple of things. She'd planned on taking a half day on Thursday—she had galas and the opera to pack for as well as her daytime activities with the delegation.

Curt was planning on picking her up at work, but she could text him to pick her up somewhere else depending on timing. Besides, anything to do with Bella was more important. "I can be there in half an hour."

"We'll be waiting."

Lizbeth neatened up the files on her desk and shut down her computer. Her hands were shaking. First, the CIA was asking about her, and now Angela and Demarco were insisting they meet. Had they seen her with Curt this morning? Were they about to change everything?

She popped her head into Katherine's office to let her know she'd be leaving early, that an important meeting had come up.

"You're out of the office tomorrow and Friday right? You'll be back on Monday?"

"Actually, I have a couple of things to do tomorrow. I'll come in around ten thirty to wrap up here before heading over to the hotel for the weekend."

"Is everything okay, Liz? You look stressed."

Lizbeth smiled tightly, but didn't give Katherine any more of an explanation.

The cab ride over to the Alstons' was excruciating. Her stomach churned and she regretted the pie she'd snacked on not that long ago—the cherry tasted suddenly bitter to her. It seemed they hit every red light on the way. After climbing out of the cab, she stood outside on the sidewalk, pretending to examine their house while gathering her nerves. Part of the reason she had picked them was this house. It was a classic two-story brick home with white shutters on all the windows. It was solid. Wholesome. She wished she had grown up in a fancy house like this, and she had wanted that for her baby.

She made her way up the walk, head held high. Deep down, she knew why she was here. They had found out about her stalking Bella almost every morning at her school. Would they punish her taking by taking away her monthly visits? The thought of not being able to visit her daughter once a month scared her.

Angela opened the door before she even got there. She had been standing by the door waiting. Angela's usual smile had been replaced with a tight frown. Lizbeth followed her into the formal study. Demarco stood at the window, a drink in one hand. He held it down low, swirling it slowly, almost as if he didn't want to admit he was drinking it. But Lizbeth took heart that whatever they wanted to talk was not something that was easy for him.

"Where's Bella?"

"Bella is at a friend's house for a playdate. We didn't want her here for this."

Lizbeth shivered and the light shifted. She dropped onto the closest chair. "What is this, exactly?"

Demarco threw Angela a look. It was clear they had been arguing. "You tell her." His voice was harsh, slightly accusing.

Angela threw back her shoulders and moved so she was standing in front of Lizbeth, close enough that she had to lean back to see Angela's face.

"We know you've been following Bella."

There was no reason to deny it or play it down. "I don't talk to her. I *only* watch her. From across the street. That's it."

"She's not blind, Lizbeth. Two months ago, she came home from school asking why Auntie Lizzie was always at the coffee shop across the street in the mornings."

Lizbeth stiffened in her chair. She thought Bella had never seen her. She'd never waved at her, or called to her. "Was Bella upset? About me being there?"

Demarco sipped at his drink. Scotch probably. He was looking out the window.

"That's not important. The point is, Lizbeth, you broke our agreement. We can no longer trust you."

Panic flooded every pore. "I... I swear. I promise to never go there again. I only wanted to *see* her. Has she been upset by it?" Her voice rose as she repeated the question.

"You expect us to believe that? You really expect us to believe you innocently moved to DC and *just happened* to want to see our daughter every now and again... and that you *just happen* to be watching her on a near daily basis?"

"I'm here for work too, you know. My job brought me here." Lizbeth had no idea what she was going with all this. She was thankful for her quick thinking, but the truth was she was there for Bella to get a daily glimpse of her flesh and blood. "And I live near there. Am I never supposed to leave my house?"

Angela let out a huff and crossed her arms. "I don't believe you. As a matter of fact, I believe you're planning to take her away from us."

Lizbeth jumped out of her chair and into a casual sparring stance. "Now hold on! This is unfair. Bella herself told you I've been watching her. That's *all* I've been doing."

Angela plowed on as if Lizbeth hadn't said anything. "As a matter of fact, we had you followed the last two months since Bella came to us about your creeping around."

Demarco spun around to face them, pointing at Angela with his drink. "Get to the point, will you?"

Angela glowered at Demarco. "I need to make our position exceedingly clear, darling."

Demarco downed the rest of his drink and poured himself another. His eyes drooped with sadness as he returned to the window.

Angela returned her attention to Lizbeth, straightened her shoulders, and took in a deep breath before speaking. "Our investigation shows you have been with four different men in the last six months."

Plenty of women who went through men at a faster rate than that. "So?" Lizbeth asked, confusion rippling over her face. *Their investigation?* Bile in the back of her throat made Liz gag. They had hired an investigator? She was being followed? How could they do this to her?

"And yesterday? You were speeding around DC on the back of a motorcycle, clinging to a man you'd met the day before. And then, you let him spend the night. *After one date.* I suppose I shouldn't have expected anything better from a girl who got pregnant while in high school."

The words were a painful allegation. Years ago, Lizbeth would have been completely cowed by someone trying to shame her like this. Not now.

Lizbeth squared off with the other woman in spite of the nausea flooding her entire body. "My dating life has nothing to do with Bella."

"Oh really? Even when you bring him with you?"

Lizbeth's jaw dropped open. "What?" They *had* seen her this morning after all. With Curt. Her instincts had been right, but she hadn't wanted to listen to them. "I was there getting coffee. It was an hour before school started."

"The fact remains, you were there with a man you hardly knew, this close to *my daughter*." She held her thumb and forefingers up to Lizbeth's face, almost touching, but not quite. "*My daughter*," she repeated through clenched teeth. "That is too close. It shows a complete disregard for our agreement."

Lizbeth would cop to watching Bella, but she hadn't even mentioned Bella to Curt. She had strict rules regarding the way she divulged the knowledge of Bella. Curt was still an unknown in her life. How could she possibly have told him about Bella yet?

"Curt, that man on the motorcycle, works for the State Department. He's been vetted by the government. This is ridiculous, Angela."

"I don't care if he's Secret Service. I don't care if he's the fucking President. You had no right to get that close to her, and you have no right to bring your *man friends* anywhere near her." Angela was red in the face, her eyes dark balls of fury. "You've been lying to us for months. We cannot trust you. We can't trust you to not take Bella from us."

Take Bella? Why would she take Bella?

Lizbeth couldn't take it all in. Everything became dull and muted around her, a rushing roar filling her head. The accusations were unfair. Wrong. Unjust. Angela was completely out of line. But, she was also completely in control of Lizbeth's relationship with Bella. It was clear Demarco wasn't getting involved in this other than to be present.

"I promise... I promise I will *never* bring another boyfriend around the coffee shop again. And *I promise* to not go there in the mornings any more. I will stick to our agreement by visiting her once a month with you in attendance."

"See, Angela? I told you it's all a misunderstanding," Demarco said.

Angela looked at him with narrowed eyes, her jaw clenching and unclenching. "It's too late for that," she said. She turned back to Lizbeth with her full wrath. "We are moving. And we are not going to tell you where. You are never going to see Bella again. Now. Get. Out. Of. My. House!"

Chapter 13

*L*izbeth stumbled past Demarco who looked at her helplessly. She made it to the sidewalk, past their little white picket fence and turned around to look at the house that had once been the symbol of home. Now it looked like a fortress. Angela and Demarco were taking Bella away from her. Her heart split wide open and it hurt like it never had before—worse than when Darius had died. She had known and loved Bella longer than she had known him. What would she do without Bella in her life?

The sky was so unfairly blue and normal. Nothing in her life was normal. It hadn't been for a long time. Not since Darius had died and she had learned she was pregnant. Everything she had done had been for Bella. Researching and interviewing different parents. Giving her up so she could have a better life.

About a block away, she wrapped her arms around herself and dropped to her knees, not caring who saw her. The tears flowed freely, bubbling out of her, cascading down her cheeks. *What was she crying for, anyway? Darius? Bella? Both of them?* She'd always dealt with her grief by refusing to think about it, pushing it out of her mind, believing that adoption was enough. Now she had to face it.

She could accept that she had broken the rules. She would understand them telling her she couldn't see Bella unless it was during her formal visits. But for them to think she would take Bella from them? After all this time? She did not understand how Angela had gone there. It made no sense.

She stood slowly, finally looking around to see if anyone had taken notice of her, but she appeared alone in her misery. By losing Bella, she'd be losing the last thread of connection to Darius. He was stuck in her memory as someone important, but he wasn't, not in any real way except to someday tell Bella who he was. Lizbeth had to let him go. She had to forgive herself, but she didn't know how.

Lizbeth walked in a daze from the Alstons' to the Justice Department Office of Asian Affairs. She needed Curt. She needed his warmth, his dragon arms around her. Curt would be there somewhere, right? She had gone there automatically, hoping to find him.

Her hands shook as she called Curt to let him know she was at his office instead of hers. He didn't answer, so she left a voicemail telling him she would wait for him in the lobby. It was already almost five, and the guard eyed her suspiciously as she entered. She didn't try going through security, but found a bench near the door instead.

Liz hid her face in her hands. She didn't want the guards to see how distraught she was. Loud strong footsteps clomped toward her. She knew it was Curt. She recognized his gait, the sound of his shoes. Had he come from outside?

He slid onto the bench pressing his leg against hers, immediately pulling her into an embrace. "What's wrong, Liz? You look like someone's died."

His words hit truer than she liked to admit. Darius had died. But that was so long ago. Almost ten years. They were taking Bella from her. Would it be much different knowing she was alive somewhere and never being allowed to contact her or see her ever again?

She leaned her head against his shoulder and let him hold her. Underneath his shirt, she knew that dragon would breathe fire for her. Calmness and strength flowed from him, grounding her back to the earth. The fuzz in her head and the roaring silence cleared. The shuffling and chatting people made as they left the building were back to a normal, every day buzzing undertone. For most of them, this was another regular day, nothing to remember. They would not be marking it on their calendars and thinking about their loss for the rest of their lives.

Curt lifted her head away from his shoulder until he could see her face. His eyes narrowed in concern as he cupped her cheeks, his thumb gently stroking her lower lip. "Where do you want to go?"

"Anywhere but home right now." She couldn't take looking at the photos of Bella's smiling face hanging on her fridge or the framed images sitting on her bookshelf.

He wrapped an arm around her waist and steered her down the steps. He hailed a taxi. "Let's go to my place then. We'll stop by your place first so you can check in with your kitties and then grab a bag. I have a really great bed..."

She stiffened. "I'm sorry. I'm probably not going to want to have sex tonight."

"I was going to say, I have a really comfy bed that is perfect for talking and sleeping."

She didn't want to be alone. Not tonight. "Okay then, Mr. Wu. Take me home with you. What about your bike?"

"I don't think you're up for a ride today. It's okay where it is for now."

When he gave the cab driver her address, she interrupted him. She couldn't face the photos right that moment. "To your house, please. I just, I can't go home right now. The kitties will be fine for a night."

He leaned forward and gave the driver new directions before settling back into the seat with her in his arms.

Lizbeth had taken different approaches when talking to men about Bella over the years. Sometimes she told them before they even went out, in a casual email exchange before a date. Sometimes, she didn't mention her until things were going well. Sometimes, she never knew them long enough or well enough to tell them about Bella. But here she was. She could hold back if she wanted to, but it would change the relationship forever. This was a crossroad. There would be no turning back.

She leaned into him. "Can we talk about it at your place?"

"Sure. Sure." He kissed the top of her head as she settled into him. "You should relax."

The buildings and cars flew by and she closed her eyes. Memories flitted through her like a silent movie, images from her past roiling together in a jumbled mess without regard to chronological order. Bella as a newborn. Her father riding a horse on the beach. Her first piano recital. Her mother's face in the dim light at an opera, eyes open wide taking in the grandeur on stage. A karate match where she had downed a boy twice her size. Waipo's gnarled fingers working soft dough in the kitchen. Her handing Bella over to Angela and Demarco when she was only a week old, the older woman's face streaked with tears of joy.

They drifted around her consciousness like tendrils of a spider web. She wiped at her face, brushing them away as Curt lifted her out of the cab. They had arrived at a Craftsman style cottage with a long set of stone steps leading up from the street. Looking around her, she guessed they were near Georgetown.

He carried her nimbly up the steps, pausing at the front door. "Sorry, I'll have to put you down to fish out the keys."

He placed her carefully on her feet. She stretched. A profound tranquility engulfed her. She was safe. Cared for. Curt pushed the door open and swept a hand gallantly to invite her in. "My humble casa es su casa."

The inside was tastefully accurate to the period in a masculine sort of way. The woodwork was rich, dark, and polished. She was pretty sure the wallpaper was reproduction because it was too perfect and fresh looking, the colors still fully saturated. The dining table was solid oak with matching chairs. The craftsman style coffee table was strewn with books and magazines, the only real nod to a human living in the house.

"Come with me." He led her towards upstairs to his bedroom.

"Curt? I don't..."

He rummaged through a drawer and tossed a pair of sweat pants and a worn Berkeley t-shirt onto the bed. They were definitely not the sweats she had given him this morning. He tugged at her skirt. "This is hot, but it's not comfy looking. Take your time. I'll be in the living room," he said.

When she finished changing, Liz settled on the couch next to him. He closed the magazine he'd been reading and handed her a glass of red wine he'd poured for her. She might as well tell him about the baggage she was carrying early on so he could renege on his wish to spend every night with her. She took a sip of the wine and put it down on the coffee table.

"I'm upset because I have a daughter. Well, not really. I had a baby girl I gave up for adoption. I was almost eighteen."

She paused. No surprise, no condemnation—his arm tightened around her shoulders a little, silently urging her on.

She let it all tumble out. How she'd loved Darius and thought she'd spend the rest of her life with him.

How he'd died never knowing she was pregnant. How she'd given Bella to the Alstons for adoption.

His steady breathing, his warmth enveloping her kept her from bursting into tears again. She hadn't even gotten to the hard part.

"I get there's more to this story?" he asked when she had paused.

She nodded, took another sip of the wine. She continued. "In college, I went wild. Completely crazy. I slept with anyone. Everyone. I guess I wanted to feel needed, but I never found what I wanted."

He stiffened against her, his fingers tightening around her upper arm. "Do you still..."

She shook her head. "Not so much. Not so many, anyway. I won't lie to you, Curt. I have had dozens of lovers. But, I... I'm done with that. You're the only person I'm interested in right now."

He let out his breath. "Right now. Great."

She craned her neck so she could look at him. "Seriously. I don't want anyone but you."

Their eyes met, his narrowed on her for a moment and then his face relaxed. She was exposed and open. Raw. This was her truth and she bared it to him willingly.

"Okay. You still haven't told me why you were so upset today. I take it you're leading up to something upsetting?"

"It's about Bella," she said. "I moved to DC largely to be close to Bella. I've told myself it was all about my career, but I was probably lying a little bit to myself. Exaggerating the career part to rationalize it all."

It wasn't until she said it aloud that she realized the full truth of it. Yes, she wanted the career, but she could have gone straight into Foreign Service and found a position in Beijing five years ago. She had waited. Given herself the excuse to be in DC.

"We have an open adoption, and originally, that meant her parents would send me a letter once a year with pictures. When I moved to DC we adjusted the agreement, and they let me see her once a month at their house."

She was at the point where she had to confess to sneaking around to see Bella. Admitting it out loud was hard, and telling Curt about it even harder. Would he think she was crazy and drop her? Lizbeth breathed in deeply, hoping to boost her courage.

"So... you know when we were at the coffee shop this morning? The playground at the school across the street?"

"Yes?"

"That's Bella's school. I started going to the coffee shop six months ago. I told myself it was for the awesome waffles. For the coffee. Not to find Bella. At first I went once a week. But then, I started going more and more often."

"Did you take me there today hoping you would see her?"

"No. I didn't. That's the irony. I thought we'd be there way too early to see her. I was only wanting to get those waffles and take you there. It's a special place."

"Is it special because of your connection to Bella?"

"I don't know. Maybe. But I didn't take you there to see Bella, or I would have pointed her out to you."

"Did they see you this morning? Is that how they found out?"

"No. Bella told them. Two months ago, she asked why I was always at the coffee shop. I had no idea she'd even seen me. That's when they hired a private investigator to follow me."

Curt stiffened briefly. "They've had you followed for two months?"

"Yeah. Apparently, they've been keeping tabs on who I've been dating. They even called me out for riding on the motorcycle with you last night."

"That's kind of extreme."

"Extreme? What's extreme is they decided to move. Take Bella away from DC and go someplace I can't find them."

Curt chuckled. "They don't know who you work for?"

"They know I work for a congressman. I never told him I have lots of friends in Intel. Still. They are taking her away from me. They won't let me see her. Ever again."

Curt's arms tightened around her. "What kind of legal agreement do you have with them?"

"They have all the control and power. They changed everything, but not in the contract, to accommodate me visiting Bella. They didn't have to do that. They could have insisted on the letter and photo deal we'd originally made."

"You know, they might feel differently in a few weeks. Or months. Maybe later, when you have children of your own someday, you can repair your relationship with them. When they no longer see you as a threat."

Someday. A nebulous day far off in the future wasn't all that comforting.

She'd told other guys about Bella, but never in this greater context of her being taken away from her. Expecting him to make up some lame excuse to get up and away from her, she watched him closely for his reaction. This would be the time for him to call her a cab and say it was too much for him to deal with—tell her she was messed up. Instead, he was on the couch next to her consoling her, caressing her with the kind hand of a concerned lover. He wanted her. Maybe even loved her. There was no feeling that he was going to use her and spit her out, or like he was going to push her away.

"You look hungry. Let's get you something to eat."

He picked up their wine glasses and led her into the kitchen. She slid onto a leather padded stool at the woodblock kitchen counter. He poured himself a fresh glass, but hers was still full.

She took a sip. "I'm not a big drinker. My parents don't drink, and I mean at all. Totally about not wanting to fuzz up their heads."

"Sometimes it's medicinal. Drink up, it will help you relax."

Lizbeth took another sip and twirled the glass around between her fingers. "Your house is pretty. It's kind of old-fashioned."

"I'm an old-fashioned kind of guy."

"Sure you are. How'd you end up here?"

The sink had a few dishes waiting to be loaded into the dishwasher. On the counter, some spotted bananas lay atop apples and oranges in a thick pottery bowl.

He opened the fridge. The interior showed a healthy assortment of condiments and ingredients for someone who might actually cook on a regular basis.

She was pretty sure she spotted green stuff in a drawer at the bottom. "I have enough in here to cobble together dinner. To answer your question... I've always loved this style of house. When I bought this place, it was in foreclosure and slated for demolition." Curt shuffled things from the fridge to the counter as he spoke. "I spent four years remodeling and restoring it. Thank god for online tutorials."

"I love this style." Earlier, she thought she'd never want to eat again, but her stomach grumbled and turned. "I guess I am pretty hungry. Can I help?"

"You collapsed in my arms not more than an hour ago. You can sit there and watch me cook."

She sipped her wine and relaxed. He turned up his shirtsleeves, one fold at a time, exposing his muscular forearms. There was something incredibly sexy about the way he did it even though it was an everyday sort of move, practical.

He pulled out the biggest damn knife she'd ever seen and chopped an onion into tiny little bits in no time. After filling several small bowls with bits of meat and vegetables and scrambling a couple of eggs into another, he lit one of the eight gas burners on the range and pulled out a wok from a cupboard. He rustled around in the freezer, emerging with a bag of rice and she understood what he was doing. Comfort food at its best—fried rice.

The man knew how to handle a wok, that was for sure. "My mom is an unbelievable cook."

"It's kinda rare for a boy to cook," she said, teasing.

"My mom taught my sisters. I watched and learned. She'd freak if she saw me cooking. She must *never know* I'm better at it than any of them."

He tossed the veggies against the scorching hot pan. After dumping them into a bowl, he made egg threads like her Waipo used to do, the thin coating of egg across the whole surface of the wok. He added the rice and cooked vegetables and seasoned it with the perfect amount of soy sauce and white pepper before splitting it between two bowls.

He put one in front of her and handed her a pair of well-used chopsticks. She lifted the bowl in one hand and placed it against her lips and scooped in the fragrant morsels. It was every bit as good as Waipo's. Maybe even better. When they were done eating, he held out a hand to her.

"What now?" he asked.

"It's too early for bed," she said. "I'm tired, but I'm sure I'll toss and turn if I try to sleep now."

"We could... watch television?" He looked as dubious about the prospect as he sounded.

"Is that a library?" she asked, moving towards a little room beyond where they stood.

He followed her. "I probably spend more time in here than anywhere else."

Floor to ceiling shelves lined every wall. Books filled them and overflowed into neat piles on the floor. A worn leather armchair with a reading lamp took up one corner. On the table next to it was a stack of books all about Chinese foreign policy. "A little light reading?" she asked with a grin.

He laid his hand on top of the pile. "I don't have time to keep up with everything at work. Part of my job is to be on top of what people think."

She took a quick inventory of the shelves and landed on a familiar edition of Jane Austen's completed works. The same set of beautifully leather-bound graced her shelves as well. "Oh... I know. Let's read to each other." She pulled out *Pride and Prejudice* and waved it in the air. "Nothing like a little Mr. Darcy, hmm?"

Now he looked bemused. "Read to each other? All right, then, Miss Lizbeth." He made a face. "Hey... You're Lizbeth. Lizzie. Elizabeth. That's the heroine in this book, isn't it?"

"Indeed, you are quite correct, Mr. Wu."

"The lighting is best in the living room. And perchance, we shall find the couch there quite service-able. After you, my lady," he said, shifting his voice into a pretty credible British accent.

He sat down with his back against the arm of the sofa and patted the space between his legs. She slid in between them, leaning her back into his front. It reminded her of their motorcycle ride, but reversed. He wrapped one arm around her and held the book off to the side to read.

It was almost like listening to a live performance of the BBC. Curt lifted his voice into a falsetto when he was reading the women's parts, lowered it to a deep baritone or a tenor for the men. Every once in a while, he'd pause and kiss her on the neck or nuzzle her with his nose. His voice resonated throughout her body, especially when he was using his Mr. Darcy voice. Could this become her new normal? After half an hour he paused to take a sip of wine. The sense of impending doom over Bella's situation loomed in the back of her mind, but she let Curt's voice take her away.

"You could narrate audio books for a living, you know that, right? You sound like Colin Firth."

His laugh reverberated through her body. "I've always been a pretty good mimic. Your turn to read."

She took the book, a little self-conscious. "I won't be nearly so entertaining, my lord."

He wrapped his arms around her waist and snuggled his chin against shoulder. He switched into Mrs. Bennett's quavering high-pitched motherly voice. "Oh, do go on, Miss Crandall. You have a lovely voice, and I'm sure you'll do an admirable job."

Lizbeth picked up the story where he left off, occasionally trying her hand at different voices. She closed the book at the end of a chapter. "Well, that wasn't so bad, was it?"

He kissed her neck. "I could listen to you all night long."

The wine and stress of the day were catching up to her. She hadn't even told Curt about the fact the CIA had been questioning the Congressman about her. It would be better to not bring it up. They were having such a nice moment. Besides, he might think she was paranoid.

Curt shifted so his back was against the couch. He lifted her onto his lap so they could see each other's faces. She linked her arms around his neck.

"Would you be happy spending your evenings like this?" he asked. "Sitting together, reading to each other?"

"I'd like to go out occasionally. Maybe dancing every now and again. Dinner. But, yeah. This is... wonderful."

He kissed her. "When I first saw you enter the conference room at the Embassy, I..." he paused and looked up at the ceiling and let out a huge breath of air. Something in his body relaxed, gave way. "I *knew*,

Lizbeth. I could sense you were the woman I've been waiting for."

"Love at first sight? An old-fashioned ideal for an old-fashioned man? That kind of stuff only happens in books."

His face grew serious. "Not true. I've fallen hard for you, Lizbeth Crandall."

He knew about her wild college years. Her problems with Bella. He was the first man to get all three cats straight with a single introduction. But, she knew about him too, his dark history selling drugs and Malachi. Was it meant to be?

She sucked in her lower lip. "It's so fast. Are you sure I'm the one? This intensity—it's new to me. I've never felt like this before."

Not even with Darius. Should she dare call it love? He hadn't said the word yet either. *Fallen hard... spend every night...* These were emotional and strong sentiments, but not love.

"I'm sure."

They kissed. Slow. Gentle. Deep.

"Is this what I think it is?" she asked, her voice barely above a whisper.

Say it, please say it first.

"Yes. I believe it is."

A shiver of fear skidded through her. This new thing she was feeling threatened to overwhelm her, to replace all markers of what she had always thought she had known. If she had thought her love for Darius was deep and intense, it was nothing compared to this. Guilt swam through her as it dawned on her that her therapist had been right all along. She would probably have broken up with Darius if he had lived. She'd clung to his memory and put it on a pedestal so high that no one else could possibly knock it over... until now.

She shivered in Curt's arms, hopeful and terrified at the same time. "Would you be offended if I still wanted to just sleep with you tonight—no sex?"

"There will be plenty of other chances for us to rip each other's clothes off and make mad, passionate love."

There. He had said it, sort of. Not *I love you, Lizbeth,* but he had asked if she believed in *love* at first sight and told her she was the woman he'd been waiting for. Surely the two together were the same thing.

Chapter 14

They climbed the wooden staircase to the upper floor. There were four doors off the small hallway. Only one of them was open, and it led to his bedroom. Across from the door was a king bed. It matched the style of the house, as if it had been made specifically for the room.

More books hid the top of the bedside table on one side. These were lighter reads than the ones downstairs. A large chaise lounge filled a bay window. On top, several pairs of pants and shirts lay discarded.

"At least you have some messes."

"I've been busy lately. I don't have the selection of ex-lover's clothing in stock like you do," he said, waggling his eyebrows at her. "I can offer you one of my pajamas if you don't want to sleep in the sweats."

He opened a drawer and pulled out a flannel top. "You'd look cute in this."

She took it from him. She didn't really want to undress in front of him right then. Everything was awkward all of a sudden. "I don't suppose you have an extra toothbrush?"

"There's one in the drawer to the left of the sink." He shifted his weight back and forth on the balls of his feet. "Take some time. I'll be back up in a little bit. I need to close up the house, wash the dishes, get the mail in—that kind of thing."

He left her alone as she curled up on one side. She'd burdened him with her whole history and he hadn't run. He hadn't even seemed surprised. Maybe he was biding his time. Maybe he really did love her. But words were meaningless without action. Even though to this point everything he'd done indicated he did love her, she wasn't quite willing to give herself over yet.

The clock on the bedside table said it was only ten thirty. Early yet. She tossed and turned, restless in spite of her exhaustion. Curt was probably downstairs in that room full of papers and piles of books. Her feet were cold and she wanted to stretch her tight muscles.

Sitting on the edge of the bed, she looked at the open closet, at the rows of jackets, shirts and pants in color order. She wasn't disappointed. There was also a rack holding seven pairs of shoes, almost identical but for their individual scuff marks. He was a neatnik. Organized. The only mess was the clothing on the chaise.

She flicked on the light and looked at the room more closely. The art on the walls were sensuous—darkly masculine. After a few stretches on the floor, she peeked under the bed. There was nothing there. Not a stray sock or a dust bunny. Vacuum marks met in the middle of the carpet underneath. He must have a housekeeper.

She opened the top drawer of the dresser. Neatly neatly rolled socks and underwear were in perfect rows. The next drawer held t-shirts, equally organized. She found a pair of athletic socks and closed the drawer.

Heavy curtains blocked out any light from outside. She opened them. She could see why he had black-out curtains. Bright street-lights shown over the whole street. It would be impossible to sleep without them. Curt's house was away from any major roads and the neighborhood was made of generous lots that were carefully landscaped to maximize privacy. Shrubs and flowering cherry trees concealed the neighbors from almost every angle. The overall situation would make for a very quiet night indeed.

Lizbeth relaxed into the bed again and lapsed into an old trick she'd learned as a child. It was a counting game designed to make her mind settle and relax. It never failed to help her find sleep. She woke up briefly as Curt climbed in beside her, cuddling up against her back. He snuggled in close to her neck, kissing her gently on the ear before slipping his arms around her, his legs pressed up against hers, two spoons in a drawer.

Morning rays came through the curtained window. She hadn't slept so soundly in ages, even at her own house. Curt's warm breath on the back of her neck tickled, but she could tell he was still asleep by the rhythm of his breath. Their bodies had melded into each other with comfortable precision.

She slowly rolled over without waking him so she could look at him. After watching him for a while, she gave into the hunger deep within. She kissed him on the nose. No movement. She kissed him on the cheek. Then his collarbone.

He moaned softly, but his eyes remained closed. She ran a finger along his upper arm, tracing Malachi's deep red eyes and a long wispy tendril of a whisker. Curt's skin twitched a little. She circled his nipple with a light flick of her tongue and grasped it between her lips. Another long moan.

She nibbled her way down his chest, teasing his belly button with her tongue and continued until she found proof he wasn't *completely asleep*. She nibbled her way back up to his neck, more insistent now. His arms pulled her in tight as his eyes opened and he grinned at her.

"That is the most delightful way to be woken in the morning, Miss Crandall."

"I'll try to remember that."

He wiggled under her, pressing his erection against her belly. "You've got me going, that's for sure. Were you teasing me awake on general principle, or are you prepared to let me take you up on your offer?"

She pushed his arms away with a naughty grin and threw the covers off them, exposing them both to the gentle chill of the room. His cock sprang upward, ready for her. She pushed his knees apart and knelt between his legs. Pressing the flat of her palm against his cock, she landed caressing kisses along his upper and inner thighs. Nibbling, tickling, licking everywhere but his cock. He shifted his hips under her, his fingers laced into her hair, tugging gently to make his wishes known. His cock twitched under her palm.

Rising to her knees, she grasped him firmly around the base and took the rest of him into her mouth. She swirled her tongue around the tip in ever widening circles, over and over again until his hips rocked slowly, thrusting upward toward her mouth.

"Wait," he said, his breathy, growling, command surprising her. "I don't want to come yet..."

Lizbeth rubbed the tip of his cock with her chin as she met his eyes, sizing him up. He had meant it. He pulled her up into another kiss while rolling her onto her back. One hand skimmed across her, tweaking her nipples one moment, the other delving into her pussy. She arched her back, thrusting her hips upward and clamping her thighs around his hand, wanting to close him in against her. Wanting him to focus his efforts on one particular spot.

He released her nipple and lay on his side, one hand propping him up, the other doing all the magic. "I want to watch you as you come."

Lizbeth sucked in her lower lip, relaxing into his scrutiny. Who was she to argue? His eyes never left her face as his fingers pumped deep inside her and all along her clit when he pulled them out.

His hot breath tingled against her ear. "Come for me, Lizbeth."

Lizbeth dropped her head back, reveling in his attention, loving the warmth of his hand between her legs. His urging, whispered need continued as he patiently brought her closer and closer to a climax.

When she came, it was swift. Focused. She clamped her legs tightly against his hand to keep it from moving and held herself against him. Her eyes squeezed shut and her mouth opened wide as she groaned.

He kissed her again, lifting her easily up, his body under her. She leaned over him, stretching his upper arms against the bed over his head, her weight on his wrists. Her hot, wet pussy found him easily and she wrapped around him in one smooth movement, sliding down quickly on him.

She rode him, letting her hips swing to feel the full measure of his hard cock inside her. She took her time, letting the pleasure from her first orgasm build up again, readying herself for a second. She refused to let herself come again until he was ready so they could come together.

"Lizbeth, I'm close. Sooo close..." His chest heaved as he spoke.

She lifted herself up nearly off him and slid back down, now going as full stroke as she possibly could get. "Together," she said, "take me over the edge with you."

She locked her eyes onto his, both of them waiting for the right moment. His low moan was a cry of pleasure, of release, of desire. His cock pulsed inside her as he came. She rode her second orgasm building into a crescendo along with his. They slowed together, her hips grinding against his, savoring every moment. His eyelids fluttered closed and his mouth dropped open.

She collapsed across his chest with him still inside her. They remained motionless until she rolled off him. She curled up into his side as he wrapped his arms around her.

"Well..." he said at last. "That's the way to start the morning."

"I hope I didn't interrupt your dreams." His skin rippled under her finger.

"This is better than any of my dreams, Lizbeth."

Lizbeth lifted herself onto her elbow and kissed him on the nose. "I'll try to remember that for next time."

"And the next, and the next," he said laughing.

Her body tingled with sexual electricity. Energized, ready for the day, she wanted to spring out of bed and dance her way across town. "I need to get home and feed the cats. Pack for this weekend. Come with me?" She traced a circle around the dragon's snout.

He stretched lazily. "Miss Busy. Let's lounge around here before going over to your place. Your cats can wait a couple more hours, right?" His voice was still fuzzy with sleep.

"That whole mess with Bella yesterday got me

behind. I have to meet Madeline about a press release, then finish a couple of things at work before heading to the hotel." He started to sit up, but she took pity on him, nudging him playfully back to his pillows. "Go back to sleep. I know you want to."

"You are the most amazing woman," he said, grinning, eyes already closed.

Watching him drift back into sleep made her want to cuddle him again. Resisting the temptation, she pushed herself out of bed and picked up the covers. She draped them over his now snoring form.

He had an enormous shower with modernized plumbing including several jets located at knee, hip and shoulder level. She found something that looked like an *on* button. She pushed it, hoping for the best. She almost screamed when water jetted out at her from all angles. It was like being run through a car wash without all the brushes. She fiddled with the controls until she had a reasonable amount of water spraying at her. She squirted a dot of his body wash onto a shower puff. The smell of tea tree oil infused the steamy shower. She lathered up, relishing his scent mingling with her own.

After dressing in her clothes from the day before, she kissed him on the cheek and went downstairs. There was a fresh pot of coffee on the counter. *Impressive.* There was yogurt and fruit in the fridge and some muesli in the cupboard. Layering prepared foods was her single culinary skill, so she used it to her best advantage. She made two parfaits in tall clear glasses—spooning in yogurt, then berries, then the muesli in even layers—and returned one to the fridge for Curt to eat later. She put a sticky on the fridge saying "Seven Layer Breakfast Delight Inside" in Chinese characters.

As she was searching for sugar for her coffee, she discovered a pile of mail on the counter that had not been there the night before. One of her favorite magazines peaked out from the bottom, so she pulled it out to look at it. When she did, an open envelope came along with it. It was addressed to Curt and had a San Francisco return address. It had to be from his mom. She held it for a second and put it back. She shouldn't read his private mail.

She returned to the table with her parfait and the magazine. When she was done eating, she returned the dish to the kitchen sink and ran some water into it.

But the letter from his mom intrigued her. She listened for movement from upstairs but there was nothing. Curt was still asleep. She found the letter in the pile again, examined it one more time. The top of the envelope had been sliced open. Unable to stop herself any longer, she pulled out the packet of papers.

She told herself she was reading it to get to know Curt's mother, and maybe a little bit more about him.

The letter was written in traditional Chinese charac-ters. The first page was about the family business followed by a tirade against Curt's youngest sister. From what Lizbeth could tell, Celina was causing all sorts of consternation for Curt's traditional mama. She was dating a man from the law office she worked in, and, apparently, he was white and didn't like Chinese food. Oh great. At least Liz had a healthy appetite for Chinese food and was fluent in the language. That had to count for something in her favor when Mama Wu was tallying things up.

Being white is bad enough, she wrote, *but he refused to eat anything other than rice. He said he didn't care for garlic. What kind of man doesn't like garlic? You must talk your sister out of this nonsense when you come. If I say anything, she will dig in her heels and keep dating him in order to annoy me. If you tell her she should stop seeing this man, she might listen.*

The letter rambled on about neighbors and family members. Business and home. Apparently, Curt's family was not wealthy. They had money problems, but she insisted they were doing fine. Curt's father owned a small business and they were making ends meet. There wasn't enough detail in the letter for Liz to figure out exactly what kind of business. In many ways, it read like a letter she would get from her own mother with the same general cares and worries a mother would have.

She paused to listen for Curt. She didn't want him catching her reading this letter from his mother. She shouldn't be reading it, but continued in spite of herself. It was a tiny window into his life. The last paragraph detailed all the things Curt should be prepared to do during his visit home in a month. He hadn't mentioned he was going to San Francisco to Lizbeth, but when would he have had time to tell her?

There were two more pages after her letter. Instead of more rambling or motherly hints on dating, Lizbeth was confronted by an information sheet for a young woman printed from a Chinese matchmaking website. The woman was beautiful, though the image reminded Lizbeth of those fancy photo shoots where you go to the mall and someone does up your hair and make-up like a model.

Her name was Eu-meh Hwang. Lizbeth choked back a laugh. In Chinese, her name meant "especially beautiful." In English, the written phonetics were kind of ironic and sort of funny.

She was twenty and currently living in Beijing. A full page was filled with specific numerology notes and predictions. Lizbeth read a couple before skimming the rest. The Chinese fascination with numbers and portents was something she'd never been able to wrap her head around in spite of living with a Chinese grandmother. Waipo would understand everything.

A bright pink sticky note was attached to the page. *Here's the info I told you about last week. Eu-meh is a perfect match! What will Americans call her—Emma or Uma? Your wedding here first for U.S. family next month, second in July for her family after you move to China. So excited!!! ~Mama.*

She'd been such a fool, fallen too fast and too hard. She was so sure everything was different with him. Her vision blurred through tears. *No tears. Do not cry over this man.* She closed her eyes. She shouldn't have looked through his things, but screw him, she was glad she had. It would be easier to approach this weekend knowing it was all they would have together. She wiped at her tears with the back of her hand, then took great care putting the letter back in the envelope and its proper place in the pile of mail. She shouldn't have opened the envelope, but she couldn't un-see any of it.

Perfect match. Wedding next month. Move to China in July.

How could he have read all that and come up to bed with her? How could he have made love to her like he had, less than an hour ago, knowing he was engaged? His mother was following up on a conversation. The postmark was last week, before they had met. He had come to bed, to sleep by her side, after having read that letter. She had no right to the information. They'd only had three days together. She had no claim on him. He had none on her.

You deserve this.

But... he had said he could spend every night with her.

You knew it was coming.

But... he had said he loved her.

They had made love less than an hour ago. It was no longer a mere fling for her. How could it be for him? The way he touched her. The way he kissed her. He told her about Malachi. She told him about Bella.

No one else would do. Even though it would hurt, perhaps even worse than leaving right now, she wanted him until Saturday night and then—that would be it. They'd no longer be working together after that. She'd never have to see him again, especially if he was moving to China in a month.

She came up with a mantra to repeat in her head.

Curt is a fling. Curt is a fling. Curt is a fling. An exciting, amazing fling. But. A. FLING. Nothing more.

This was how people did things in DC. They had short and intense romantic liaisons. A good time. No commitments. Nothing more than good sex and companionship. She'd done this before. She could do it with Curt. She was forced to work with him for the rest of the week, she'd make it what it was. It would be worth it, though. Even only a weekend, it would be worth it. And, if she managed to keep her cool, she could still get him to help her with her application. She'd managed to keep Randy as a friend, why not Curt?

You never felt this way about Randy. Who are you kidding? Curt is special, but he is engaged. Get it into your head, girl. There is nothing more.

It stung, but there was something freeing about accepting that whatever was going on would end in a few days. She could relax about things and simply be herself. There was no need to worry about what his mother might think of her. Or, for that matter, what he might think of her. She was free of any pretense. She'd take everything from him she could and give back equally.

It will be okay. I'll be fine.

She had to get out of his house before Curt woke up again. She couldn't look at him straight in the face without losing it, not yet. She needed some time to adjust her emotions to fit the mantra she was screaming in her head. She pulled the custom wood door firmly behind her, the automatic lock clicking loudly into place. She was a block away and waiting at the closest metro station when she remembered she'd left the magazine open on the table.

izbeth made it home, fed the cats, and packed her clothing and gear for the weekend. She walked to her office, taking a different route to avoid the waffle shop entirely, glad she'd gone with the more expensive suitcase with better wheels. She used the time to figure out how she was going to approach the weekend. She couldn't be openly angry at him unless she'd admit to her snooping. No way was she going to do that. She hoped he would assume she'd pulled the magazine out and left it on the table without noticing the letter from his mom. Let him bring it up if he wanted a confrontation about ethics.

Lizbeth headed straight to the coffee shop to meet Madeline Asher, the Communications director. Madeline actually had the audacity to ask if she was playing

BINGO. Hadn't she made it clear that she wasn't going to play?

Afterwards, there was a short meeting with staff to discuss the various press releases for the Chinese visit. Madeline would release something new every day to highlight the various trade implications of the meetings on the Hill and the good relations between the two countries. She was sending a photographer to both the Dragon Boat Festival and the gala.

After reviewing the calendar with Madeline, she had another couple of hours of work to do before she left for the hotel. At her desk, she used her headphones and a recording of a South American rainforest to block out all the blips and clicks from her office mates. She wanted to leave behind a clear desk.

As she wrapped up an email to Michael, putting him in touch with her mother, she realized that it was up to her to make changes in her life. She would make new contacts, and she already had Michael and her friend Randy as a resource. She would stop dithering around on the Foreign Service job application and call more regularly to move things along. Maybe Link would be willing to push things along. She didn't need Curt. She could do it on her own.

With a new job in the foreign service, she'd be able to leave DC. She'd tell the Alstons she would move so they didn't have to. She brightened at the possibility.

Bella wouldn't have her whole life uprooted. Liz would be willing to do that for her, she would do anything Bella.

She clicked off her white noise and took out the ear buds. Real life appeared so distant suddenly, like it was something she wasn't a part of. The whole office was like that. She poked her head in Kat's office to let her know she was heading out and would be back on Monday. A deep melancholy threatened to drag her into an abyss from which she might never escape. It was as if a part of her was already saying goodbye by making the decision to forge ahead. Kat waved at her while still talking on the phone, barely acknowledging her.

Lizbeth's phone beeped with a text message notification as she climbed into a cab. The Chinese plane had been delayed by forty minutes. She could head over to the hotel anyway and get settled early.

C: I'm looking forward to the evening together

She sighed. No matter what was going on in their personal lives, she wouldn't let it impact her professional one. He was going to be married soon and she wouldn't get any more of his texts. She put aside her mixed feelings, the longing for him. The knowing that he was the one. If she was going to have fun for the weekend, then she was going to make it memorable.

L: Thanks for the update and... me too. Called the hotel. Our rooms share a door

C: Good. Unlock it when you get there?

L: I'm blushing

C: Love it

There was that love word again. But it was never an I love you. Only make love to you. Or a general 'do you believe in love at first sight.' Or referencing a stupid text. Liz pitched her phone into her purse. She was going to fuck him so good, he'd cry when she left.

Enjoy the weekend Curt Wu. It's just beginning.

The Pembroke Hotel near Mt. Vernon Square wasn't far away, but she'd already lugged her suitcase enough for one day, so she hailed a taxi. There weren't a lot of beautiful hotels near the Chinese Embassy, so they'd chosen one closer to the actual activities and events for the weekend. The only exception was the gala, which would be held at the Embassy.

She loved the architecture and glass windows of the Pembroke. The hotel took up an entire city block and was one of the coolest in town. Her job was to be at the hotel in order to verify security protocols and make sure the check-in went smoothly as well as coordinate the huge translation team.

Normally, the large group would have stayed at the Chinese Embassy, but there was not enough room. The Embassy was still under repair from pipes that had burst during last year's freeze. It was ninety percent repaired, but even the best contractors hadn't been able to work fast enough to finish the guest wing in time for this visit.

A hotel stay would be required. As a courtesy to the People's Republic of China, the State Department had rented the entire hotel for the added comfort and security of the Chinese delegation since their Embassy was unable to accommodate them all.

She checked her watch. The plane should be landing at Dulles International soon. The delegation would take about two hours to get through their expedited customs and immigration transition and another hour for traffic. They would be escorted via a motorcade that would close down the streets. Nothing unusual in this town, really. The only difference was the motorcade would be flying the Chinese flag and not the American flag. The honor escort was in place.

She had organized a shuttle service to move people back and forth between the Embassy and the hotel hourly during business hours and every half hour during the gala. Mostly, though, the delegates would be meeting with U.S. officials on the Hill and their spouses would be off site-seeing.

The Chinese had been very clear that they didn't want their visitors wandering off on their own. This super-controlling organized guard over their people was stereotypical old-school Soviet-era stuff to Lizbeth. The Bureau of Diplomatic Security folks had their own SUVs and drivers for the high-level officials who needed more flexibility.

She paused as she stepped into the lobby to admire the sheer beauty of the place. It wasn't the largest hotel in DC but it had an old-world elegance. There was both strength and beauty to the architecture. The interior had been refurbished not too many years ago and had managed to retain its old-world charm while incorporating modern amenities. The furnishings were modern while still in keeping with the Art Nouveau feel.

She loved the Pembroke Hotel and was pleased they had managed to broker a deal to ensure the entire building was catering to this one event. The managers went above and beyond to help other guests find alternate lodging elsewhere in the city. People were politely informed that the State Department required the use of the hotel that weekend and were given an equal or better set of rooms nearby. Only a couple of people complained, but the hotel manager did what was necessary to satisfy them.

The security teams were already set up by the time she arrived. Check. The manager, a gorgeous blonde wearing a navy-blue suit gave her a quick tour. Each room had a packet that explained logistics, had a master events schedule, and a phone number to call for questions. For meals, they had reserved seating in the restaurant serving Chinese, and they had routed a special room service line which would allow them to order food with a Chinese speaker. The hotel had sent over a list of their employees months ago. Individuals with a felony were given paid time off courtesy of the U.S. government.

The manager pointed out the signage in both English and Chinese that would help to direct people, along with a Chinese speaking concierge to help with directions and other questions. Several of the interpreters were already in the conference room, waiting. Lizbeth thanked her and welcomed the interpreters.

In the conference room, Lizbeth started with the usual speech about translating and confidentiality. They might overhear things that were state secrets, American or Chinese, and they were to forget any such comments immediately. Nothing, not even what the representative had for breakfast, was to be discussed.

Each interpreter had a complete schedule and was assigned to stay with a delegate during all pre-planned activities. She handed out cell phones with her number as well as everyone else's on the team programmed into the phones. This was done for security purposes, to assure that no other recording devices or other apps had been loaded onto the phones. Everyone, including herself, would be expected to remain at the hotel or be with their assigned delegates until Sunday afternoon when the delegation left Washington and was out of U.S. air space.

To make matters even more complicated, the Chinese delegation would be bringing their own staff of twenty translators as a safeguard to make sure the American translators were being accurate—one for each delegate but not for spouses. The Americans would not be allowed to debrief them.

Liz sighed; that detail made this event even more complicated to coordinate, but she was good at her job, and could handle the extra work with ease. The Chinese clearly didn't trust anyone, and wanted someone listening in on every conversation, but the U.S. frowned on that level of scrutiny. It would be impossible to monitor everything that was said between everyone involved over the course of three days and all the various activities.

Lizbeth ran through the list of activities with the translators. Basic orientation would be first after everyone was checked in. The Chinese staff was running that. Then, the Embassy was hosting a private dinner for their staff and the delegation. The Embassy had hired a Chinese band to provide entertainment, raucous entertainment, for after dinner. This would force the visitors to stay awake until ten o'clock to prevent severe jet lag.

The hotel would set up an American and Chinese buffet to make everyone feel more welcome. Friday morning would be spent in meetings or on the tour around the mall and memorials. Friday evening was split into two groups. One group would be attending the season's final performance of Il Trovatore at the national opera house. The second group would be attending a special hockey exhibition Lizbeth had set up just for this occasion. Katherine had dated one of the players on the Washington Capitals and helped her set it up.

She was a fan of both but made sure she was put in the opera contingent. Curt knew nothing about opera, but he was interested. She had been so excited when he had shown interest. Had that been a lie, too? Had he been playing her the whole time?

Nothing but another weekend fling. Fucking him hard would feel so good.

A ripple rolled down her spine at the thought of him on his back at her command.

Saturday morning would be spent at the Dragon Boat Festival on the river. Saturday night would be the gala. Even the interpreters were expected to dress in black tie and formal gowns. Lizbeth had carefully planned her outfit weeks ago. It was spectacular, to be honest. Oh god. She was going to be seated next to Curt. The idea stung a little. She'd make him pay anyway. There was no way she would let her personal feelings create havoc during this event. She was in control.

Curt texted her that the delegation was about five minutes out as she was wrapping up the room changes. She used to be an expert at weekend flings, and dammit, she was going to show him how it was done.

She'd break up with him first. That way she wouldn't be disappointed when he told her about his plans. If he ever told her. He owed her nothing. She owed him nothing. The good thing about Curt was that he reminded her who was in charge—she was.

Then she'd be gone. He had given her a push to move on with her life. There was no way she could stay in DC, not after him. Soon, she'd be the one standing behind the leaders as they negotiated their trade deals. She would be the one brokering trade deals or calming political tensions between nations. Lizbeth would be the one on the dignitary list. Curt could do whatever the hell he was going to do in Beijing with his brand-new wife.

Chapter 16

*L*izbeth greeted each group as they arrived. By the time everyone was squared away and the orientation she was in charge of was over, she was tired. As the delegation settled into dinner and all the last-minute stragglers were now in the right place, Lizbeth headed to her room. She was exhausted. Her brain ached in spite of being fluent in Chinese. It was rare for her to speak it for six hours straight. All she wanted was to watch a movie and order room service.

She texted Curt to see if he wanted to join her and unlocked the door. She had taken her clothes off, tired of the constricting clothes and the smell of them and stretched out onto the bed in her bra and panties.

Scrolling through her phone, she stopped at a picture of Bella on the playground. She wondered if she should reach out to Angela and Demarco in a gesture of good will. She was already planning a move, but she had no specifics, nothing concrete to tell them.

If she made the first move, maybe they'd relent and let her see Bella on their monthly schedule at least until she moved away. It would be so much less disruptive to their lives. She carefully worded a text making the offer and held her breath as she hit send.

She'd find her way into the Foreign Service. It was likely they'd send her to China with her qualifications, but she doubted she'd get her first posting in Beijing. She'd be away from DC and away from Curt, on her way up the ladder. That was all that mattered.

Lizbeth stared at the door. He wasn't coming. *So much for being in control.* She removed the lacy bra and panties—they were useless to her now. Her body longed for the soft comfort of cotton sweats and a t-shirt. She shrugged them on and flopped back down on the bed, annoyed at herself for being disappointed he wasn't there.

As she was about to shut the lights off and go to sleep, Curt knocked at the door and pushed it open.

"Oh hey, am I too late?" Curt gave her one of his boyish-dangerous smiles, but didn't skip a beat. "Look what I found," he said holding up a bottle of wine. "A 2008 Didier Dagueneau Pouilly-Fumé Silex. One advantage to having access to the kitchen."

Liz reached for the plush hotel robe as she slid

out of bed. She played right along with him. "You didn't steal this, did you?" After securing the belt of the robe around her, she looked at the bottle with appreciation. "Hmmm... Bottled in Loire, France. I'm impressed. I'll probably get tipsy after one drink, you know."

"Yeah, I don't like getting drunk. People do stupid things when they're drunk."

Curt did not seem like the kind of guy who would do stupid things, drunk or sober.

Lizbeth pointed to the room service menu. "I bet it will take some time to get food if we order now."

"I suppose we could find a way to kill the time," he said, pulling her into his arms and kissing her gently.

There was an underlying urgency to the kiss, but also an exquisite familiarity as if they had been kissing each other for years and knew each other on an intimate level. She didn't want to feel this way, so she kissed him back hard to break it.

He pulled away and pressed his forehead against hers. "How was your day?"

"Good. Where'd you disappear to? I thought you'd be here earlier."

"I had something come up." His hands slid along her back down to her bottom. He cupped her gently and squeezed.

Desire for him quickened at his touch as he

pressed his erection against her. Oh yes. *He* was defi-nitely going to cry when she left him.

"Didn't you want to wait and order dinner?" She wriggled her bottom suggestively against his hands.

He kissed her again, sliding his hands down to her thighs and lifting her up. She wrapped her legs around his body. Lizbeth breathed in his scent, memorizing the traces of lime and ginger. She kissed him behind the ear and tugged at his earlobe with her teeth. *Make him cry.*

He moaned as he lowered her onto the bed. He kissed her again and rolled onto his side, propping his head up on his elbow to look at her. He cupped her cheek and turned her to face him.

"I've got something I'd like to talk to you about."

Lizbeth's breath caught. *Okay... all hot and heavy—now talking? That was pretty abrupt.*

Was he about to tell her he was engaged and moving? Or admit that he was here for the week-long sexy times?

"Sounds serious." She put on a mask of innocent neutrality.

"I'm kinda into some kinky things. Not that I have any fetishes, but I honestly need to let you know before we go very far in this whole dating thing."

This was not at all what Lizbeth had expected. "What do you mean by kinky?"

Curt caressed her breast and pinched her nipple between two fingers. "I like being a little... dominant."

"You didn't seem to mind me being in charge this morning," she said, wanting to lure him in, wanting him naked, wanting to be on top.

His smile widened. "I don't always have to be in charge. I like to spice things up sometimes. Nothing too crazy."

Lizbeth's heart skipped a beat. What kinds of things did he want to do to her? Part of her thrilled at the possibilities, the other part recoiled. She loved that he talked to her about sex before actually doing it. He was a man of consent—one of the good guys. Too bad he was engaged to another woman. She held up a hand. "I'm not into pain."

"I'm not into that either."

"You want to fuck with my mind?"

He grinned. "A little, maybe. In ways that are fun. Teasing. Light stuff."

"Like that whole orgasm denial the other night?"

Curt sucked in his lower lip. "Just thinking about it, " he pulled her hand against his pants, "has gotten me rock hard."

"You *are* a talker. Don't forget, I'm a goat. It isn't my nature to be submissive all the time."

He stopped laughing. "See. This is the thing. I

enjoy the idea of... say... tying you up, but I don't *need* it. I am fine without it."

"Curt, what are you talking about? Are you saying you want handcuffs and whips or are you talking about something else?"

"Oh, no, more like pretending we're strangers and meet in the bar downstairs, then throwing you on the bed... maybe silk scarves to tie you up... that kind of thing."

Lizbeth had read plenty of books where the hero throws the woman on the bed or otherwise ravages a heroine who started off fighting him away only to end up with her having a scream-inducing orgasm by the end of it. Or books where a virgin was taken by force by a rich boss or Sheik and turned into a sex slave. They never rang true to her.

And yet, she'd always been slightly embarrassed at her own proclivity to be turned on by these stories.

"So... you want to pretend we don't know each other for a hook-up?" She fought the urge to tell him to piss off, to tell him that she *knew* everything. But she didn't. She wanted him. For now, anyway.

"That, or..."

"I'm willing to try anything once," she said. "But it feels kind of fake to plan it out ahead of time. Do we write it out first?"

Curt shook his head. "Scripting it out would be

tricky. The easiest thing to do is for us to... agree to try it, and then if I do anything that is really not working for you, you let me know. Immediately. This kind of thing requires good communication."

Lizbeth thought about this for a moment. *Good communication. Like the one you and your future wife are going to have. Oh, you are going to pay, Curt Wu. Pay with your heart. Even your dick is going to miss me.* She ran a few scenarios through her head. "No means no, right?"

He nodded.

"There was this Jane Austen rip-off I read where a man had kidnapped a woman and taken her to a remote country estate. It turns out that she was really in love with the man, but he wasn't her husband and she had to pretend to not want the man's attentions. He was really saving her from an abuser, but propriety wouldn't allow her to accept him openly as a lover. I loved it. I loved it so much, I totally got off on it."

He drew a heart on her bare stomach with his finger. His fingernail left a pink line that disappeared within seconds. Heat blossomed between Lizbeth's clenched legs.

"Let's forgo the kidnapping part, unless you want to get dressed and go down to the lobby and have me throw you over my shoulder like a caveman."

She laughed. "No. We can skip straight to the part

where she's tied up on the bed and he has to assert himself over her."

Curt dipped into the voices he played the night before while reading to her. "Perchance, dear lady, have you any rope with which I might secure your delicate and frail wrists to the bed?"

Was she really going to let him tie her up? She wanted to be on top so bad, but it was such a mindfuck at this moment to be submissive. As if she were being submissive to her feelings. Submissive to the weekend. She took a deep breath. "I have a scarf that goes with the dress I'll be wearing to the gala."

He kissed her and rolled off the bed to search her closet. She sipped at her wine. Then she gulped at it. She was getting pretty good with play-acting, might as well step it up a bit. She was excited and a little anxious about admitting she could enjoy the scenario, the odd way her fantasies and real-life dove tailed together.

He came back holding up two pieces of fabric. "Are these okay?"

She had forgotten about the shawl she'd brought for the opera. It was thin, almost transparent, gossamer silk. The other piece matched her gala dress. It was a neck-drape scarf placed across the front of her neck with the two sides draping down her back.

"I'm going to tie you up and then re-enter the

room. You'll pretend to not want my attentions, and I'll pretend you are saying you don't want them to protect your honor."

They say men think with their dicks, but women have a similar inability to think straight when their bodies are directing them to fuck. And her whole body thrummed with excitement and expectation. She'd read her fair share of dirty books, seen some movies that had sent her to her room to masturbate behind the backs of her lovers, unwilling to admit she secretly wanted to be touched a certain way. Had she finally found the right man to trust with those conflicting desires?

Right now, she didn't have to do that. She could be free. And in some ways, the scenario was a better enactment of reality. She didn't want him in her life as a lover, not a real lover, not a forever lover, but she was willing to consent with him in a sexual escapade that satisfied her fantasies.

Curt drew her up to him and kissed her. Their lips were hungry for each other. They had found their rhythm, the dance between their tongues. A familiarity that normally came with lots of time and trial and error, but this was only after two days.

"What kind of secret desires do you have, Miss Crandall?" he asked when they finally broke their kiss and came up for air.

She blushed, suddenly self-aware. "I... would like to be tied up. There's something vulnerable about it."

"Like in your novel. The lack of choice means you can't be held accountable for what happens."

"And of course, I'd never admitting to enjoying it."

"Stop whenever you decide to." He kissed the top of her nose and held up the scarf and shawl. "Ready?"

"Yes."

His lips twisted as he considered her and the bed. "Wait. Two isn't enough. I'll be right back."

It dawned on her that he meant to tie her arms *and* her legs. She'd be unable to move—at all. He could do anything... She downed her wine and poured herself a second glass. She took a sip and set it aside. Being tipsy would not help. She couldn't drink more than a glass without getting sick. He returned holding up two of his ties.

"Voila!" He looked at her critically for a moment. "Do you have any clothes that don't care about?"

Waving her hands along her body, she said, "You think this is my glam outfit?"

His eyes twinkled. "I want to cut them off you."

Her eyes widened, but she saw the sense of it in terms of the role-play. "Do you have scissors?"

He lifted an eyebrow. "No, but I do have a straight edged razor. That will do the trick."

A tiny piece of her thrilled at the idea of the cold

blade sliding up her skin, closely dangerous, without actually cutting her, the threat so imminent yet unrealized. *Did she trust him? Could she?* She sucked in her lower lip. He might not *be* a dragon, but there was definitely an edge to him.

He smoothed his hands down her arms. The touch grounded her, making her feel safe. *How the hell did he do that? No time to think. Just do.*

"No. No razors tonight, buddy. I'm not ready for that." Lizbeth ripped her clothes off and stood before him naked.

"All right then. No razors, *tonight*," he said, the last word implying a promise for the future. He slid a hand against her pussy, and she leaned into him as he pressed two fingers into her.

"Mmmm... you are enjoying this, aren't you?"

"Should I have a safe word or something? People are always talking about that."

He paused, eyes narrowing on her. "In case I go a little too far into this rogue character?"

She doubted Curt ever lost control. Surrendering herself to his touch as he took his time tying her to the bed was freeing.

"I think cantaloupe would work."

The look he gave her was one of such utter confusion that she burst out laughing.

"Cantaloupe?"

"For my safe-word, silly. If I want you to really stop, I'll say cantaloupe. That way I can scream *stop* or *don't* or *no* and you will continue doing whatever you were doing. If I say cantaloupe, that's your signal to stop whatever you're doing and make sure we're good."

His shoulders relaxed, and he laughed. "Okay, got it. Cantaloupe. I was trying to figure out what you wanted me to do with a cantaloupe. Cucumber? Maybe. Cantaloupe... no way."

Cucumbers? Lizbeth sucked in her breath. Just how kinky did this man like to get?

He kissed the entire length of her arm as he stretched it toward the corner post of the bed. These kisses were different—deliberate, and without the frenzy of get-your-clothes-off sex. His fingers moved with ease as he wrapped her wrists in the fabric and then fastened her to the bed. He repeated the moves with the other arm.

Liz tugged at the bonds to test them out. They gave just an inch, no more. Slight panic sent new shivers of excitement through her. He ran a tongue along her inner thigh to her knee before restraining her leg. He worked his way back up, teasing her madly by skipping over her pussy to her other thigh. He licked and nibbled all the way down the other leg before securing that one, too.

When he was finished, there was nothing she

could do to free herself. She was his to do with as he willed. He stood beside the bed looking at his handiwork, fully clothed. Lizbeth waited for him to go into character or whatever was supposed to happen next. She'd never pretended to be someone she wasn't with another lover like this before. Role playing with intent was new to her.

He rolled his shoulders back. "I am sorry, my dear, for the restraints, but I could not be wholly persuaded by your argument earlier, that you would not flee the moment we arrived at my castle," he said in a rich British accent.

Lizbeth tugged at her bonds. She didn't want to do the accent. He was so sure in his role, and she would sound silly trying. She swallowed hard, choosing to be in the moment. This scenario was of her making. "But, my lord, why have you brought me here?" She started off whisper soft and then found her courage. "I will never be yours. I am intended for another."

"He is a swine, a scoundrel, a villain. To have your father choose him over me is utterly maddening. Even knowing your wishes..." Curt placed his palm against her ankle and slid it up her leg as she spoke. His fingers stopped short of actually touching her pussy. "Unless you've changed your mind?"

Lizbeth shifted her hips, willing his fingers to find her. She didn't want to answer him.

He shook his head, wagging a finger in her direction. "You must answer me before I touch you. I won't take a maid wholly unwilling."

"My lord, I promise you. The engagement was all my father's doing. Lord..." she searched for a name and lighted upon a name from another Austen novel. "Thorpe... is wealthy, and my father cannot see beyond the money."

"Ah... yes... money. It is always the answer for some, is it not?"

"But, please, sir. Tell me how you think tying me up and ravishing me will work? My father will not succumb to such rash threats." Lizbeth was having way more fun with this than she thought possible.

"Once certain of our congress, your father must relent and allow us to marry."

"But I would give myself willingly to you, surely you must know that."

Curt pretended to look shocked. "But a lady of your stature would never do such a thing. You must hold onto your virtue, guard it like the golden treasure it truly is." He cupped his hand around her mound for emphasis. "Truly, it should be under a lock and key. For your own protection."

A squeak escaped Lizbeth. She squirmed as much as she could under his hand, wishing for more pressure. All her thoughts about the future vanished. She only wanted him. His fingers skimmed across her stomach and up to her nipples, which stood hard and erect in her excitement.

"If your father thought you were complicit in the venture, my dear, he would never forgive you. Knowing you have no say in the matter, he will be able to forgive you."

Lizbeth pulled ferociously at the ties. "No. No, he won't ever forgive you." She paused for a moment, playing up the scene and relishing the way the words of the game reflected her emotions. She would never forgive Curt for lying to her. "You must let me go, please. Sirrah, please. There must be another way. I can talk to my father. You don't have to claim me like this."

"But I must. Upon taking your virtue from you, your father must cast Lord Thorpe's offer aside in favor of restoring your honor by marrying me."

"How, sir? How will my father even know that I was not complicit in this venture? Unless... you plan for him to catch us in the act?" Lizbeth rounded her eyes in mock surprise. She was having fun getting into this. Her body was reacting to the new sensations. She liked not having to think about love. She wasn't beholden to anyone but her own decisions, her own voice. Being tied down and spread wide like this left her feeling vulnerable and incredibly sensual at the same time.

Unable to move, Liz's other senses were heightened. The smoothness of the sheet against her back, the way the knots around her wrists and ankles held her firm without pain, the way Curt's hands were hot against her skin. His scent, usually heady and sensual, was intoxicating. The slight constant underlying buzz from the alarm clock on the table.

"My dear, I won't let him see you naked like this, but we must be convincing in our efforts. My servants have ears, and they can bear witness to your struggle. It must be obvious to him the deed is done."

Lizbeth tilted her head back into the mattress. "Please, my lord, my virtue is intact. If you take it from me, I will have nothing."

Curt slowly undressed, placing his clothing carefully over a chair. At length, he stood at the head of the bed, his cock erect.

He climbed onto the bed between her legs, placing a hand on each of her thighs, spreading her open with his thumbs. "Ah... my sweet, sweet, lady. I can contain myself only so long."

Curt spread her pussy wide as he lowered his mouth to it. She pulled at the restraints, the shock only too real.

"My lord, what are you doing? This is not at all what I was expecting."

He didn't answer. Instead, he sucked her clit into his mouth, giving it his full attention.

Liz wanted to run her fingers through his hair, to push or pull at his head to guide him, but she couldn't. She pulled at her arms in real frustration.

He laughed against her, the buzzing feeling reminiscent of their motorcycle ride. She relaxed, giving up on fighting the restraints and finding what little movement she could in her hips. She wanted more and pressed up into him, but his hands moved to her thighs and pushed her into the mattress.

He held her there, insistently lapping, taking her higher, but not enough to let her come.

"My lord," she panted, pretending she'd never had an orgasm before. "I don't understand what's happening, is this normal? I feel so hot. So shaky. Is something wrong with me?"

He responded by redoubling his efforts, insisting on her coming into his mouth.

"Oh, oh... oh..." Lizbeth let it go when she came. The closest guests in the hotel were at least six doors down, and she was certain no one could hear them. As the orgasm ripped through her, she pulled hard against the restraints, trying to move with it, but she couldn't.

Being tied up restricted her from moving to dissipate the intense orgasm. Everything focused on her pussy.

She wanted to beg Curt to fuck her now, but she stayed in character. "My lord, this is not what I had expected. My mother prepared me for something... unpleasant, and that was most... wonderful indeed. Now, should my father find us, will our plan have worked?"

"Ah, innocent beauty. I have yet to take my fill of you." He pressed his cock meaningfully against her thigh. "You see, this is what will seal our fate together forever."

She widened her eyes, feigning surprise.

"Now, my love," he whispered, "Now, my dear, is the time for you to cry out for me to stop before I ravish you. Let the servants believe you are being taken against your will."

"Please. My lord, no. My virtue, oh, please, do not take it from me. I beg of you," she grinned as she said it.

He plunged into her.

Liz gasped as he filled her, unable to contain her actual pleasure at finally having him inside her again. It had been less than a day, and she was hungry for him.

She moved as much as she could, struggling against the bonds. "Stop, my lord. Please, my lord, don't do this. My lord, you must STOP!" The panic in her voice shocked her, she was really getting into this.

She must have sounded convincing, too, because Curt paused, fully inside her, eyes intent on her. She nudged upward with her hips with the tiny amount of freedom she did have.

"I said stop, not the other word." *No way was the word cantaloupe going to come through these lips anytime soon.*

He laughed a little in spite of himself. "My dear, the servants will most assuredly find your reticence entirely convincing. I know I almost did."

"My lord, please..." She writhed under him, soaking up the pleasure he gave her, completely forgetting the game they were playing. "Don't stop," she begged, her voice ragged. "Whatever you do... keep going."

He buried himself deep inside her, his whole body tensing above her and inside her. Liz exploded underneath him. She'd never had an orgasm with a man on top of her like this. She always had to be on top, in control of the movements. He kissed her neck and continued until he, too, came. After, he collapsed on top of her, his face pressed against her neck.

Lizbeth still couldn't move, she wanted to wrap her arms and legs around him, holding him inside her forever. *Damn it. Her resolve to burn him kept drifting away*. Curt reached out and tugged at a loose end of the scarf holding her arm, then at the other. He lifted himself off her, the cooler air of the room whooshing in between them.

He untied her legs and tossed all the bindings off to the floor. Pulling the covers up over them both, he snuggled in next to her. "I've never done that with anyone. It was fun."

Lizbeth wrapped her arms and legs around him, a full reversal of the position she'd been in for the last twenty minutes or so. She fit into his torso perfectly. Soon, they were both asleep in each other's arms. It was as if they'd always been together. She was too tired to think anything else. The weekend would end soon enough, but for now, she wanted to be with him. To pretend that they were one.

Chapter 17

*L*izbeth woke with a start. The dream she'd been having flitted away from her, leaving only the slightest trace of something scary behind. A general sense of wrongness. She ran her tongue along her teeth. Curt's face was relaxed in sleep, his breathing quiet and deep.

She stretched and sat up, letting the bedclothes fall into blanketing pools around her waist. Curt didn't move. It would take more than that to wake him, and she *had* promised him more delightful awakenings the previous day. She kissed his ear. His forehead. Ran a finger along his lips and studied the dragon tattoo. *I wish you were mine.* When he breathed, it looked like it was moving. The man could sleep through anything. Finally she bit his earlobe and tugged. With his eyes closed, he chuckled and vaguely swatted at her.

She giggled into his ear as he rolled onto his back, pulling her over him to straddle his morning erection.

"I thought you liked me to be in control," he said.

"Well, that was last night. Right now, I need it hard and fast."

Grabbing the headboard on the bed for balance, Lizbeth reached for the anger she needed to keep herself from falling any harder for him. Last night was last night. And she'd come dangerously close to forgetting he was leaving her, to forgetting he was engaged to another woman. The cold light of the morning had reminded her it was a short-term gig. She would use him over the next few days, but she had to work to break her emotional attachment.

She'd take her orgasm from him and hit the shower, not caring if he came or not. She used his body hard, fucking him fast and furious. Riding him like there was no tomorrow, *and maybe there wasn't*, she closed her eyes and focused her body. He gasped and bucked under her, his hips thrusting up to meet her own, driving himself deeper into her. He groaned in pleasure as she thrashed on top of him, relishing the taking of him.

As soon as she came, she removed herself from him. No lingering this morning. "Gotta get going." She launched into the bathroom, slightly confused by her own emotions. Love him. Don't love him. Fuck him.

Fuck with him. It all jumbled around in her head. What had she done? He probably hadn't even noticed her attitude. There was no way he could read her mind. He was probably thinking she was hot for him.

Argh. Why did she care?

Lizbeth ran through the day's events as she lathered the hotel's free shampoo into her scalp, pulling the suds through her thick hair. She was looking forward to the entire day, but especially the walking tour and opera.

She rolled her hair into a towel and drifted back into the bedroom to dress. Curt lounged against the headboard staring at his phone and muttering.

"Everything okay?" she asked.

Curt looked up. "Yeah. I'm annoyed at my sister. She's being unreasonable."

"You have three? All married, right?" She dressed while they spoke. An image of the letter from his mother invaded her calm. She knew he had three sisters, the two older ones married, his youngest sister, the baby of the family dating a guy who didn't like Chinese food. Lizbeth had to do her best to pretend she knew nothing about the situation; she didn't want to give away that she had been snooping.

"Nope. Not all married. My youngest sister is dating a white guy who doesn't even like Chinese food. My mom is having a fit."

"Ouch. Is your mom okay with half-Chinese girls?"

Curt looked up and gave her an odd glance. The moment was gone in a flash as he went back to work. She shouldn't have asked him that. He was going to get married. They already had someone picked out. Someone fully Chinese.

Once she was dressed, she returned to the bathroom to finish her hair and make-up. The twenty minutes of non-stop hot air to get ready was a welcome respite. She had to center herself before she saw him again, to put on her game face. It was turning out to be harder than she thought to keep her emotional distance.

When she was finally ready for the day, she returned to the bedroom to find Curt standing at the dresser, his face set and eyes focused on a piece of paper in his hand. He turned to her in slow motion, his normally kind eyes edged in anger, his jaw clenched shut. His upper body was rigid, muscles bound tight.

Her purse was on the dresser, most of its contents spilled out.

"Curt?"

He thrust the paper at her face, holding it too close for her to be able to read it. "What the fuck is this?"

She brushed his hand aside. "Were you going through my purse?"

"Your phone was ringing. And then pinging texts. I thought something important might be going on." He held the paper up again. "This? You're saying you don't know what this is?"

She tore it out of his hand. It was the BINGO card she'd been given the other night and stuffed into her purse. The title across the top *Monument Bingo—five guys, five monuments, five kisses* made her cringe. "It's a stupid game." She shook her head, still trying to figure out why he was so upset. So angry.

He ripped it out of her grasp and put his finger on a square. "State Department. Roosevelt Memorial." He spit out the words.

"I'm not playing the game, Curt."

"*You* insisted we go to the Roosevelt Memorial the other day. I work for State."

"Yeah, but..." she stopped short. But *what?* If he wanted to believe that she had dragged him there as part of a stupid game, what could she do to convince him otherwise? The title was pretty descriptive. It made sense he'd jump to that conclusion.

"I'm not playing this game," she said, crumpling the card up and lobbing it toward the wastebasket. "It's stupid and childish. And I'm not playing."

She could hear his teeth grinding against each other. His eyes remained cold and angry.

She reached out to touch him, but he shrugged out of her reach.

"Curt?"

"You only pretended to be interested in me to get a kiss at that memorial. How many memorials have you been to? How many men have you kissed?"

"You are overreacting. I only have the card because they gave it to me; I shoved it into my purse and forgot about it."

Curt turned away.

"Oh. My. Fucking. God. Don't you dare turn away from me."

His muscles bunched as he turned to face her. "Me?" His eyes were as dangerous as she'd ever seen. Even so, she wasn't afraid of him. Naturally, from years of karate, she moved into a defensive position.

"You're one to talk. You're worried about me playing an innocent kissing game—which I'm not— when you're engaged to be married? Exactly when were you going to bring that up? Huh, Curt?"

An icy cold fear zipped down her back as he lunged at her. She blocked his move with ease and jumped away from his grasping hands, real fear at the danger this man posed pulsing through her.

The twinkle in his eye had switched into an inter-rogator's spotlight—piercing and frightening at the same time. He held up his hands, giving up the physical battle and stepped back.

"What are you talking about?" His voice was low. An animalistic growl.

Who was this man?

"Eu-meh Hwang? I read the letter from your mother."

He looked down her body, assessing her weak spots. She clenched her hands into a fist. He inched closer to her, and she could feel his quickened breath against her cheek. He examined her intently and in utter silence, like he was trying to read her mind.

"How much of that letter did you understand?" he asked.

"I am fluent in Chinese, Curt. I could read it all."

"But what did you *understand?*"

She shook her head, completely confused now. "What was there to not understand about the fact you're getting married and moving to China? You think that might have been something you'd want to mention before fucking me. Multiple times."

"Fine." He stormed into his own suite, slamming the connecting door between them. The heavy thunk of the lock sounded so final.

Chapter 18

A text chimed as Liz still stared at the door. She had no idea where her phone was and didn't care. She had no intention of going after Curt. The bastard lied to her then had the audacity to call her out? She was tired already and had a long forty-eight hours ahead of her. With utmost concentration, blocking thoughts of him, she calmed her body with five deep breaths. She had a job to do. And it would be spent in this sudden stranger's company.

Another text chimed in—the reason he'd gone pawing through her stuff to begin with. She had four phone calls and six texts. Three of the phone calls had been from last night, but she didn't remember hearing them come through. She'd been busy. The texts were all from this morning.

The phone calls ended up being easy enough to

tend to. Various small problems that their guests were having with the hotel directly. Fortunately, she hadn't missed anything critical. The texts were mostly nothing—one was from her mom, one was from Michael—he had connected with her mom in San Francisco. No need to do anything with those. The last was from Demarco.

Her thumb hovered over the screen, terrified they'd turned down her offer to move without thinking it through. Breathing in deeply one more time, she pressed her thumb against the screen and closed her eyes. She counted to ten and looked at the message.

M: Our plans have not been made. Your offer to move was received rather well, given the circumstances. Let's talk next week, after Angela has had some time. We'll call you.

Lizbeth was uncomfortable that Demarco had responded directly to her and not included Angela in the loop. But whatever worked. Right now, she had the Chinese delegation to deal with. Personal calls would need to be set aside.

Once the working dignitaries had been escorted off to their meetings on the Hill, Lizbeth joined their families at the buffet breakfast. She piled her plate with eggs, sausage, and hash browns and hadn't even started eating when Curt waltzed in. He grabbed a croissant and threw her a sharp look. Glaring at him, she stabbed blindly at her sausage and bit into it with a vengeance. He pretended to ignore her and stalked out of the dining room. The plate of food in front of her was no longer appetizing, and she pushed it aside as she choked down the meat.

He was the one who had lied. She refused to feel wounded. He had a fiancée and a wedding looming in the future, and he had willingly pursued her. With a drink of water, she tried to quell her emotions. He had won her heart and soul. How could he believe she was playing a stupid game with him? Maybe it was because he had lied to her all along. Liars had a hard time finding the truth.

She had to get through the day without falling apart. *He doesn't deserve my heart... or my tears.* Her job demanded that she be professional for the delegation. In five minutes, she had to be on. She closed her eyes and imagined her happy place, focused on it and breathed deeply until she was sure she wouldn't explode. Usually she was able to do it within a couple of breaths. But this morning put her whole world in question. It was as if she was teetering on the edge of a skyscraper. The sense of calmness she needed didn't come for a long time.

In the lobby Lizbeth greeted interpreters and dignitaries, hoping her fake smile didn't betray her actual emotions. She led them to a private coach bus parked out front and politely let her guests board first. They boarded the bus, translators mostly sitting near the front, leaving the members of the delegation to themselves behind them. Curt was already seated. He barely glanced at her as she climbed aboard.

Two can play this game, asshole.

She held her head up high. In the back of the bus, Liz sat next to a dignitary's wife. As usual, Lizbeth found people were much more interested in practicing their English than speaking Chinese. Figuring out what they were trying to say in English was difficult. She tried to focus on the conversation, but couldn't stop glancing up to the front. Curt had not turned around. He wasn't talking to anyone; he was stone cold silent. Someone in the delegation had tried to get his attention, but he wasn't paying attention.

Be a professional, you jerk.

As the bus pulled up to let them out near the Ellipse, the official starting place for their walking tour, Lizbeth stood up to make an announcement. She made it to the front of the bus with all eyes turned to focus on her, including Curt. She couldn't bear to meet his hard gaze, and plastered on a smile for the Chinese guests. "The tour is about three hours. Take your valuables. Once we are finished, we will convene at Old Ebbitt Grill for lunch. The bus will pick us up there when we are done eating."

She had left her purse in her seat, so she had to go all the way back to pick it up. When she finally exited the bus, she scanned the crowd for Curt. He stood with a group of the guests and was actually speaking in a pleasant voice to others around him. The stiffness he'd exhibited earlier was shaken off with a thin veneer of good manners. The tour was something Lizbeth had been looking forward to and she wasn't going to let Curt take that away, too.

She rubbed her hands together, excited to be going with a group of people seeing the monuments for the first time. And from such a different perspective. The Chinese weren't likely to talk much about democracy or freedom in the same way that Lizbeth was used to, but she wondered how people from China really viewed the American version of heroes. They had Mao, of course, but did they venerate him or did they celebrate him because they'd been forced to?

They followed the bright rainbow umbrella the guide held up for them. The view of the White House from the Ellipse was the classic one people think of when they think of the White House. After the first round of photos was complete, the guide led them to the Washington Monument.

Unfortunately, the Washington Monument was closed so no one could actually go up inside. Lizbeth didn't pay much attention to the tour guide. Curt walked around with a group of people, motioning and talking to them. *Curt and his hypocrisy.* She didn't play games. He was the player.

The tour leader announced in Chinese that they would be walking to the Reflecting Pool and the Lincoln Memorial. The tour guide led the group flanked by Diplomatic Security. As it was, the people they were guarding now were dressed in shorts and flowered shirts and jeans or simple dresses. BDS agents looked like Secret Service agents—anything but secret looking with their plain black suits and giant white ear pieces. Even the FBI knew how to blend in way better. CIA agents were invisible by comparison.

CIA operatives were not supposed to be working in the States, but Lizbeth knew better than that. The various spy agencies stepped over each other's toes all the time, and the intelligence committee had so many groups it oversaw, she wondered how anyone ever got any work done. They spent so much time bickering over jurisdiction and funding, she wanted to throw the proposed budgets in their faces. She wanted to tell them to get the fuck to work and play nicely.

Sudden panic rose in her belly and she stopped suddenly. The CIA had been investigating her. How in the world had she forgotten about that? Between Curt and Bella, she was getting flaky. Why had they been to see Congressman Pierce about her? She had way too much stuff swirling around in her head. One of the dignitaries bumped into her. She turned quickly and apologized. If she didn't focus, she'd mess up the entire program.

Once there, the guide spoke in rapid Chinese with a detailed spiel about the history of the Memorial, including a brief description of Lincoln's strengths and the reason people in this country revered the man. They paused for a while so people could get plenty of photos. The pink blossoms on the cherry trees practically glowed with color and their heady scent was almost sickly sweet—better than gardenia and not nearly so cloying.

After the allotted time at the Lincoln Memorial, the tour guide announced they would be moving to the Roosevelt Memorial next. Lizbeth froze at the words. *Their first kiss.* The group shuffled along, everyone pointing and chattering as they went. Lizbeth made sure she stayed away from Curt. She wanted nothing to do with him right now. And yet, whenever she saw his head bob up ahead of her, her heart tightened and her stomach twisted in fresh knots.

She could have been less defensive about the bingo card. She could have brushed it off and laughed at it. She'd been caught in a bad moment. And she was feeling guilty about snooping. All she knew was that every time she saw him ahead of her, she wanted to run up to him and make things right, but hell would freeze over before that happened.

"Do you think we will have time to visit the Smithsonian?"

Lizbeth turned toward Minister Zhou, the Chinese Secretary of the Interior and the only acting official who had opted out of meetings on the Hill to attend the walking tour. Like many Chinese men, his age was hard to tell, but the white stripes at his temples gave her a little clue. Minuscule crows' feet crinkling at the corners of his eyes were another. He was probably between fifty and sixty. He dressed casually, in khaki trousers and a polo shirt. His wife was up ahead with another woman, their arms linked together amiably. Zhou had sidled up to Liz nonchalantly and spoke rather quietly. The museums were a popular tourist destination, but most people didn't know that the Smithsonian was made up of a dozen different museums.

"There's a couple of free hours late this afternoon. I could see if we can get to a specific exhibit if you know of one you specifically want to see."

"I would like to see the Spruce Goose."

Lizbeth blinked a couple of times and shook her head. "I'm pretty sure that's out on the West Coast somewhere. Oregon, I think. The Spirit of St. Louis plane is at the Air and Space museum, though. And there's a special exhibit somewhere in Reston, I believe."

Zhou started a bow and stopped himself short as if he were practicing not bowing. He pulled himself up and smiled politely. "I must be confused, then. Sorry to have troubled you."

The man left her side and worked his way further up the row of people and blended into the group. Lizbeth hung toward the rear of the group, as far from Curt she could get, to catch any stragglers.

The tour was going well, but as they approached the Roosevelt Memorial, the still hot memory of the other day filled filled Lizbeth with apprehension.

Holding onto him while riding the motorcycle. Her shaky legs when she got off. Her raging desire.

As the group stopped to listen to the guide's lesson of the moment, she caught Curt looking at her. She didn't see any emotion in him at all. When their eyes met, his remained dull and distant, as if she didn't exist. His lips twitched and he looked away.

Her eyes welled up with water and she brushed her face to keep her composure. *Didn't he feel anything?* She focused on the task at hand by speaking to the security agent closest to her. The agent checked in with his companions, and the group was given the go ahead to enter the memorial proper.

The guide gave a ten-minute description of the memorial, pointing out the features and the reasons behind them. Liz focused solely on his speech, blocking out her thoughts. After the guide's spiel, the group spread out to explore the monument. The memorial had many side exhibits and encompassed several acres. She paused near the alcove where she had first kissed Curt. Her lips buzzed in excitement at the memory.

It hadn't been an ordinary kiss, it had been *the kiss*. The kiss every girl dreamed about, the one she pretended was happening as she kissed the back of her hand before she ever got her first kiss. The kiss that made every other kiss forgettable. The kiss that sent your heart into fast motion pitter-pats. The kiss that defied words.

Darius never made her feel that way. A pang of guilt flooded through her as the realization struck her. Curt was what she had been missing from every rela-tionship she'd ever had. The fact that she could be her true self with him. Her Chinese self. Her sexual self. The thought of being without him caused her skin to hurt as if it had been burned.

She sighed and leaned against the wall in the shade around the corner from the alcove where she could sneak a few minutes of privacy and clear away the tears.

"Do you think we will have time to visit the Smithsonian?"

It was the same question. And, she was certain it was Minister Zhou again. Why was he going around asking people the same thing?

"The Smithsonian is rather extensive. Do you know which exhibit you would like to see?"

Lizbeth craned her neck to listen. The other voice was Curt's.

"I would very much like to see the Spruce Goose."

"The Spruce Goose is a magnificent plane. I would love to help you see it."

Lizbeth was confused. If she knew the Spruce Goose was in Oregon, she was pretty sure Curt would know that too. Zhou's response was even more confusing.

"Ah. Good. It is you then."

The voices dropped low, and Lizbeth couldn't hear anything else. She moved closer to the corner, not wanting to step into their view. But their words were still whispered. She tiptoed away from the corner in the opposite direction and pretended she was approaching the alcove from the other side with a loud clumping step, hoping they would hear her approach.

She paused at the entrance of the alcove, pretending she'd just stumbled across the two men. Curt narrowed his eyes on her. They were dark, but she couldn't gauge his emotion. It was more than anger at being interrupted. Minister Zhou bowed grandly to Curt and patted the bronze statue. "Thank you for explaining these... these... fireside chats to me. I do miss the days of radio. Television leaves nothing to the imaginations."

"Ah, gentlemen, there you are," Liz said, pretending she'd been looking for them. "We're about to head on to the next memorial, and then lunch. We should get moving so we're not left behind."

Curt could not have looked at her with more venom and suspicion. A cold chill ran down her spine as she realized being on Curt's dark side hung close to the surface. He motioned for her to lead the way as they followed. He spoke a few words to the minister, but she couldn't hear what he said. The minister stepped up his pace to catch up with the group.

Lizbeth was about to follow when Curt grabbed her by the upper arm. She looked down at his hand until he removed it.

"What did you hear?"

Lizbeth was almost startled to hear him speak English again. Everything around them had been in Chinese for hours now.

"Nothing. Curt?"

He glanced toward the group, his eyes roving over

the crowd, his jaw working silently. He looked more worried than he did upset.

"There's nothing to be worried about. Zhou came up to me and asked me about the Smithsonian and the Spruce Goose. He didn't seem to like my answer. I think it's weird he asked you the same thing. Why would he do that?"

Curt shifted his shoulders and looked at her coldly. "I think he couldn't accept that the Spruce Goose isn't in DC. I diverted his attention by talking about the chats."

Suddenly, other questions and inconsistencies about Curt niggled at her, making her completely uncertain about what she thought she knew about him. Had he been planning ahead to meet Zhou? Why? And, if that was true, he'd wanted to come to the memorial as much as she had. His calling her on the game was even more hypocritical. She crossed her arms and narrowed her eyes. "The other day, when we were here, you asked if anyone could see us in that same alcove."

He grabbed her by the elbow again, his fingers dug into her. "We should get back to the group. They're moving on to the Jefferson Memorial now."

She pulled herself free. "We need to talk, Curt. What is going on?"

His jaw tightened. "Not now." His words came out

clipped, cold, hard. He walked fast ahead of her, his face shifting into that of a gracious host as he approached one of the older women in the group. He offered her his arm and shifted easily back into Chinese. "You're looking tired. There's not that much further left in our tour."

The woman smiled up at him with obvious relief and took his arm. Lizbeth was furious that he had walked away from her. No matter what she did, she could not get him alone the rest of the tour. Eventually, she hung back with one of the BDS agents. She kept her eyes on Curt while she went over every minute she'd spent with him.

First, had he been scoping out the memorial to talk to Zhou privately? If so, why? She scanned the group. It was impossible to tell which, if any, of them were there as actual guests or possible watchers. The memorial had been a perfect opportunity as the group dispersed across the site. Okay. So Curt had to talk to Zhou alone, and she was pretty sure it wasn't about Roosevelt's fireside chats.

Then, there was the way his hips snapped into place during tai chi. She was certain he was proficient at martial arts. But he hadn't answered her question about it. Why be vague if there wasn't something to hide.

He had studiously avoided meeting at his office at

State, too. He had come to hers for their first meeting, saying that there wasn't space at his office. She had assumed he had taken over Michael's but that wouldn't necessarily be the case. When she showed up after learning about Bella's move, he hadn't come through the lobby, but from outside. Did he even have an office there?

Then this weird shit with Zhou. Spruce Goose? Could that have been... some sort of old-fashioned meet-up code? Was Curt actually from State? He had appeared out of nowhere to take Michael's position. He was extremely well-versed in all the operations for the weekend. It had seemed a little odd to her at the time, but his level of knowledge must have come from more than a quick study with Michael over the phone.

Curt had to be intel of some sort. What in the world was Curt doing pretending to be State? She almost slapped her head when it came to her. Was he BDS? No. FBI? Maybe, but the profile didn't fit. *CIA agents were invisible by comparison.* He blended in seamlessly, except for the weird quirks only she had picked up on. He had to be CIA. There was some link between their visit with the Congressman and her—Curt. What the hell was he up to?

Chapter 19

Old Ebbitt Grill was a staple of Washington, DC and literally across the street from the White House. Chances were you would see someone famous or see White House personnel out for happy hour. The tour had taken them in a large loop so they ended not far from the Ellipse where they had started.

Once they were checked in, the host led the group back to their tables. Lizbeth had not set up any official seating charts, but the restaurant had reserved ten large tables in one corner of the restaurant near the back bar. The plush seating and classic interior combined with a history of being the oldest saloon in DC would make lunch an authentic experience. The food was American steak and seafood, but she'd had a translation made of their menu so that their guests would have a better idea of what they were ordering.

Curt avoided her and led an older woman to the table near the corner and seated himself next to her, his back to the wall. Wasn't that the way cops and spies always sit? So they could see everything around them and no one could sneak up on them. She sat at a table where she was facing him directly so she could keep an eye on him. What if he worked for the Chinese? She hadn't even looked at his credentials all that closely. He was moving to China soon.

Lizbeth, you are being paranoid. Maybe he was giving Zhou some information back at the memorial. What kind of information could Curt possibly have, anyway? No. Something else was going on.

When the waiter came, Lizbeth ordered the jumbo lump crab cakes. Old Ebbitt was known for its oyster bar, so several people eagerly ordered several varieties. When the food arrived, she only took a few bites before it was achingly obvious her stomach did not want any. She made small talk, answering the many questions of the people sitting near her. They were completely oblivious to her personal drama and she meant to keep it that way.

She slipped into a mask of 'professional cool.' Curt looked directly at her once, causing her heart to hammer hard against her chest. Whatever warmth had been between them was hidden behind his cool and impassive face. Was he sizing her up the same was she was him? If he was CIA, had Curt actually sent those two goons to investigate her? But why? It made no sense.

The rest of the lunch was spent in a daze. She managed to function, slipping in and out of suspicion and curiosity about Curt while managing to be sociable. She knew he had to be something other than he was claiming to be. What exactly had he said about that? Only that he was taking Michael's place. Had he actually said he worked for the State Department, or had he only implied it? Or had Jiang introduced him? She couldn't remember.

What she did know is that he had been absolutely livid with her about the stupid BINGO game. There was no doubt about how real his anger was this morning. Yet, he was playing some spy game with Zhou and hiding the fact he was getting married from her. She would have to corner him later and have it out with him.

As she climbed onto the bus for the return to the hotel, she was ready to collapse. They had almost five hours for dinner and to prepare for the opera. Only yesterday she'd imagined this time being spent in a very different kind of rejuvenation with Curt. Now, she didn't dare hope he'd ever speak to her beyond what might be necessary to get their job done.

Curt took his seat at the front of the bus. When

she passed by him, he smiled at her with a fake, too bright grin while his eyes remained cool and hard. When they got back to the Pembroke, Curt stayed at the front door of the bus offering every person a helping hand off the bus. When it was her turn to get off, he held out his hand to her with a perfunctory coldness. She held her hand close to her chest and nimbly helped herself down, glancing at his hand, without touching it.

"Suit yourself." His eyes were guarded. Maybe he was hurting, too.

"We need to talk," she hissed.

He didn't answer her, but turned to help the next person behind her off the bus. She waited for him at the entrance to the hotel. They could go up to their rooms, talk there. As he turned toward the hotel, he saw her, paused and looked around. There was no doubt in her mind that he was avoiding her when he called out to one of the BDS agents and approached him.

She headed toward them, but Curt and the agent strode past her together as if they had urgent business. She watched them, dumbfounded, before following them inside. They went straight to the manager's desk.

Fine. Let him play his dumb spy game. She was tired and needed to relax. They had five hours before they needed to leave for the opera. He would have to talk to her then. She had made sure they would sit next to each other at the opera so she could give him her interpretation of the story and music. Whether he cared or not, she was going to tell him all about it.

The hotel bar was at the far end of the lobby. Several of the Chinese visitors were sitting there, the smell of sake and whiskey rolling through the room. She ordered an iced tea and walked through, checking in with the dozen or so of her guests. They had enjoyed the tour. They loved the quaintness and ease of American history—*such a young country.*

Could they go shopping this afternoon before the opera? What about museums? Did they have time for that? She helped them figure out how to get where they wanted to go and gave them advice on what to do with their free time. One hour down, four to go.

Lizbeth set her glass on the bar and stifled a yawn. Her body was tight and sore. All the adrenaline and constant stress had worn her down. Maybe she could do a few tai chi moves before the big event to loosen up.

Would she see Curt before? Probably not. Or would he be absent until they were seated at the John F. Kennedy Center for the opera? *Chicken shit. He doesn't even have the guts to face me.* He'd made it pretty clear he was avoiding her.

She told the bartender to give her something that

would calm her nerves, but nothing too heavy. He suggested a cosmopolitan. The combination of lime and cranberry made a nice contrast to the heavy ache in her heart. The bartender slid over an elegant martini glass filled with pink liquid and a curly orange slice. She eyed it dubiously. Her first sip confirmed the bartender was right. It was light and refreshing. It helped her feel marginally better right away.

She ordered two more to take to her room. He raised an eyebrow but put the order together anyway. He placed the drinks on a tray with a bowl of a roasted and herby peanut mix. She popped one of the nuts and the rosemary flavor mixed nicely with the cranberry aftertaste. She placed the first drink next to the other two, suddenly aware she must look like a complete lush. They were so small, though, what harm could they do? She carried the tray up to her room using the service elevator to avoid contact with anyone.

Once inside the room, she set her phone alarm for six thirty. Lizbeth stripped in front of the connecting door and put the plush hotel robe on. She pushed at Curt's door, but it was still locked from his side. Some of this had to be real. She dropped onto the edge of the bed and finished the first cosmo. Had she really been tied up here, pretending to be ravished by a handsome rogue less than twenty-four hours before? She ran her hand along the bed, conjuring up the feelings she'd had for him the night before. How could things change so suddenly?

Lizbeth opened the faucets. The thick rush of water flowing out of the tap reminded her of the shower at Curt's house. The next three hours were hers. Relaxing with the booze and a nice bath would be exactly what she needed. A very rare treat. The giant jacuzzi tub was built for two, but she would savor it, even if she was alone.

She sipped at the second cosmo, marveling at how good it tasted. It was *unbelievably* refreshing. Each sip was a little happy zing against her tongue. How had she never discovered this drink before? It was amazeballs.

Did she actually use the word amazeballs? Amaze-balls, amazeballs, amazeballs. What a fun word.

She tipped her glass upward and licked around the inside rim to get every last drop. Setting the empty glass down with a solid smacking noise, she suddenly realized how angry she was at Curt. She'd given him everything when she'd been tied up. Let him do things to her. Trusted him, and still... he was the one hadn't said anything about getting married or moving. He had no right to be angry at her for a game she wasn't even playing.

She swayed as she reached for her phone. For some reason, it took her a long time to get the text out.

The little keyboard on her phone was a lot harder to see than she remembered. For some reason, everything required intense concentration.

L: GET UR ASS UP TO MY ROM. WE HAV TO TLK!!!!!!!!!!!!

She wasn't much of a yeller on text, but, hot damn, it was freeing to be so candid, to yell and shout with capital letters like that. And the exclamation points, too. It was one punctuation mark she hardly ever got to use.

She texted him again, but this time she sent nothing but a whole string of exclamation points. Every time her thumb tapped the phone she grunted with satisfaction. *There, take that, Mr. Wu.*

She stumbled out of the bathroom to stand in front of her window, not really taking in the view. The last cosmo was on the nightstand. She really shouldn't, but it tasted so darn yummy. So what if it was making her a little tipsy? The unusual sensation was pretty damn nice, too. It took the edge off the pain. Focusing carefully on her hand in order to pick up the third drink, she commanded her fingers to open up and then close around the stem. It was like playing that stupid carnival game with the giant claw that never caught anything.

She giggled as some of the still cold liquid dribbled off to the side. If she had known booze could taste this good, she'd have it a lot more often. She wiped at her chin and licked it off her fingers.

Her bath must be filled by now. Except she couldn't quite understand why she wasn't moving toward it. She looked down at her feet and ordered them to walk.

"C'mon now. Bath time. Feet. Move." All her words came out sloppy. She translated them into Chinese and giggled. Drunk Chinese was even more hilarious than drunk English. "Move, I said."

How was it she had never realized how absolutely ridiculous feet look? And, really, how grotesque? She pointed at her toes in emphasis. If aliens were hideous to humans, aliens must point to human feet and run away screaming. The third cosmo went down smoothly and her feet suddenly lunged her toward the full, hot bath. *Ooo! There ya go.*

She placed her phone on the counter so it faced her. Any incoming call or text would be studiously ignored. She was going to ignore everyone for three hours. Everyone. Angela. Fuck her for trying to take away Bella. Demarco. Fuck him for not doing enough. And Curt. Asshole spy man. Fuck him. Fuck him. FUCK HIM. Of course, that was the problem, wasn't it? She giggled. She wanted to fuck him. In spite of it all.

Lizbeth opened the jasmine bubble bath and held

it under the roaring water, entranced by the rush of bubbles as they exploded and grew across the tub. *So pretty. Smells so sweet and yummy, too.* Lizbeth climbed into the tub. It was deeper than she had thought and the water went up to her chin. Perfect. The warm water would cover her whole body.

She leaned her head back and hooked her neck over the back of the tub. Her lower body floated upward as if she were swimming and pulled her head away from the edge. She shrieked. Her feet thrashed in the water, unable to find the tub wall. Her arms swung around uselessly trying to find the edge and she kicked at the water. She might as well be in the ocean. Drowning. She was drowning in a fucking bathtub, screaming like an idiot.

Suddenly Curt was in the tub with her, fully dressed and lifting her into his strong arms. She'd rather drown than be saved by him. Flailing out at him, trying to remember how to do a karate chop, wasn't working.

"I jus' slipped. Go 'way."

He hit the plug so the tub would drain and wrapped her in a towel even as she struggled uselessly against him.

"Nooooo. Not my bath." She renewed her struggles and reached for the plug. "Ugh. You meanie-pants."

"What are you thinking?"

"Baths are nice. You are not."

The tiniest of smiles played at his lips, and his eyebrows wrinkled together in the damn cutest way imaginable. "You're drunk."

"Yes. I suppose I y'am. And I think I might stay this way forever."

She had no control over her body as he struggled to change her into the fluffy hotel robe. When she was fully ensconced in white terrycloth, he stripped out of his wet clothes.

"Oh, jeezo-peeter, Curt. You're naked. That is soooo mean. What a tease."

He put on the second robe and tied the belt around his waist. "I saved you from drowning."

"Ha." Lizbeth tried to wink at him, but instead blinked slowly, "it's a good trick."

He picked her up and carried her to the side of the bed. She was suddenly very, very hot and very, very tired. "I don't feel good."

Curt grabbed the ice-bucket and put it on the bedside table next to her. Curt tossed aside the extra pillows and turned back the covers and helped her into the bed. He perched on the edge of the bed at her waist and wiped the hair away from her face. "You have about three hours before you have to be ready for the opera."

Going horizontal helped right away. "I *love* the opera. Are you going to the opera, Mr. Meany-pants?" She looked up at him, a finger lifting the edge of his bathrobe. *He is so handsome. Even if he is a jerk.*

Curt picked up the phone without answering her, gently grabbing her hand and putting it back at her side. "I'd like to order whatever you can have up here the fastest, please."

He paused for a moment, listening, and she ran a finger down his arm. He shrugged her off. "Make it two orders of that. Can you add a cup of coffee?"

"I know what song you would love." She laughed and belted out a warbling version of "La donna e mobile."

Curt hung up and put a hand on her mouth. "Oh, please, Lizbeth, you are not a singer."

She licked his palm, and he pulled his hand away looking at her in horror. Or was it amusement? She couldn't tell.

"Oh my, is my daddy," she said, hiccuping loudly, "coming soon, my lord?"

Curt sat next to her, his warm hand on her shoulder. He had such lovely hands. Had she noticed them before? They were glorious, sweet, beautiful, smooth, fabulous hands. Even after everything he'd said to her, after how he'd been so mean to her, she still wanted him. Badly. She giggled and hiccuped.

"I thought you said you don't drink."

Liz blinked sleepily. "I don't. A glass of wine here and there."

"What did you have just now?"

She opened her eyes wide, remembering what a terrific discovery, a gift really, that the bartender had given her. "Um. Cosmo..." she paused, tripping on the rest of the word. "Amazeballs. Amazeballs." She giggled again. "Cos-mazeballs. So tasty."

She put a hand on his and squeezed it. His expression softened. She moved her hand to his thigh, her fingers slipping under the flap of his robe and walked upward toward his delicious cock. His lips twisted into a smile, and she leered back at him.

Curt picked her hand up off his thigh and kissed her fingers. "You're drunk, and I don't have sex with drunk women."

Lizbeth pulled her hand away and stuck it under her cheek. "Fine. Go way, then. You're a big old lying jerk anyway. And I don't sleep with jerks, sober or drunk." She closed her eyes, feigning sleep, but it was really to hide her embarrassment.

A KNOCK at the door woke her. She must have fallen asleep for a little while and was now in the middle of the bed. She had no memory of getting into bed, but clearly, she had gotten there somehow. Her hair was still wet. Her tongue filled her whole mouth, thick and fuzzy. She was thirsty, and her stomach roiled.

She stretched and opened her eyes. Curt was opening the door. When had he come in? A vague image of them splashing around in the tub rolled in, like a nasty wave ready to sweep her into an undertow. His disappointment at her being drunk. His refusal to sleep with her. *Ouch.* Had all that really happened? She could taste the sticky remnants of the cosmos. She wished she could disappear. She'd been ridiculous.

"Forty-five minutes," he said. "That's how long you've been resting."

He adjusted her pillows and she got herself into a sitting position propped up on them. Something smelled scrumptious. Curt rolled over the room service table and took off the top.

"I got some plain pasta for you with a little butter and salt. Here," he said and held out a fork towards her. "What all did you eat today, anyway?" His eyebrows met in the middle.

"Breakfast. Lunch." Actually, nothing. He didn't need to know that. She grabbed the plate from him and ate the rest on her own. She didn't want to talk to him about this morning; she wasn't ready to confront him.

The food was doing its job already. Her head was beginning to clear.

"I've got to get ready for the opera. I can take it from here." She used her fork to point towards the door.

Curt stood up, his hands held up in surrender. "Fine." He waved at the tray of food. "I'll see you later. Don't be late. I hate it when people can't act professional."

As soon as his back was turned, Liz gave him the double bird, two middle fingers thrust at him. *God damn fucking jerk.* He left through the shared door and shut it behind him, locking it. She knew she needed to finish the pasta if she was going to have any chance at feeling better by the time the opera started. Cheesecake was on the tray and she delved into the sweet gooey richness. After a few bites, she headed into the bathroom to look for aspirin. *Tell her to be professional. Ugh.* A cold shower would do her as much as the food and coffee to wipe away any straggling cobwebs. She stuffed her hair into the flimsy shower cap and let the cold water bite into her skin. She had only thirty minutes. Thirty minutes to shower and then inch her way into a smokin' hot dress that would make Curt absolutely sorry.

Chapter 20

The shower got her halfway where she needed to be. She drank as much water as she could stand and took the complimentary package of aspirin provided by the hotel. Lizbeth dressed nicely for this event, not as fantastic as she planned for the gala the next evening, but she wore an ankle length dress that swished around her ankles when she turned quickly.

She had chosen a gown that covered her breasts without entirely hiding them. Her single strand of graduated pearls had been a gift from her mother when she graduated college. It was a set that had been passed down from one generation to the next on some special day in their lives—Liz was the eighth generation to own it. She was the first to receive it on a college graduation day rather than a wedding day.

"I don't want that tradition to continue. You might get married at some point in your life... but let's celebrate something that is all about you, and not you and some man. Or woman."

Lizbeth had laughed. "You know I'm into men, Mama."

She'd smiled at that and looked to the side as she surely thought about Bella, the grand baby she'd held for a short three hours one early spring morning.

Lizbeth touched the pearls at her neck. Proud of what they represented—all the women who'd come before her and who would follow.

Opera was something Lizbeth had grown up with. Her parents had season tickets for them as a family as long as she could remember. She had attended her first opera when she was seven years old. From the first moment, she was hooked. It was one of the few things she got to do with both her parents. There was something about the grandness of it—the huge stage, the amazing costumes, the big music—that drew her in every time. It went beyond being a family tradition, and became a passion.

She had season tickets at Kennedy Center, and had already been to this production of Il Trovatore. One of the best things about DC opera is that it is a veritable who's who of DC. Plenty of people made the effort to go simply to be seen in public.

The full-length mirror in the room showed her she had nothing to worry about. The dress looked fabulous, and her earlier debauchery was nowhere in evidence. Her outfit was missing something. In the corner of the room was one of the scarves Curt had used to subdue her. She picked it up and threw it on. Let him sweat.

Before she left, she popped another aspirin just to make sure she didn't get a headache. At the elevator, she checked her phone for any new text or emails. Suddenly Curt appeared at her side as the doors swished open, almost like he'd been waiting for her. He stepped in next to her. Embarrassment at having flung herself at him earlier kept her from meeting his eyes. She focused on her insanely gorgeous Louboutin shoes instead.

Inside the elevator, she glanced at him in the reflection of the mirrored interior. Damn. He looked good in a suit.

"You going to be able to manage tonight?"

"None of your business, Curt. I don't need you to take care of me."

"Sounds like you're feeling better."

The rest of the silent ride to the lobby was the longest elevator ride on the planet. Not wanting to sit next to him on the chartered bus, she hung back as others boarded, greeting them and complimenting them on their outfits. He had taken a seat near the front, but the old lady he'd sat with at lunch was already in the seat next to him making it easier for her to walk on past.

The group had seats all in private boxes mostly in the same part of the theater. She'd managed to procure them only after the Congressman had made a personal phone call. It was embarrassing that he had to do it, but it was more important that the seats were available to her group than that she be the one getting them, but it had impressed the Chinese delegation.

They gathered as a group near will call so she could hand out the tickets. She sorted them by box numbers, and handed them out in groups. Their assigned security officers would escort them to and from their boxes as needed.

When she was down to the last six tickets, she and Curt were left standing alone.

He grabbed the tickets from her and looked through them. "Where is everyone else?" he asked, waving them in a fan at her.

"Some people backed out of coming tonight. They wanted to stay in. Looks like we'll be all alone in our box. If that frightens you, you can leave."

With a subtle twitch of her shoulders, she dropped the shawl she was wearing, letting it drift to the floor, a delicate silk gauntlet. Curt lifted an eyebrow and followed its billowing path. He bowed his head in mock gallantry and swooped his arm out dramatically as he bent over to pick it up. He shook it out and draped it over her shoulder, gathering it together in the front. His eyes lingered at her neck and her breast, but he caught her eye before letting go of the fabric. She could read his mind on this one. *Challenge accepted.*

"Let's find our seats, shall we?" he asked, holding out a formally stiff elbow for her.

She put a light hand on it, equally formal. They kept a stiff distance between them as they climbed the stairs to their seats. They sat waiting for the lights to come down in complete silence.

Once the overture began, Lizbeth was sure she would sit and relax, allowing herself to be mesmerized by the music and the colors on stage. Before she had a chance to get immersed into the opera, Curt grabbed her wrist and leaned in close. "We need to talk. Now."

He stood up and dragged her into the furthest corner of the box where they would be mostly hidden from view. The dim lights, the loud music, and the thick curtains all provided excellent cover. No one could see them or hear them from this little space.

He searched her face with the same inscrutable intensity that he had earlier in the day. "It's safe to talk here."

"As opposed to?"

"The hotel. Around the delegates."

She shook her head, weary of the rollercoaster. "Curt, what are you implying? Is the hotel bugged?"

"Of course it is."

"And my room?" Lizbeth thought about their first night together. The noises and promises they'd shouted, and moaned, and groaned. Who would be listening to that?

Curt's fingers relaxed around her arms, and he smoothed his hands down her shoulders, gently taking her hands in his. His eyes searched hers in the dim light of the box.

"We need to be honest with each other, now. Liz. It's important. Who do you work for?"

Lizbeth didn't understand the question. Shouldn't she be asking him who *he* was working for? The CIA had come to interview the Congressman about her. What did he mean? The way he was looking at her scared her.

"Liz, I need to know the truth. I swear, I'll find a way to protect you. I will do whatever I can to make sure you don't take the fall if things go wrong." He hit the wall next to him in frustration. The music swallowed up whatever sound it might have made.

Lizbeth was up against a wall, literally, so she couldn't back away from him. She instinctively placed her feet in a karate stance. He was not going to intimidate her. She breathed in deeply and calmed herself.

"Protect me? Curt, from what?" She pressed the palms of her hands against his chest and shoved. "Who do *you* work for, Curt? Why was the CIA talking with my boss for two hours? Tell me exactly what is going on."

Curt enclosed both of her hands in his own and pulled them in tight against his chest. "You swear you're loyal?"

"Loyal? To you?" His look intensified on her and she understood his question. "You're the one getting marr... Wait. Are you actually asking me if I'm loyal to the United States? Seriously?"

"Of course to the U.S." His eyes were boring into hers, frantically searching. "You swear on all that you love, that you are not MSS?"

"MSS? Wait..." Lizbeth's head swam. The CIA and MSS served the same function; one American, the other Chinese. Her work on the House Intelligence committee had given her a very broad understanding of all the intelligence agencies of the world's governments. This was not what she had been expecting from him. Not at all. Her mouth dropped open and she struggled for words. "You... You actually think *I'm* Chinese Intelligence? Me? MSS? Seriously."

Curt's entire demeanor changed as he studied her.

After a long moment, his whole body relaxed. "No. I don't. Not now. But I had to check you out."

"Why? What have I done to make you even wonder?"

Curt placed his hand over her clenched fist and squeezed. "I had to be with you when I asked. To see your reaction."

"And now that you've seen me? You believe I'm not MSS because, why? Because of some magical thing between us allows you to intuit whether or not I am lying right now?"

Curt kissed her. It was sudden. Surprising and intense.

She kissed him back, her stance and her mouth letting him know who was in charge. Her hunger for him easily ignited with his own desire. She pulled away. He looked at her like a great challenge had been initiated.

"If I were with the Ministry of State Security, do you think I would admit it?"

Curt shook his head. "I'm trained to detect people who lie. Since I know you more intimately, it's easier for me to read your cues."

"Really? You think you could detect a trained spy lying to you?"

"So, you're claiming to be MSS now?"

Her jaw dropped open, and she gaped at him.

Gaped at the absurdity of everything. "No. I'm not. I'm not MSS, and I'm not lying. I can't believe you believed that of me."

Still, if the CIA had been questioning Congressman Pierce about her because they thought she was MSS, there must be some reason. You don't randomly accuse people of being a spy without some amount of evidence.

"Why the *fuck* would the CIA think I am a spy?"

"You spend a lot of time at the Chinese Embassy. More hours than required for this delegation. About four months ago, you spent the night with Liu Wei fourteen times. Eight times at his apartment. Six at yours." His mouth clamped shut and he colored.

Was he thinking about her in bed with Liu Wei? In the bed they had shared at her house? Liu hadn't managed to remember her cats names at all, let alone which one was which. Curt had no reason to be jealous, but she wasn't going to tell him that.

Lizbeth knew from his expression he already knew that she had spent the night there because she and one of the Embassy staffers were hooking up. It had been a fun few weeks, but that was it. Nothing more. Nothing spy-like about it. "And?" she asked, demanding more from him as proof. "It's not illegal for me to date someone who works at the Chinese Embassy. You can't judge me for it. It was before we met."

"Liu is MSS. Did you know that? We thought he was recruiting you."

Lizbeth's jaw dropped open and she blinked her eyes. This was crazy talk. Liu was a clerk, nothing high level. At an Embassy... who had a really nice apartment. He had asked her a lot about her relationships with her family. But she had thought it was because he cared about her, wanted to get to know her. Maybe she'd missed some critical clues about him. Maybe he was more than a lowly clerk.

"He never tried to recruit me. Not that I'm aware of."

"I believe you," he looked sheepish, almost guilty.

"Job related work time at the Embassy and a boyfriend I dumped months ago? That's not much to go on."

Curt's jaw tightened. "You read the letter from my mother."

"Did you know when I read it, or did you only find out about it when I told you?"

"I knew before. You left the magazine on the table and I figured it out. The letter was put back into the envelope upside down from how I had left it. But you didn't say anything to me last night. You acted like everything was fine. It made me suspicious. If you really loved me... my getting married... you would have said something. Been angry. But you didn't until I confronted you this morning."

"Finding out that you are getting married about killed me."

"That's how I felt when I thought you were playing a kissing game with men. That I was literally a mark on a scorecard."

"I can only give you my word on that. I would never use you like that."

He kissed her forehead and sighed, obviously relieved. "The letter? All the wedding stuff? It's code."

"From your mother? Your mom is CIA?"

Curt's lips formed a thin line and he looked away. He ran a hand through his hair and blew out some air. "No. It's not really from my mother. Well, it is, but it isn't. The handwritten part is all hers, but the rest, the actual dating site report is code. We've swung back to an old-fashioned set of codes because online stuff can't be trusted."

"But your mom wrote the letter, and then how did the code get in there?"

"It's complicated. But we have our ways," he said wiggling his eyebrows for emphasis. He waved his hand around the theater. "All of this, my taking Michael's place. It's a setup for me to gain visibility with the Chinese. All these delegates? They got know me today. They'll get to know me even better tomorrow at the races and at the gala."

"Why all the anger this morning then?"

"Monument bingo."

"It's a stupid game. I told you I wasn't playing."

"But, if you were, and a spy... it would mean you hadn't actually fallen for me the way I've fallen for you."

"But..."

He put a finger to her lips to shush her. "Let me finish. So, you get me to play the game, then you go through my mail. I was worried you had copied or memorized the messages on the matchmaking sheet."

Lizbeth cringed. "Oh, that. I only glanced at that part. Numerology crap makes my eyes cross. My waipo used to talk to me all the time about that, but it's nothing but mumbo jumbo."

"You said you read the whole letter."

"All I cared about is the part about your upcoming nuptials."

"You have to believe me when I say it is not a real marriage."

"Eu-ma looks real to me."

"She's real, all right, but I'm marrying her as a cover."

"When?" Lizbeth tried to remain cool, but she didn't want her dragon lover to be at the hands of anyone else. And if she remembered CIA, they didn't take undercover lightly. It had to look real, it had to be real.

"Soon. I have to." He clenched his jaw.

Something about the way he said it sent a new chill down her back. "Does *she* know she's a cover? That it's a fake marriage?"

Curt leaned his forehead against her shoulder. With a sinking heart, Lizbeth was sure she knew the answer. No. She didn't. That meant the marriage would be real to the other woman even if not to Curt. How cruel—for both of them. Worse, he would have to consummate the relationship to keep up the ruse.

Jealousy stung at her even more, knowing the truth, knowing that she would not put up with this kind of life. There was no way they could be together. Not long term. Not with him carrying on with another woman. It was so unfair. She would have to enjoy the next few days with him. Get the most out of him while she could. Once the gala was over, so was he. She had been telling herself he was a fling; she needed to believe it.

She pressed her lips into his neck. Lizbeth wrapped her arms around Curt, and they moved back into the darkest corner of the balcony, hidden by the shadows. The opera played out in the background, the words and music a meaningless mass of sounds.

"It's an arranged marriage. She's not expecting... love. Even so, I don't think I can pretend a whole fake marriage to her. Not when I'd be thinking about you every moment I am with her."

"I don't want to think about that right now." Lizbeth wasn't sure how much more she could stand this particular emotional rollercoaster. She grasped his face on either side. It was her turn to try to read minds. "We have tonight. Tomorrow... and then... who knows anyway, right? Let's take it one day at a time."

"But," he said.

She pressed a finger against his lips. "Shhh. One. Day. At. A. Time."

She stepped out of his arms and scanned the crowd. Everyone sat entranced, their eyes glued to the stage. Except them. Their own little drama overtaking the one playing out in glorious harmonies below.

Curt held out a hand to her, an invitation or a question, she wasn't sure.

"I'm still a little tipsy from the booze earlier."

He wrapped his arms around her. "I'm so relieved you're not MSS."

"There's a great qualification right there," she said, lifting her fingers as if she were holding up a sign over her head, "not a spy."

He chuckled. "Okay. So what now? Sit and explain what is going on down on that stage to me?"

She tugged at his tie. "I'm sober enough to know I don't think I can concentrate on the opera right now."

"Oh, really?"

"Did you really think I was playing that game?"

"Yeah... for a little while."

"Even after I told you I wasn't?"

"I'm sorry, Liz. I didn't trust you."

"Do you trust me now?" She pushed on the door to the hallway making sure it was securely shut.

A smile played at his lips. "What do you have in mind?"

Lizbeth unzipped Curt's pants and reached inside through the opening. His eyes widened, and he looked around as if they would be caught any second.

"This time I get to be in charge." She stood behind him and took off her shawl—the sheer fabric he'd used the night before to tie an arm to the bed. She looped it around itself until it was a band of fabric and tied it around his eyes. "Don't touch me until I instruct you to do so."

As she walked in front of him, she touched the tip of his dragon tattoo, right where a tendril licked against his neck. She grasped his lengthening cock by the base, stroking him until it was full and thick. And hard. She squeezed her legs together, but that wouldn't stop the flow of her ready juices from dripping down her thighs. She rubbed her legs together before turning from him so she was facing the stage. Everyone in the audience was focused on the stage.

She slid her dress up so it was over her waist and leaned over her empty seat, pressing her backside against him, letting his cock feel her wet pussy. He groaned, and his arms started towards her, but held himself in check. She rubbed up and down against him a few times first, making sure her juices were all over his hard dick and hearing his grunt of unrequited satisfaction.

"You may touch me now."

Even though she had whispered it, he heard her. He placed his hands on her hips and ran his hands along the curve of her waist. His pressed the lace of her panties into her dripping pussy and against her aching clit.

"Oh my god. This is amazing. I've never touched a woman this way. Blindfolded." With one hand, he found her opening and massaged it, his fingers working at her clit. "You're mine, Liz. Mine to take."

"I'm yours because I want to be." With the sweet caress of a blind man, his fingers traced her spine, dancing across her upper back and along her arms. Her biceps tightened as she gripped the sturdy back of her seat. With the other hand, he guided his cock inside. Once he was in, he grabbed her hips and delved deeply into her, hard. His movement was a perfect counterpoint to the bombastic music on the stage.

His finger worked in rhythm with the music as the chorus belted out what was probably one of the most famous pieces in opera history. He thrust into her with each strike of the anvils. Liz couldn't help but grin at the half-naked men on stage and their bulging muscles hammering away. Curt caught onto the rhythm and moved with it like a dancer.

She'd never had sex in such a public venue before. It had nothing to do with being an exhibitionist so much as wanting and needing Curt so badly right that moment. She pushed back against him ensuring the deepest and most intimate connection.

He never let up pressure against her clit. Curt buried his face against her neck and she could feel the deep rumble of his moan. The music was so loud he could have been screaming like a banshee and no one would have heard him.

"Come with me, Lizbeth. We can do this. Together..." His words buzzed against her ear.

He was holding back, waiting until she was ready to join him. The music had shifted into one of the quieter moments and she bit her lip to keep herself from moaning. The chorus would strike up the anvil again soon. When it did, Curt renewed his energies, found her clit with one hand and revved up his efforts, fucking her double time to the music.

She struggled to hold herself upright when she came, her pussy tightening around him. Her knees weakened and buckled, but Curt caught her at the hips holding himself deep inside her, leaning over her so his chest pressed against her spine. He kissed the back of her neck, staying inside her until they both caught their breath.

When she regained her senses, she scanned the audience to make sure no one was looking their direction. As far as she could tell, no one had noticed their little make-up session. Curt pulled out and smoothed her panties back into place. Still blindfolded, he ran his hands along her body, stretching her dress back down over her hips. She turned around and removed his blindfold. He put himself back in order.

He untwisted the shawl and draped it carefully over her shoulders, his finger tracing a heart around her throat. He kissed the back of her hand before intertwining his fingers with hers. This was one of the most momentous performances of opera she had ever experienced, and it had nothing to do with what was happening on stage.

She leaned into him, feeling whole again. She wouldn't let herself think beyond the next couple of days, and she'd be okay. She'd maker herself be okay with it.

They sat next to each other holding each other's hands. Her mind wasn't on the opera at all. He turned towards her and took her chin so that she was looking at him. He kissed her. "I love you, Lizbeth Crandall. Head over heels. I'd quit my job before I let them make me marry someone else."

"I love you, too," she said, surprising herself with how easy it was.

WHEN THE OPERA WAS OVER, they walked arm in arm to the chartered bus. They didn't flaunt their couple status, but kept it low-key. They maintained a more professional distance while on the bus, sitting next to each other without any kissing or groping. Their guests had a lot of questions about the opera, and Lizbeth happily answer them all.

Booming laughter from the bar rolled into the lobby. A mixture of Chinese and English rolled out into the lobby. The older woman Curt had helped at Old Ebbitt Grill called out to Curt as they walked by. She wanted to thank them both by buying them drinks. She smiled at Curt in a motherly way.

Lizbeth didn't think she ever need another drink,

even a cosmopolitan. Curt made their excuses for the evening so that they could go up to their rooms, meaning her room. Both of them were exhausted. In her room, they stripped naked and got into bed together. He pressed his body in close against her and she wiggled her hips against him. She loved the way his skin glided against hers. Once she was comfortable, and about to go to sleep, her eyes bolted open. Certain details they hadn't discussed suddenly bothered her.

Like, exactly what was Curt doing taking Michael Hong's place anyway? Was that a cover-up for getting close to her? Had she been the target of his mission and now that he was sure she wasn't a spy, would he be free to leave? Why had he talked to Minister Zhou in private? What was he trying to do? Was he getting information from him?

How would he get out of his mission to China? And if she wasn't the target of his mission, what was? There was something very vague about it all. He had said something about getting on the good side of the Chinese. Was he going double?

Curt had said he loved her, and she loved him. If he could get out of this assignment without ruining his career, they could probably be together, assuming this thing was real. Would he send for her later? In years to come, would he grow to hate her for giving up on the opportunity to go to China and completing his assignment? Would she hate him for leaving her?

She peered into his face wondering if she could tell if he was lying. Curt's quiet and steady breathing told her he had no problem getting to sleep. His conscience must be clear of anything sneaky. He was a spy. Maybe he was used to questions not being answered. Her hand was poised on his shoulder, about to wake him up. The only reason she didn't was due to her level of exhaustion. If she asked him now, they'd be up all hours of the night.

And the Dragon Boat Festival was the next morning, bright and early. There would be little time in the morning for anything other than getting dressed and eating at the buffet. Another look at the dragon tattoo and the expression on his face soothed her. She was completely sated from their make-up sex at the opera. All she needed now was to be near him. To touch him. To smell him. To hold him. She trusted him even if she wasn't sure she should.

Chapter 21

"Have you ever considered moving to China?" Curt asked as they walked the perimeter of the delegation pavilion. Until the actual races started, the delegation members would be able to mill about as they liked in the pavilion. They had private catering and their own portable bathroom trailer with running water and flushing toilets. No porta-potties for these VIPs.

Crowds crammed in along the riverbank. The many blankets made a crazy quilt of wild plaids, stripes and company logos. A tingle ran up her back and along her neck. She was pretty sure she hadn't told him about her offer to Angela and Demarco—that she should be the one to move, not them. "It's been a dream of mine to be part of the U.S. ambassadorial service, so yes. Why?"

Curt shrugged. "I honestly don't know what will be happening over the next month or so. I'll be talking to my superiors on Monday. I'm going to insist on a change in plans. I can't do the fake marriage."

"Would you really quit for me?"

He grabbed her hand and squeezed it briefly before releasing it.

"Looks like things are ready to go," Curt said, glancing at a BDS agent who was giving him a signal.

Minister Zhou had been invited to open the races. Two of the nondescript Bureau of Diplomatic Security agents escorted him to the starting pavilion. He looked happy to be in such a position of honor.

"You come to this every year?"

Dozens of the boats were lined up along the pier. Half a dozen were already out on the water, lining up for the first heat. They were essentially brightly painted giant canoes with elaborate dragon heads and tails.

"Yeah. I love it."

"Look at them all." Curt was pointing at a team climbing into a boat. His finger bobbed up and down as he counted them.

"Twenty-two people per boat," she said. "Twenty people paddle. Then there's a drummer to keep them all synced up. And one more person who stands in the back and steers the boat. Steerer doesn't sound right. Probably has a special name."

She pointed toward the team that was loading into a green and gold boat. "The dragon on that one looks like Malachi. But with a sweeter disposition."

He laughed. "The colors are similar. I haven't been to this before. I hadn't realized how big a deal it was here."

The crowd was large, but had mostly gathered toward the river to view the races. Two large bleachers had been set up next to the starting pavilion, and they were filled.

Minister Zhou was given a horn to sound off the beginning of the race. He held it out in front of him like he was aiming a gun. It blared out, and Curt winced. "Wow. My head is still ringing from the anvils last night."

Liz back handed him with a playful slap at the jibe. "You loved the opera. Admit it."

"I am betting they're not all quite so magnificent as last night."

She blushed. The boats lurched away from the starting line and zoomed past the formal pavilion, the drumbeats of each boat pounding a slightly different pace. The crowd cheered them on, urging them forward. Lizbeth almost got caught up in the excitement and cheered along, but kept herself in check.

The crowd went wild when the green boat crossed the finish line.

"Look at that Wu. Dragon wins," she said laughing.

He smiled, but she could tell he wasn't paying attention. He was scouting out the entrances. The second heat lined up and Zhou's official duties were over. His security detail flanked him on both sides, but he pointed toward a food vendor. The three stopped for a second while the two agents spoke to each other, then they proceeded cautiously on toward the stall.

Lizbeth nudged Curt. "I think we might have a problem."

"Let's keep an eye on it. Maybe the guy has never had a corn dog before."

"Bleh. Why they even allow corn dogs into this festival is beyond me. It's not at all culturally appropriate."

"Who cares? They're delicious."

"You are kidding, right?"

Lizbeth kept her eyes on Zhou. It was her responsibility, after all, to make sure everyone made it safely back to the hotel. The large gala tonight was going to be the big shebang at the end of three long days of meetings and gatherings.

"Curt, look closely at the security on Zhou," she said. She recognized them from somewhere, but they were not on her roster for this. They were not the men who had escorted Zhou over to the starting podium.

"What's wrong? What are you seeing?"

"Look at their faces. Do you recognize them? Blanchard and Manning were on him, weren't they?" Lizbeth had spent a good deal of time reviewing the faces of all the BDS officers assigned to the detail this morning, not to mention that she had talked to everyone this morning at least once about their assignments. The two guys heading off with Zhou were not Blanchard or Manning, she was sure of it. They looked like the real thing, but were definitely different guys than fifteen minutes ago.

"Blanchard's tall. Manning had a fresh buzz cut. Those two guys are neither," she said.

"Holy hell."

Lizbeth and Curt looked at each other for half a second before sprinting after the trio that was rapidly disappearing into the festival crowd.

She caught a glimpse of Zhou being herded out of the area between the two men. They looked vaguely familiar, but all wrong at the same time. Maybe it was the suits. As they got closer, the three picked up their pace and started running. Zhou continued to look back over his shoulder as if he were being chased by demons.

Was he happy to be going off with these guys? Was

he being kidnapped? Why Zhou? He wasn't even that big a deal in the Chinese government over all. He certainly seemed cooperative.

Curt edged past her, and she pushed herself harder to catch up, glad she'd worn a pair of tennis shoes with her cherry blossom dress.

They caught up to the trio as the suits were ushering Zhou into a taxi-cab. Suddenly, Curt was on top of one of the guys. Zhou hunkered into the taxi with his head in his lap his hands crossed over the back of his neck.

The third guy pulled out a gun and pointed it at Curt, completely ignoring Lizbeth as a threat. She pulled an old, well-practiced, karate move out of her personal arsenal and had him screaming and on his knees holding a dangling wrist protectively against his chest. She kicked the gun out of the way like she'd seen it done in movies, hoping that it wouldn't suddenly go off and hurt someone.

She was breathing hard from the run, but taking the guy down had been a piece of cake. Holy shit. She kicked this guy's ass without even thinking twice. She grinned over at Curt who was sitting on the chest of the other kidnapper. He had a dark look on his face. They had plenty of help within seconds from the security detail, but Lizbeth was feeling a particular charge from using her karate for the first time in a practical situation. Tai chi was fun and made her feel good. But, karate? Man. That made her feel useful. And she hadn't even consulted a safety manual. She chuckled. What the hell was happening to her? She didn't know, but she liked it.

Zhou's original security were found unconscious on a blanket, ten feet outside of the podium. Their black jackets had been removed and replaced with Capital hockey shirts. Zhou was shaken, but he was adamant about staying with the rest of the delegation and not going back to the hotel. As they walked back to the group, Curt and Zhou dropped behind her and had a whispered and urgent conversation. She tried to listen in, but the cheering was too loud. She couldn't hear a word of it.

Zhou was asked by one of the Chinese interpreters to return to the pavilion where he was surrounded by other officials of the delegation. He told them how he was asking to try a food he'd never seen before when he was being pulled through the crowd by the strangers. He hadn't realized they were different men than who had escorted him.

Everyone knew he was lying. But no one was willing to turn this into a diplomatic crisis, so they accepted Zhou's story in the public light of the pavilion. Lizbeth hung around and listened in on conversations throughout the tent. It was clear there was going to be some sort of private consequence for Zhou when he returned to China.

Lizbeth shuddered as she considered what might happen to him. When things had returned to what seemed like a normal festival, she pulled Curt aside, dragging him behind the Chinese pavilion and next to the fancy bathrooms.

"Tell me what's going on here."

Curt shook his head. "I have no idea what you are talking about."

"I swear, Curt, you can't leave me out of this. Not now. And there's no way that little stunt back there was a kidnapping. What the hell was that about?"

He shrugged and tried to look innocent.

She leaned into him. "We're intimate. I know your cues." She slapped his upper arm with the back of her hand as she remembered where she'd seen the two guys who'd tried to take off with Zhou. "Those two guys? The so-called kidnappers?"

Curt's face became hooded, guarded again. "What about them?"

"They are the same two CIA agents who came to my office to talk to my boss three days ago. They practically ran me over when they were leaving my office so I got a real good look at them."

Curt's lip twitched into a half smile. "Damn. You

are amazing. Not only do you remember faces, you can put two and two together."

Lizbeth was taken aback by the compliment. "Why did you stage a kidnapping?"

Court shook his head as if he'd given up entirely any ruse. "Keep this to yourself, or you will blow the entire operation."

"Please clue me in so I don't blow whatever it is you're trying to do."

"The kidnapping was supposed to fail. I was supposed to be the one to notice the security switch. You beat me to it." He had a big grin on his face now.

"But, why, Curt? I am trying to understand what is going on."

"I helped returned Zhou to the People's Republic of China by thwarting a kidnapping. I am now going to be seen as a trusted comrade."

"What difference does it make what they think of you? This must be all some part of a much bigger plan. Isn't it? Does this have to do with your moving to China?"

"Something like that. But this is more about getting the eyes off of Zhou for the rest of the day."

Lizbeth was trying to put things together, but nothing was adding up so easily for her now.

Curt pulled her in for a hug, but it was more so he could whisper in her ear. "Zhou is defecting. After one foiled attempt, he's the defeated comrade. At least in their eyes."

"The *actual* defection will take place later. I get it. Why not take him now? Why the subterfuge?"

"We wanted certain members of the delegation to see me in action, in front of the crowd, bringing him back to his people."

"So who takes the fall when he does defect?"

"It's going to happen at the gala tonight. On the Embassy's own grounds."

"This whole thing is a huge deflection?"

Curt wobbled his head side to side. "More or less."

Lizbeth put a hand up to her mouth and her eyes went wide. "Oh my God... I broke a CIA agent's wrist."

Curt kissed her quickly on the lips. "That, my dear, was beautiful."

Chapter 22

Jiang Hu called a meeting at the hotel directly after they returned from the festival. The visit task force decided to move Zhou and his wife to rooms at the Embassy. The guest quarters there could house up to fifty people, and the Embassy made it clear they wanted Zhou and his wife under Chinese watch. They said protection, but Lizbeth was pretty sure they were under house arrest.

The task force did not want to deal with an all-out diplomatic scandal. Jiang pronounced the event an attempted kidnapping by people unknown, though he slyly suggested Russian agents had something to do with it. He stated the Chinese government did not want to embroil themselves in a petty squabble with the United States, especially since Curt and Lizbeth had been instrumental in saving Zhou.

The CIA certainly wouldn't be announcing their part in it. They weren't supposed to have any operations on U.S. soil. Lizbeth was sure that there was going to be some fall out about this. She could tell Jiang Hu wanted to investigate further, that he wanted to interrogate Zhou, but agreed to accept his version of kidnapping as the truth. No doubt there would be ample opportunity to question Zhou once he was inside the Embassy walls.

Would he be at the gala that evening? Perhaps they would wait to interrogate him until after the event. Lizbeth didn't think Jiang was the kind of man to implement torture, but there were stories. But there had been a coldness to him at the meeting she'd never witnessed before.

Lizbeth and Curt returned to her suite after the impromptu meeting. They had three hours to kill before they had to get ready for the gala. Curt ran the bathtub, the loud water and jets giving them enough cover to whisper to each other. As they floated in the tub, Curt went over the plans for the gala-based defection with Lizbeth. She would take no part in the plot itself, and he didn't want her interfering. He told her the basic plan. That the defection would take place during the gala and from the Zhou's rooms at the Embassy. There was something about secret tunnels built during the recent reconstruction and hidden walls and corridors that would only be there until this defection was over. She had a vague mental map of that part of the Embassy in her head, but had never been in the actual quarters. It was a lot of planning and work for one person. Zhou must have some pretty important intel.

"Promise me you will stay out of things tonight," Curt said. "When I disappear for a while, mingle. Dance. I should be gone for less than ten minutes."

"I promise. Besides, my dress is so tight and my heels so tall, I won't be doing any running tonight."

"I can't wait to see you all dolled up."

"I think your plan is kinda improbable. And messy. And weird."

"Glad you have so much confidence in me."

"I didn't say it's not going to work. Even the basic plan is crazy and overly complicated."

"The crazy ones always work."

She kissed his forehead and lifted herself up in the water so she could pull his face toward her. He caught the offered nipple between his lips and sucked it in, swirling his tongue around the areola until her whole body tingled. He tugged at the other with two fingers, twisting it.

She leaned her head back, moaning loudly into the steaming room.

He shifted under her and suddenly she was on her

back in the water floating. He was grinning down at her. "Trust me?"

"Yes?"

He kissed her lightly on the lips before floating her over above one of the jets, steering her through the water like a toy boat. "Bend your knees and spread your legs wider."

"Hmmmkay?"

He pressed a button. A jet of water hit her right on her clit. He held her close, keeping the jet on target. He continued to tease her nipples with his free hand as the other held her firmly in place, her head supported by his shoulder. She closed her eyes so she could focus on the intensity of the sensation between her legs and accept what he was doing.

It wouldn't take long for her to climax like this except for the fact Curt was watching her, that he had ordered her to come. If she'd been alone, she'd already be done. They may have had sex in the shadows in front of thousands of people at the opera the night before, but this exposure was more raw, more vulnerable.

He held her head up with his shoulder, but she kept her eyes closed. "Come for me, Lizbeth."

Pleasing him by showing him her pleasure was a new one on her. Curt would make sure she got her fill of her pleasure and him. She relaxed every part of her body trusting he would keep her pussy aligned with the jets. The steady torrent of warm water was more intense than any of her vibrators. As she relaxed and let it take her away, her body responded naturally. Her hips moved upward hungrily, seeking more. Curt kept her lined up with the steady stream, constantly pulling her back in alignment so there was no reprieve from its onslaught.

The intensity of it was too much, painful even. Curt held her against the jet as her body jerked against him, completely out of control. When the orgasm hit her, she lost all sense of embarrassment. As she came, as the powerful wave of orgasm rolled through her body, she lifted her head off of his neck and elongated her spine like she was going to fly. Her arms slapped against the water looking for something to hold onto, but he kept her pinioned against the jet. A noise she had never made before burst out of her—animalistic, loud, joyous.

It could have been ten seconds, or it could have been ten minutes, but she was unable to move on her own. Curt turned her away from the jets and held her, caressing her cheek as she leaned in against him.

She found a strange new space in her head she'd never been to before where everything was calm, serene, and perfect. The combination of floating, completely trusting him to hold her in the water, and the intense orgasm followed by his arms around her was incredible. She was completely safe in arms. Warm. Loved.

This zone was one where she was hyper aware of everything and completely unaware of everything at the same time. Curt was still holding her in the cooling bath.

"Wow. That was intense. It's like I went away—somewhere else. I have never had that happen before."

Curt held her chin up and kissed her lips. "You were beautiful. Thank you."

She had no idea what to say to that. He didn't seem surprised by her description of it, but she didn't press him for more details. "How long has it been?"

Curt shrugged. "Maybe twenty minutes since you went all spacey."

"That's a good word for it. I wasn't sleeping, or dreaming. It was... is... hard to describe. I'm sorry. You didn't..."

"It was enough, for now. It's a different kind of pleasure."

"What is that supposed to mean?"

"I'll give you a full lesson some day. For now, we need to get ready for the gala. I suspect it will take you a little longer than getting ready for work."

Lesson? What did that mean?

"You got that right, buddy," she said, stepping out

of the tub and rubbing her hands down her side. "I'm going to look so amazing you're going to have a hard time keeping your thoughts on the job tonight."

CURT GAVE her a kiss and left the room to get ready. Liz pulled out her dress and hung it over the door. In her everyday life, Lizbeth had little option in terms of style. She had to dress professionally, and that usually meant boring. She could add a pop of color with a scarf or some interesting jewelry. Even then, she had to stay on the modest end of things. She had been shocked to learn she couldn't enter certain areas of government while wearing a sleeveless shirt.

Because this gala was officially a work gig, she had to maintain modesty, but it being a gala meant she could go for something couture—something lavishly expensive, and yet tasteful enough that she couldn't be faulted for showing some skin. She had found a vintage Dior dress that fit her perfectly. It was stylish in a way that never went out of style, yet suited her love of vintage clothing she could never indulge in at work. They knew how to construct beautiful garments in the 1950's.

She had found the gown at a tiny thrift shop that specialized in high end vintage. It was backless in a rich ruby red that made her skin glow. To show off the cut of the back, she put her hair up into an elaborate braided, curled design. Lizbeth had always done her own hair; she'd learned how to braid, twist, and knot it into complicated patterns by watching YouTube. Her mother asked her never to cut her hair, so she only went for a trim every six months. When she was twenty-two, she had almost chopped it short in order to piss her mom off, but she'd chickened out in the end.

She dropped the dress down over herself, enjoying the silky hiss of the fabric slinking over her body. There were no zippers or connectors on the dress. It was elegant in its simplicity and indulgent fabric. She put on a pair of paste gemstone earrings that reflected the beading along the neckline and looked like they had been designed specifically for the dress. Lizbeth slipped into her custom Louboutin shoes which lifted her an easy three inches. She stepped back to admire the entire effect in the full-length mirror.

Curt came into the room, his eyes on his cufflinks as he fiddled with them, trying to get them to snap into place. "Damn shirt. I hate these..." He stopped short as he looked up from his wrists.

"You like?"

His mouth dropped open in mute appreciation before he nodded. "Umm... like doesn't even begin to describe what I'm thinking right now."

"It's real vintage."

He circled her slowly, his eyes moving up and down her body. He drew a finger along her back, above the cleft in her buttocks. "Wow. You are going to have every man in the room drooling over you. Some of the women, too."

"Don't tell me you'll be jealous?"

He pulled a curl near her ear gently and released it. "I like the curls. It's different, but pretty."

"It won't last. It's fun for a few hours."

He kissed the nape of her neck. "I seem to recall a very special piece of fabric that goes with this dress."

He found the scarf in her closet and draped it around her neck so the fabric became a thick choker.

She shivered under his touch. They didn't have time for anything more than a chaste kiss at the moment.

"You think anyone will figure out what we used this scarf for the other night?" He tugged at the two ends, teasing her.

She pushed at him playfully. "You came in here about your cufflinks."

He held out his wrist for her.

She set his cufflinks into place and adjusted his bowtie. "You don't look complete without the jacket."

"I hate wearing tuxes. The cufflinks. The tie."

She followed him into his room. "Men are so lucky. What did it take you to get ready, five minutes?"

"I napped while you did your hair and makeup. It was nice."

Lizbeth hadn't really thought much about the realities of dating someone like Curt before. The chase earlier in the day had been exciting, even before she knew the gun she'd knocked out of the agent's hand was a fake. The reality of what could happen to Curt in the real, everyday world was scary.

He held out his arms as if unsure if they should touch. She moved into them, not worried about a little wrinkle or two. "Don't let the fear get you," he said, holding her hands, caressing her wrists. "I'll be fine."

"I'll believe that when I see it."

Chapter 23

Hundreds of red and gold paper lanterns hung from the ceilings at different heights. The sheer number of them filled with twinkling lights gave a magical feel to the space. There were forty or so standing height tables draped in gold and red fabrics, traditional colors of luck and good fortune. The Embassy staff circulated the room in gold brocade, trays laden with drinks and hor d'oeurves.

The Chinese Embassy was known to be an architectural gem, designed by M.E. Pei. The interior was clean and composed, elegant, even, but Liz thought it was kind of boring. The transformation of the space from simple and bland was magnificent. She hadn't believed it possible. They had dedicated two large ballrooms to the event. The first was for a cocktail hour meet and greet before the banquet and a second for the banquet itself. A string quartet performed in a corner of the room. The music was background and not at all intrusive.

Lizbeth held on to Curt's arm lightly as he escorted her inside very much like they were playing out a scene in one of Jane Austen's novels. All the guests were in formal wear, tuxes and long, glittering dresses. Many of the delegation had chosen to wear elaborate, floor-length cheongsams—their intricate embroidery and high-mandarin collars a throwback to history but with varying degrees of modernization.

One woman had a backless version, but the front had the traditional high neck with an open circle at the center and buttons angling from neck to arm. It was daring in a modern, almost snarky way. A few even had fishtail swishes at the bottom of the skirts. Several wore western style ball-gowns, but all of those were younger women.

Madam Zhou wore a shapeless cheongsam that dropped straight from her breasts down to the floor. It was fairly plain fabric as well with only a tiny bit of embroidery along the collar. Lizbeth got the sense that there was a statement in the woman's choice. Curt had confided in her that Madam Zhou was part of the defection. Maybe the Embassy had spoken to the Zhous about their loyalty to China and her communist party issue dress was an effort to mollify any suspicions Jiang might have.

Lizbeth passed on the Champagne. Getting tipsy tonight was a very bad idea. She found a waiter and asked her to bring her some sparkling water instead. That way she could still blend in with a cocktail glass without the boozy effects of Champagne. She glided from group to group, checking in on them.

"Lizbeth? Don't you look amazing."

It was Lincoln Pierce. He had a beautiful woman on his arm. Lizbeth was under orders from Opal to take notes on Link's date for the evening. Her dark, shoulder-length hair was sprayed into place. A level three hurricane might not even dislodge it. Lizbeth thought she might be about thirty-five, possibly forty. Her beaded dress showed off a curvy figure. There was an elegance about her that would work well for a First Lady.

"Lizbeth Crandall, this is Erica Mitchum. Lizbeth is my staff liaison to the intelligence committee. She helped put this shindig together."

"Lincoln, you never mentioned that you have such stunning staffers in your office."

Lizbeth smiled demurely at the compliment.

"It's amazing how smart she is, too," Link said.

Getting praise from Lincoln Pierce was better than getting a gold star in school. She hoped Erica wasn't offended at his praising her so candidly. No one liked being on a date with a man who was paying attention to another woman.

"Erica, it's wonderful to meet you. I hope you both enjoy the gala. The banquet will start soon, and, after a couple of speeches, there will be some dancing." She was nice enough, but didn't feel any zing between the two. There wouldn't be much to report to Opal.

She left the couple alone and went in search of Curt. Her initial attraction to the Congressman was juvenile in comparison to her feelings for Curt. Liz found him in a group of men talking about the upcoming art exhibit at the National Gallery. He drew her in close and held her lightly around the waist, quietly claiming her in front of everyone.

The group continued their conversation, unbroken as if she hadn't joined them at all. Curt's fingers dug into her waist, signaling her for an extraction from the group.

She whispered in his ear. "I love the way you look in a tux."

He pretended surprise as if she'd said something urgent. "Excuse me, gentlemen. We are needed elsewhere."

After they were well clear of the group, he kissed her lightly on the ear. "You're pretty good at reading cues."

Liz gave him a side glance. "I think the Clay Warriors exhibit is going to be amazing, actually. Why were you so anxious to get away from them?"

Curt waved down a server and popped an appetizer into his mouth. "I'm starving. I'm wishing I'd grabbed a corn dog at the river today."

"Not corn dogs again."

A gong rang loudly announcing the beginning of the banquet. The doors separating the ballrooms were thrown open to reveal an even more elaborate interior. If Lizbeth had never seen the ballroom in its original, functional state, she wouldn't have believed they were in the Embassy.

Lizbeth drew in a breath of surprise as she entered the dining room. It had been transformed from the almost stark modern hall into something that reminded her of a modern English countryside. On the center of each table stood a massive vase with long branches of cherry blossoms. Each vase was different, and the branches were all artfully arranged. The table cloths were gold and somehow didn't look cheap. Instead, they brought a rich warmth to the room and contrasted with the deep blue of the vases and china.

To add to the effect, thousands of white lights had been strung around the room and crisscrossed overhead to give the space a twinkly airy feeling. It softened the space considerably. People found their way to their assigned seats. As they made their way through the room, Lizbeth saw a number of people making angry eyes at each other. The seating program appeared to have been worth its weight in gold. She would have to take Eleanor out to dinner to thank her and convince her to make a fortune selling the program to wedding planners.

The Embassy had taken over every detail of the gala except the seating chart. She had seated herself next to Curt in the back of the room. They were with the rest of the visit task force, except for Jiang Hu. He sat at the head table in a place of honor. Lincoln and Erica were up near the front along with other notable Congressmen and Senators. The President hadn't been required for this visit, thank goodness. That would have been a logistical nightmare of its own.

Lizbeth didn't mind being in the background at the moment. One day, she would be the up there as part of the American Ambassadorial entourage. The first course of the banquet was already on the table waiting for them—a cold dish to whet the appetite. She picked up her chopsticks with ease and put the delicate sliver of crispy pork belly into her mouth.

She settled into the rhythm of the banquet. Servers moving from the front of the room to the back in efficient waves of black and white. From first bite to last, every morsel in the banquet was perfection. The head chef had outdone himself. She looked down at the last plate as the waiter removed it from in front of her.

"You look sad," Curt said.

"I am. I've been coming to the Embassy a lot. Well, I guess you know that, but I am going to miss the food. It's so good here."

"You eat a lot."

"And the problem is…"

"Oh, no problem. The moment you put sesame balls on your plate, I knew you were perfect for me." He put his hand on her thigh under the table. The speeches were about to start, and, finally, the dancing would begin.

"Will you have time to dance with me?" she asked.

"Once. Probably."

That 'probably' of his set her nerves on edge. He didn't really know what was going to happen. *Ugh.* The speeches were all in Chinese. The Americans who didn't speak Chinese held little earpieces against their ears for the translation. Nothing new was said, and there was a lot of boring platitudes. But soon enough the speeches were over.

Another wall opened like magic to reveal a dance floor. People could stay in their seats to continue conversation or they could dance. It wasn't big enough for everyone, but it could hold fifty or sixty people easily. It looks like she would get her dance. Curt stood up and held out his hand to her. She took it lightly and he led her to the dance floor.

"You think we're okay dancing while working?" he asked.

"Dancing tonight is part of my job. I don't think anyone will complain if we have one dance."

It was a moderate waltz, and she followed his lead easily. She made a mental note to thank Katherine, once again, for making the entire office staff take a ballroom dance class as a work-related team event.

"Oh, you can dance, Mr. Wu," she said, teasing him with her best British accent.

"Why, so can you, Miss Crandall." He led her through a series of simple turns, pulling her in close against him. "Perhaps Mr. Thorpe is awaiting your return?"

Lizbeth blushed and whispered back, "You rogue! How dare you!" She pulled herself away and established a formal dancing stance with a look that appeared as if he had offended her propriety.

His eyes sparkled with humor as he led her across the floor to the corner of the room. He bowed formally over her hand, kissing it like an old-fashioned gentleman.

"My lady. I shall return," he said, using his Mr. Darcy voice.

She held onto his hand when he tried to turn away.

Their eyes locked as he dipped his head in silent question. "Don't leave me here for long."

"Of course not." He glided away from her, his strong shoulders back in a confident swagger.

Lizbeth almost jumped when Lincoln Pierce appeared at her side. "Well, now. He's a good looking young man, Lizbeth. Would you honor me with the next dance?"

Lizbeth was a little freaked out to be in the arms of her boss. She twisted around, looking for cameras. Realizing there were none, she relaxed and pretended she was dancing with her dad. Or any other older gentleman on the dance floor. She wasn't in his arms... they were dancing.

"I want you to know I got an interesting report from this morning's races. I'm concerned that your young man there might not be who you think he is."

Lizbeth tried to put together what Lincoln must know from the top-level security access he had with what he might think she knew. On the surface level, everyone believed Curt to be a State Department rep who had jumped in to stop a kidnapping, not knowing that he was preventing a defection.

She wondered what Lincoln knew about tonight's operation or if he knew Curt was actually CIA.

"I know exactly who he is, sir. He's a charming

State Department rep who was in the right place at the right time. Why are you so concerned?"

"I don't like the CIA meddling with my staff, Lizbeth. Stirs up the shit that cows don't crap. I certainly told them I trust you when they came to the office."

"I appreciate that, sir."

Lincoln leaned in close, pretending it was part of the spin of the dance. "There are things you are unaware of and I cannot tell you. Trust me when I say, you should stay well clear of Curt Wu."

Lincoln swung her out wide into an underarm spin and drew her back in. How did he know who Curt was, let alone to warn her away from him? "Thank you, sir. I'll take that under advisement."

His smile was attractive. His personality and charismatic draw was even more potent this close. Lizbeth wanted him to succeed whether she was part of his team or not. But she didn't want to be romantically involved with him. That was a life for someone else. There was only one man for her.

As the Congressman danced her around the room, Lizbeth kept her eye out for Curt, but couldn't find him. Minister Zhou and his wife were also gone. When the song was over, Lincoln led Liz over to the table where Erica sat. Opal would be all over her on Monday asking for details about the evening. From the looks of it, Erica and Lincoln were doing okay, but she didn't sense any strong attraction between them. Cordiality. Politeness.

"Lincoln," Erica drawled. "You're back from your dancing. How sweet." Three empty glasses sat in front of her. She lifted a hand and a waiter came over with another glass for her. Lincoln sat down next to his date. She swayed toward him, leaning heavily on his arm even though they were both seated.

"I think it's time for me to check in with the Embassy liaison, sir. I'll see you later." How in the world did someone so elegant turn into someone so, so... she almost smacked her forehead. Three glasses. The woman was obviously drunk. She made a note to let Opal know that Erica Mitchum would not last long with Lincoln Pierce. He probably only put up with her being tipsy if not drunk because sending her home in the middle of the gala would be embarrassing for both of them. Opal would have to look elsewhere to find Lincoln a suitable future First Lady.

Lizbeth made her way over to Jiang Hu. He looked a bit tense, but that wasn't entirely unusual. She hadn't had much chance to be alone with him since the incident at the races, and she wanted to check in with him about it. She bowed to him when she approached and he bowed back.

"Ms. Crandall, it has been an honor to work with you on this most wonderful visit."

She looked away and then down at her feet showing humility. "I am sorry about the incident this morning. I trust you have been able to calm Minister Zhou's fears."

Hu's lips twitched. "If not for you and Mr. Wu, we might have lost him."

"I am glad to have been of service."

Hu took both her hands in his. "Have your people been able to determine who those men are? What government they work for?"

"I acted out of instinct this morning. Zhou is a guest I feel responsible for. I thought he was being taken."

Jiang Hu put his hands behind his back. "My thoughts are it was the Russians."

She returned her gaze to her feet to hide her surprise. It would be a good face-saving alternative. "You may be right, sir. The one certainly looked Russian to me." They seemed as good an alternative as any, and she certainly wasn't going to offer up what little she knew.

"Minister Zhou seems quite recovered. He was at the banquet, at least."

Jiang Hu quickly scanned the room.

Oh, No. Maybe she shouldn't have brought up the

minister with Jiang. His eyes narrowed, and his lips turned into a thin straight line. "Excuse me, Ms. Crandall, but I feel I should check in with the Minister. I need to be sure he is feeling well. Especially after the excitement this morning."

Hu excused himself and moved gracefully through the room, in as straight a line as he could manage toward the bathrooms. Lizbeth bit her lip. She'd stupidly pointed out Zhou's absence to the one man that actually might be suspicious of a defection. What had she been thinking? She'd sent Jiang straight toward the operation.

Chapter 24

ext Curt. Her purse was all the way across the ballroom. She had to warn Curt that Jiang was on his way. What if Jiang got there in time to stop the defection? At the very least, she could warn Curt he was coming. Then again, what was he going to do? Stop whatever he was doing to look at his texts? He probably had it turned all the way off. Fighting her way through everyone would take too long. She had to do something and changed directions to follow Jiang.

Liz was able to catch up to Jiang but remain hidden. He glided past the bathrooms and opened a door that had been invisible in the woodwork. If she hadn't seen it move, she wouldn't have even noticed it.

She waited a few seconds and followed him, taking a few seconds to figure out how it opened. The door opened onto a narrow corridor that ran both directions.

She placed it in the mental map she had of the Embassy. It must link the ballroom to the lobby and the guest quarters directly. Maybe it was used for servant access. Interesting.

Jiang was ahead of her by twenty feet in the corridor. Her first few steps clicked loudly against the linoleum. She swore to herself before removing her shoes and leaving them in a potted palm next to the door. The shoes would make too much noise, and she didn't want to carry them. She might need her hands.

Hyper-focused on Jiang, she watched his every move to see if he would turn around, but he never did. He moved purposefully and without any concern. At the end of the hallway, he opened a steel door and exited. She had a pretty good mental map of the Embassy, and she was sure he'd gone past the main lobby and was now at the guest quarters.

Halfway to where Jiang exited, there was a utilitarian looking door with a small window in it. She glanced briefly inside and saw stairs going both up and down off a small landing right at the door. That was curious. She'd been to the upper level of the Embassy. But she was pretty sure the Embassy didn't have a basement. Where could that second set of stairs be going to? At least there wasn't a basement in the official plans. There was no time to explore now, however. She'd definitely ask Curt about it. Maybe the basement had something to do with the tunnels they were using for Zhou's escape.

Lizbeth scampered quickly to the door Jiang had used, hoping she wasn't too late. She cautiously pushed it open, hoping he'd still be in view. It opened into another hallway in the intersection of a T. The dark wood accents and finish of the walls told her she was back in a regular part of the Embassy. She could hear voices to the right of the T.

She poked her head around the corner and could make out the lobby to the Embassy's guest wing. Certainty calmed her. If she turned left, she'd be headed toward the Embassy's formal courtyard garden. Her back against the wall, she peeked around the corner toward the guest wing. A guard to the upper floor of the guest wing straightened upon Jiang's approach and saluted.

The guard and Jiang spoke in rapid Mandarin, loud enough for Lizbeth to hear them. The acoustics in this particular lobby acted like an amplifier. They obviously hadn't seen her.

"The Zhous," the guard said, "passed by earlier on their way to attend the gala but neither have returned to their rooms, sir. They are the only people staying here. I would have seen them, sir."

That was strange. The plan had been for the Zhous to leave the gala early to 'retire to their rooms' for the evening, complaining of exhaustion or headaches. Then, the team would extract them both from their rooms. During the renovations to the Embassy, the CIA had managed to infiltrate a secret tunnel system in the Chinese Embassy that appeared as a sewage system. The plan was to remove the Zhous through the tunnels once they returned to their room. That plan had almost been ruined when the entire delegation was moved to the Pembroke. The CIA wanted the defection to happen on Embassy grounds for a variety of reasons. If Zhou disappeared while under the Embassy's protection and on their own turf, they would never lose face by admitting it.

The fake kidnapping attempt at the Dragon Boat races had been to ensure the Zhous would be removed from the hotel into one of the Embassy completed suites. If they hadn't gone past the guard, where had they gone, and why had they chosen to go elsewhere? It didn't make sense. If they had left the ballroom, the only other place they could be was in the front main lobby, the administrative offices, or... outside. The courtyard. On the opposite end of the corridor.

Jiang did not come to the same conclusion. He pressed past the guard, obviously intent on doing his own search of the guest wing. He strode purposefully up the stairs, the guard calling out after him that they were on the west side of the wing.

How long did she have before Jiang had finished his search of the guest quarters and figured out they'd be in the courtyard? Two minutes? Five? She ran for the courtyard at full speed, hoping her bare feet wouldn't slap against the cool stone and draw the guard's attention. As she took off into a sprint, the sixty-year-old stitching on her dress give way at the knees and the slit was now mid-thigh. *Shit.* At least she could run more freely.

The glass doors opening to the outside were closed. She opened them quickly but with precision, praying for silent hinges. She ran down the four steps leading to the rectangular courtyard and paused, trying to decide which of the three gardens that led off the courtyard they might have gone into.

The courtyard was a formal Chinese garden. It was small, but had all the traditional elements—stones, water, and plants. The only lights on now were the regular soft lights that provided barely enough illumination to not trip. Her eyes to adjusted to the darkness, and as soon as she could see the paths, she veered left, closest to the Embassy. The bottoms of her feet screamed as she hit the pebbles of the pathway, but she forged ahead. She wished she'd kept her shoes. But then again, Louboutins wouldn't do well on gravel, either.

A harsh laugh from behind her made her swivel

around. She ran to the garden closest to the Embassy's tall wall. Maybe they had climbed over the wall. That was completely off kilter with the original plan, but just as sensible. The whole point of having Zhou disappear from *inside* the Embassy, seemingly without a trace, was to freak out the Chinese in a strange game of political non-diplomacy.

Curt was supposed to come out of this appearing to be 'helping the Chinese' and amenable to maybe switching sides and acting as a double agent. This courtyard business was not part of the plan.

Three figures standing in the gazebo in the middle of the garden. Curt and the two Zhous stood in a triangle, about ten feet apart from each other. All three had guns drawn. Curt and Minister Zhou both had theirs pointing at Madam Zhou. She had her gun pointing at Zhou. Then she pointed the gun at Curt. Liz froze. She couldn't breathe.

Madam Zhou glared at her husband, but kept the gun pointed at Curt. "My decision is final. I am not leaving," Mrs. Zhou said. "I refuse to go along with this plan."

"Please. Reconsider. My dearest love...You must come with me. I don't know what they'll do to..."

Lizbeth found her breath again as she listened to the argument. She couldn't quite follow what was happening.

Madam Zhou spit at his feet. "You weak, little, insignificant man. I was never your dearest love. I am not going to let you ruin our good reputation by selling secrets to the Americans."

Selling secrets. Hm. She adopted her karate stance and instinctively wanted to kick out Madam Zhou's gun, but she knew that wasn't the way to handle the situation. Curt didn't even look fazed that a gun was pointed at him.

"We will have a better life here—in America. Please, wifey... put down the gun and come with me. Before it is too late."

"You would let them kill my parents, my brothers? Everyone? You would do all that so you can live a bourgeois life, *Hubby*? You let your true dog-self show." She spat again in his direction. "You have no one to lose. It is my family that will pay. I can't allow that to happen."

Zhou shoulders slumped and he closed his eyes, but his gun stayed pointed at her. "You are right, woman. Always so right. They would take this out on your family. They probably still will."

They exchanged a look with some profound understanding between them. His face took on a sharpness that hadn't been there before as he raised his gun again, pointed at his wife. There was no love between those two. They had used the terms to hurt each other, to poke at their lack of relationship. *Hubby*. *Wifey*. Both had been verbal arrows launched at each other.

There was a lull in the conversation. Madame Zhou was completely concentrated on her husband. Why didn't Curt make a move?

Madam Zhou's mouth pinched closed for a moment. "You are a selfish bastard, hubby."

"I am. I am very sorry, Wifey. It must be this way. At least you will never see them suffer."

Curt's weapon was steady on Madam Zhou. Where had he gotten a gun? Wouldn't she have noticed it when she danced with him? How clueless was she?

"Both of you," he said, "put down your weapons."

"Wifey, come with me." His intonation for the usually loving diminutives was snarky, ironic.

Minister Zhou pulled the trigger on his gun, but there wasn't even a click. Zhou swore and hit the gun against his hand as if it would unjam something. Madam Zhou glanced back to Curt and fired. His gun hand wavered for a moment, but he didn't seem to lose his composure. Lizbeth's heart stopped beating.

Had he been shot? She couldn't see any blood, but she knew she had to get to him. But not while Madam Zhou had her gun; Curt would never forgive her for doing something that stupid.

Madam Zhou aimed her gun at her husband. "Well then, Hubby. You should say…"

But her final word was eaten up by the blast of Curt's gun.

Madam Zhou's face widened as a dark hole appeared in her forehead. Her expression shifted into one of confusion, then understanding. She took a step forward, her arm lifting a couple of inches before she dropped to her knees. She bent over backward, slowly as if stretching into an exaggerated yoga position.

Lizbeth broke her silence, screaming, "Curt!"

Curt hadn't known she was there; he pivoted in slow motion on one foot to look at her. Blood seeped through the fingers of his free hand against his stomach. His gun hand dropped limply to his side, anger and confusion on his face.

"Oh, Liz… So sorry…" he said as he stumbled toward her two steps and then twisted to land on his back.

Minister Zhou ran to Curt and dropped to his knees, apologizing. He looked up at Liz as she approached, surprised at seeing her, thinking she was there to help. "What do I do now?"

Lizbeth wanted to tell him to go shoot himself. To leave her alone so she could tend to Curt, who might be dying. She didn't say any of those things. She knew something important must be at stake, even if Curt hadn't shared why this man's information could be very important to their country. She had to trust Curt that Zhou was important enough for him to be shot over.

"Go on with the plan. You were supposed to be up in your bedroom by now?"

Zhou nodded.

"The problem is Curt and your wife shooting each other will prove she was not going to run away. That Curt was helping you, not trying to stop you."

Liz darted over to Mrs. Zhou and grabbed the gun from the dead woman's hand. She wiped the woman's prints off the gun with the bottom of her torn dress. She pressed the gun into his hands. She did the same with Curt's gun and handed it to Zhou.

"Take your wife and Curt's guns. If you get caught, you shot them both. You overpowered Curt. You took his gun. Got it? *You shot them.* Now, run back into the gala and yell for help. Then, as soon as people go crazy, *continue to the meet as planned.* Go to your room and *continue with the plan.*"

Zhou looked doubtful.

Liz looked over her shoulder toward the Embassy, surprised that no one had come running. The music for the dance must have kept anyone from hearing the shots. How long had it been? How much time did Curt have?

She stood up and pushed Zhou towards the gala. "Run inside and yell, *there's a shooter, there's a shooter,* and pandemonium will break out. When it does, go back to your room."

She was surprised at how calm she remained in this situation. Almost like she was out of her body. Almost like she knew instinctively how to handle it. Liz dropped to her knees next to Curt, her hands lightly running across his chest, pushing his jacket aside. Zhou looked at the two of them, still immobile.

"NOW. Do not waste this moment. Do not waste what he has done for you."

Zhou stuffed one gun into his suit jacket and the other gun into his pants pocket. He took off towards the ballroom. Liz dropped to her knees. She got close to his face. "Don't leave, Curt. Stay with me." Her fingers shook as she fumbled toward his neck for a pulse.

She rifled through his jacket to find his phone. She swiped for an emergency button that auto-dialed 911, completely unsure if the Embassy would allow an emergency crew on scene. If they didn't let a gurney through, she'd find a way to drag Curt to the ambulance if she had to.

Lizbeth leaned over Curt, cupping his cheek with one hand. His pulse was faint to the touch and getting weaker. The entire front of his tuxedo shirt was crimson now.

Sorry? What had he said he was sorry for? Sorry for getting shot? Sorry for involving her? Sorry for loving her?

She tore off her scarf, balled it up and pressed it where she thought it might help. "You're gonna be okay, honey. Hold on, please. Don't leave me. You'll only be sorry if you die. You can't. Not now." She cooed into his ear. Willing him to stay alive. Promising him things she'd never promised any man. If you stay alive... if you come back to me... if... if... if...

She could hear people coming out into the courtyard now, running away from the building. She screamed for help, sure the cacophony they created would eat up her cries. "Over here. He's been shot. Help!"

She kissed Curt on his lips, his forehead, his cheeks. "Stay with me, baby, stay with me."

Bright flood lights suddenly replaced the twinkling-charm of the regular courtyard lights. They were bathed in full light. Lizbeth hunched into Curt, shielding her eyes from the brightness by pushing them into his shoulder. Sirens screeched, but they seemed millions of miles away. The crunch of running steps approached her. Maybe Curt had a chance.

Embassy guards surged out of the Embassy, pushing through the crowd that had come from the ballroom.

Lizbeth was lifted away from Curt. As she realized they were being separated, she kicked out, flailing her arms and screaming, "Let me go. I need to be with him." She was being held firm by two guards, and there was nothing she could do against them as they held her up off the ground between them. She was yanked backward away from Curt, who remained lying on the ground.

As they dragged her away, she met the eyes of Lincoln Pierce, who stood in the crowd, his arm protectively around his date, waiting with everyone trying to figure out what was happening and what they should be doing. He started to push his way through the crowd to her, but there were too many people.

"Help him, Link. Help Curt," she screamed, trying to get out of their grasp. "He's been shot and needs help."

The guards held her arms tight. She couldn't wrestle free from the tight grip. Jiang Hu appeared at her face, his eyes narrowed in suspicion. "What happened?"

Lizbeth struggled against the men who held her firmly. "Minister Zhou. He's crazy. He shot them both and climbed over the fence." She pointed in the direction of the garden fence. Opposite of where Zhou had actually gone.

Jiang snapped his fingers, and she was hauled into the building. They dragged her into a service corridor and through the door with the funny window. Down she went, down three flights of stairs into that basement level Lizbeth didn't even know the Embassy had.

Chapter 25

She was thrown into a small room, onto her stomach, and the door slammed shut behind her. It was pitch dark inside. This was beyond bad. If the Chinese Embassy had a dungeon, she might never get out. Liz slammed up against the bolted steel door and pounded her fist against it, but the soft thuds of her wrists against the padding on the door were hardly audible to her, and she was inside the room.

No one cared. Lizbeth blindly groped for the wall. It was a small space. She could reach from one side to the other if she held her arms out. The walls were padded. Great. A looney bin room? There was no light within reach, and certainly no switch on the wall.

She dropped onto the floor in a corner opposite the door and pulled her knees up to her chest. Was Curt dead? She couldn't see anything in the darkness. She wrapped the shreds of her vintage Dior around her legs. It was ruined, ripped, and probably blood-stained beyond repair.

"Let me out!" she yelled one last time. She had done nothing wrong. Well, okay, she'd conspired with a CIA agent to help a Chinese citizen defect, but she hadn't actually *done anything*. If she stopped to think about it, she *had* messed with evidence in a huge way when she'd had Zhou take the guns. And lying to Jiang as she was being carried away to send people on a wild goose chase over the fence could be counted as "doing something."

There was no fixing any of it. She pulled at the fabric until it covered her bare legs pretty well. The room was cold and she wrapped her arms around her legs. She rested her head on her knees and wept. She had no idea if Curt could survive his wound. *All that blood.* Curt's blood. Had an ambulance come? She shook uncontrollably, unable to stop, visions of red soaking across his white tuxedo shirt.

What had gone wrong? The plan had been simple. The Zhous were to leave the banquet early. They were supposed to return to their room at the Embassy and Curt would meet them in their room. Curt would lead them to the tunnel the CIA had hidden under the Embassy, and another agent would direct them through to a safe house.

Lizbeth hadn't believed a secret tunnel possible, but she also hadn't believed there was a basement under the Embassy no one knew about. And yet, here she was.

Curt was supposed to hand the Zhous off to another agent. That person would navigate the Chinese couple through the hidden tunnels and to safety. In the process, Curt would do something to make it appear as though he were helping the Chinese more than the Americans.

Lizbeth had never been clear on the details about what was supposed to have gone down. Now that everything was totally messed up, she hoped her sudden revisions at the end worked. Curt being shot by the escaping defector could definitely be considered as service to the Chinese. Lizbeth hadn't worn a watch to the gala, and her phone was in her purse on the table upstairs. Well, it had been, anyway—however long ago. She was sure it was in the hands of Chinese security now.

She racked her brain to think of anything incriminating on the phone. They'd have gone through all her texts by now, and she was relieved she hadn't sent Curt a warning about Jiang leaving the gala. All they'd find were scheduling texts and the slightly embarrassing flirting they'd been doing.

She was in a darkened padded room. Lizbeth

rolled onto the floor in a little ball and closed her eyes. She was so tired from everything. Maybe it was all a bad dream, and by going to sleep she would wake up to reality. She closed her eyes and tried to use the counting trick, but sleep, of course, had other plans.

She ran through the evening and developed a plausible narrative that would explain her actions and everything that had happened in the courtyard. She prayed that Curt would keep his mouth shut until she got to him to give him her version of events. If he was alive.

Please, let him be alive.

Unable to sit still, she paced the perimeter of the room, walking in a slow circuit with one hand on the wall, before stopping at the door to listen. Muffled and indistinct voices filtered through the padding of the room. She couldn't make out anything they were saying though. Lizbeth was an American citizen. She pounded on the door, alternating her screams in Chinese and English.

"I have rights, you know!" The words were eaten up by the sound-proofing in the room but yelling gave her a sense of power, as if she was doing actually something.

After what seemed like hours, the door opened, and a light clicked on overhead. After the darkness, even this single fluorescent was enough to hurt her eyes. A set of dry grey sweatpants and sweatshirt were thrown at her.

"Dress in these. Quickly."

The gown looked worse than she thought it would. She peeled it off, trying not to look at the twin spots of darker red at the knees and the rips along the sides. She tossed the dress in the corner. She never wanted to see it again. The evening was supposed to end with her and Curt back in her room with him taking his time unzipping the delicate fabric and kissing her shoulder as he helped her out of it. This was not how her night was supposed to end.

She took all the pins out of her hair and stashed them in her bra cup, finger-combing her hair. Having a couple of bobby pins handy seemed like a good idea. Supposedly, a bobby pin could be used to free yourself from a pair of handcuffs. As if she'd be able to figure that out, but she couldn't try if she didn't have any.

She sounded a little bit crazy to herself, and she'd only been in this cell for a couple of hours at best. Or had it been longer? She had no idea. Two guards in standard Chinese Embassy uniforms dragged her out of the room.

"Where are you taking me?" she asked in Mandarin. No answer. She tried again in another dialect. No answer. She tried a few more times in different dialects, and still they refused to speak, not even a nod of the head.

They led her through a set of corridors she'd never seen before in cold silence. Lizbeth breathed a sigh of relief as they moved up three flights of stairs, away from whatever was behind her. She was suddenly thrust into the very conference room she was familiar with. The one that usually had a pile of sesame balls and warm doughnuts. Tonight, there wasn't anything on the buffet. The cool light of dawn was barely peeking through the window of the conference room. She must have been held for about six hours then.

Lincoln Pierce, Jiang Hu, and three other people she didn't recognize were seated at the table. Lincoln and Jiang both still wore their tuxes from the gala. Their jackets were unbuttoned, and their bowties hung open along with their shirts which were also open and loose at their necks.

Lincoln jumped up, leaned his weight against the table. "Lizbeth, thank God you are all right." His face looked strained.

Jiang Hu was pale in the face. He held up a hand and pointed to a chair for her, a slight smile on his face.

"You see, Congressman. We were holding her for her own safety."

"Thank you. I appreciate that. Now, if you will

allow me to take her home, I'd appreciate it," Lincoln said.

"After we ask some questions." Jiang's usually friendly eyes had taken on an icy, stone-like quality. "Ms. Crandall, please have some tea. I'm afraid those clothes are all we could find at such short notice. I am so very sorry though, I do not have shoes that will fit your large American feet."

Lizbeth took the offered cup and held it in both hands for the warmth. "Thank you for the clothes, sir. How is Curt?" she asked, her voice quiet, almost inaudible.

Lincoln looked at her with his kind eyes and shook his head.

Panic filled her.

He held up his hand, shaking his head vigorously. "No, I meant to say, we don't know. We won't know for a while yet. He's alive. He's being operated on."

Lizbeth closed her eyes and bowed her head over the cup of tea, breathing in the floral notes of sweet jasmine. She sipped at it before giving them her attention again.

Jiang Hu was looking at her differently—as if she were a threat and not a colleague. She withheld a shiver as she wondered if Jiang was an MSS agent. If the CIA loaded the U.S. embassies with spies, surely it was the same for the Chinese. She focused on Lincoln instead.

"You don't have to answer any questions, Lizbeth," Lincoln said. His eyes bore into hers with an unmistakable message. "But, I want you to meet Spencer Watson and Quinn Bennett. They work with Curt closely at the State Department."

Lizbeth was tired of talking in code, but this one came through rather clear to her. Watson and Bennett were definitely CIA. She smiled at them, wondering if Curt had had any time to dissuade them from the notion that she was MSS. If he hadn't, they weren't necessarily friendly to her.

"Ms. Crandall," Jiang said, "You are the only witness to tonight's events. I would like to know exactly what you saw."

What was it they say about lies? Tell the truth as close as you can.

"At the gala, we were talking about the Zhous. You seemed concerned about them and left the ballroom."

Jiang nodded.

"I realized that I hadn't seen Curt for a while either. I followed you, thinking maybe you knew where they'd go."

"Through a secret doorway?"

"Yes. I didn't think it was secret like that, more like a secret for kitchen staff to use."

"And leaving your shoes at the door?"

"Well," she took a sip of her tea, trying to think. "This is kind of embarrassing."

"Please continue."

"My toes were pinched all night. They look amazing, Louboutins, but they are so uncomfortable. I thought I could take them off for a few minutes."

Jiang looked as if he wasn't sure whether or not to believe her. He eyed her feet dubiously. "Your feet hurt?"

"Yes. Would you like to walk in them, to see if I am telling the truth?"

Jiang let out a single laugh. He steepled his fingers together and gave a slight bow, a tiny smile at his lips.

Jiang had seen her follow him! Lizbeth breathed deeply, glad she'd chosen to tell as much of the truth as she could. "After you got to the stairs, and the guard said the Zhous hadn't been past him to leave the gala, I assumed they must have gone somewhere else. Given the way the building is set up, I thought maybe they had gone out to the courtyard. So, when you went up to make sure they weren't in their room, I went directly to the courtyard."

Lincoln sat with his hands on the table, his knuckles white from holding his hands together so tightly. Was he angry with her? Had that been an order, not a polite suggestion that she not talk?

"When I got to the courtyard, I heard them arguing—the Zhous. They were having a fight. Minister Zhou wanted to leave, but Mrs. Zhou wanted to stay. Curt pulled his gun, but Zhou was faster. He shot Curt and then he shot his wife. Before he shot his wife, he said *if you are dead, they can't hurt your family. They will know I won't care and they can't hurt you.*"

The first story a person heard about an event was often the one people will most likely believe. Had they caught Zhou and already gotten a different story out of him? Had Curt regained consciousness enough to say anything? She had to take a chance on this one. And, she needed to make sure no one debriefed Curt before she could get to him. Only she and Curt knew what had happened. Unless, of course, they had Zhou in another room and he had been broken.

"I think Curt was worried about Minister Zhou. He didn't want anything to go wrong during this visit. Having Minister Zhou disappear during such a public event would be embarrassing for everyone. State. Your government. He would do anything to stop him from leaving. He noticed that the Zhous were gone and went looking for them. He must have found them in the garden, arguing, before I got there."

"Why didn't Zhou shoot you, too, Ms. Crandall?" Jiang asked.

Lizbeth hung her head. "I honestly don't think he ever saw me. He looked shocked after shooting his wife, but he ran off. I was intent on making sure Curt was alive. I called 911 with his cell phone. Then there was a bunch of commotion inside the Embassy and everyone started coming outside. I was crying, screaming for help when you had me dragged away from him."

She looked at Jiang, legitimate anger clouding her face.

Jiang held up his hands. "I am sorry, the Embassy guards were perhaps a little too hasty."

Lizbeth knew better than to remind Jiang he had stopped them on the way. He could have had her released when he asked her what had happened earlier. Instead, he had let them drag her down to the basement.

"I don't believe there is anything more that we have to discuss," said Jiang. He nodded to the guards who turned tail and left the room. Lizbeth squeezed the cup. She knew it had been close, and was lucky to be in the conference room with Pierce. She looked down into the cup, at the dregs of tea leaves. She barely remembered drinking it. The leaves shifted into a shape at the bottom. It was a heart.

"Lincoln, you have to take me to Curt."

izbeth fell asleep in the chair next to Curt's bed when they wheeled him out of recovery and into a private room. She pushed the chair up close and put her feet up against his feet underneath the sheets. The steady beep of the machines he was attached to as effective as any sleep-inducing trick she'd ever learned.

Her dreams were strange repeats of the crazy night. She kept finding herself dancing with other men and not being able to get to Curt or call for help. And they shifted around to her and Curt doing tai chi in the park. Eventually she settled into a deep sleep unencumbered by dreams.

Curt poked her awake with his foot. "Hey, aren't you supposed to be watching me? I'm the one who was shot."

In spite of the levity, his voice was still weak. She opened her eyes slowly, afraid of looking at him. It was noon.

What she wanted to do was jump up and launch herself into his arms, but she held back. "And, exactly, how did you let that happen?"

"Madam Zhou was definitely not down with the plan."

"I was in the garden when... you were shot." She leaned over the bed, gripping the rails so she didn't touch anything but his lips, and kissed him. Then she shook out her legs, working out the pins and needles that jabbed her muscles.

"I am so glad you are alive."

"Me too. It would have sucked if I had died."

"You're making light of a very serious situation."

"Zhou got out?"

"Yes, he did. I don't get why he was so important. I mean, the Interior Secretary? Parks?"

"The title is a deflection. An intentional one. He has information about Chinese nuclear production facilities. He handed me a sample of his documentation at the Roosevelt memorial on Friday."

Things were beginning to make sense to her. "You're leaking some pretty top-secret stuff to me."

"Shhhh. Don't tell, m'kay?"

She looked at the bags hanging around him,

attached to him via little tubes and needles. "Yup. Drugs. That one says morphine."

He shifted and grimaced from the pain. "Don't suppose you could squeeze me some more?"

"No way am I touching anything but your lips." She kissed him again, but he was already asleep.

Three more times, he woke up hazy and confused before falling back asleep. The drugs they had given him had some memory stuff in it, and he never remembered waking up before. On his fourth awakening, she told him her version of events, knowing he'd be debriefed on it soon.

"I'm embarrassed about being shot."

"You could have shot her before she shot you. Why didn't you? And where did you get a gun, anyway? I swear you didn't go into the Embassy with one tonight."

"I brought the gun in during the meeting on Monday morning. It was hidden in my motorcycle. The guard in the garage was easily distracted." Curt closed his eyes and winced as he shifted a little in the bed. "Madame Zhou refused to go. They both had guns. They were arguing; I thought maybe the Minister would have talked her into leaving with him. They were married, you know?"

"I heard the whole thing—*hubby*. An arranged

marriage maybe?" Lizbeth asked, as casually as she could.

Curt's eyes clouded over. "I'm not going to do it, Liz."

He reached his hand for hers and found a way to her amongst all the machines. She kissed him again. "Sleep, silly man. You can worry about your fiancée later."

She settled back into a chair as he fell asleep again when Spencer Watson entered the room. He placed a vase of flowers next to Curt's head. Without changing her facial expression, she knew she'd check later to see if the vase was bugged. When Lincoln had given her a ride home from the Embassy, he had confirmed the two men he'd brought with him were both CIA, not from State.

She nodded but said nothing. Of course they were CIA. She had already figured that part out even though neither one of them had spoken at the Embassy. As he dropped her at home he ordered her to take the week off work.

Spencer Watson stood next to Curt looking at him for a long while before turning to Lizbeth. "You almost fucked up everything, Crandall. Curt was set for this assignment, and you walked into his life and messed with his head." He walked over to the machines and his hand swooped over Curt. "You did this. If you really love this guy, you will walk out that door, get on a plane to San Francisco back to your mommy, and never look back. Leave him a note telling him you are not cut out for this kind of life. Leave before you get him killed."

Lizbeth wasn't about to go anywhere. She eyed the helpless, sleeping Curt on the bed. She'd never leave his side. Not like this. She stood up and squared off with Watson, hands on her hips. He wasn't a slight man; he could have tossed her down with his pinkie. He was probably well trained in the art of hand to hand combat, but she didn't give a flying fuck.

"Tell you what, Spencer Watson, you can take your opinion and shove it straight up your ass. I am going to stand next to him no matter what. You don't scare me."

Watson narrowed his eyes on her, studying her intently. She didn't back down.

Then he laughed. A big belly laugh, and his smile changed him into a decent looking man. "I wasn't expecting that. Man, Curt was right about your, um, brevity. Anyone who sticks up for Curt like that is a friend of mine." He held out his hand.

She smiled at him, but that didn't mean she trusted him. Even so, in the spirit of good will, she shook his hand in return.

izbeth became a fixture in Curt's room, leaving him only to feed her cats and change her clothes. Each day, Spencer Watson came for a visit. He still gave her the side eye, but treated her with respect. Soon enough, he warmed up. He brought in different games, insisting they play backgammon, checkers, and chess. He made small talk, asking her questions about her family and her job. After a while, she found herself at ease with him.

She shoved aside the last of her doubts and told Spencer about the situation with Bella and that she had offered to move so Angela and Demarco didn't feel threatened. Demarco had finally texted back saying they wouldn't move, but Angela wasn't willing to let her visit for now. They would send an update every six months for now. Lizbeth's heart ached over the loss.

She'd messed it up and would have to live with the consequences. She'd work to find her way back into Bella's life somehow.

Watson called Curt's mother daily, giving her updates on his progress. She had decided not to fly out when it was clear he would survive. Liz eavesdropped during their conversations while pretending to be busy reading a magazine or playing a game on her phone. Liz never heard her ask about the wedding plans, and Watson never brought them up. Watson insisted that it would be better to not mention Lizbeth's presence until Curt had a chance to talk to his mother directly.

"I've met Mrs. Wu, and she does not like surprises. Let him bring you up with her directly. When he's strong enough to withstand her questioning."

He promised to sit with Curt so she could go see Lincoln Pierce. Lizbeth didn't know what her future plans were, but she tendered her resignation anyway. Lincoln, Carleen, and Katherine were at the meeting and, at the end, Katherine offered to take her out to lunch. Watson sent her a text that Curt was sleeping and wouldn't miss her for another hour, so she agreed.

On the Friday, almost a week after the gala, Watson brought in a challenging crossword puzzle and pestered her for the answers. Curt woke up from his nap when Watson had given her a particularly hard clue to solve.

Curt pointed an IV laden arm at Watson. "I know what you're doing, here. How did you get to the cross-word stage? Seriously?"

"You were right about her, what can I say? I owe you that beer. And bro, you have been sleeping twenty hours out of every day."

"Wait, Curt, he's not hitting on me. Even if he were, I would not be into him." Even as she said it, Liz understood she'd totally misread the situation.

Watson responded as if she had wounded him.

"Ouch. You know how to hurt a guy's ego," Watson said, shaking his head and placing his hand over his heart dramatically. "Okay," he said, turning to Curt, "Mr. Smarty-pants, why don't you tell her."

Lizbeth didn't like being the only person in the room who didn't know what was going on. The other two were grinning with their shared secret. She couldn't hit Curt, so she balled up her fist and back-handed Watson lightly on his gigantic bicep. "Okay guys... Give it up."

Curt moved his bed into a full sitting position and grimaced. "Are you sure?" he asked, looking at Watson. "It all worked out? We got the go-ahead?"

"Yep. All the backgrounds checked out. She just has to do the final testing on site."

"What final testing? What are you talking about?"

"They'll need to ask you some questions at Langley. Unless you fail that miserably, I'd say you're in."

"Curt?" She grasped his hands, anxious to hear what he had to say.

"I asked to get you fast-tracked into a job at the CIA. Beijing might not happen, but it's looking good."

She looked over at Watson, eyes wary. "This whole week. All these games? All those questions? You've been evaluating me?"

He shrugged. "I also happen to be a good friend of Curt's so, my being here wasn't all about you, Crandall."

"You want me to be a CIA agent?"

Curt nodded toward Watson. "Not an agent. That's a year long training process. But, there are some other ways to get you on the team. Watson's been working to readjust the operation. And fast-track you in. You have the language skills, and enough physical prowess, we'll be able justify you somehow."

"You don't have to go through with the fake marriage?"

"We'll see how it goes with the final stages, but it looks good, Crandall."

Lizbeth threw her arms around Watson's neck and kissed him on the cheek. "Well, I guess I like you a little bit after all. Was all that 'leave now before it's ruined' bullshit some sort of test?"

"Curt is my friend, as well as a fellow agent. I had to determine how strongly you felt about him."

Lizbeth should have been angry at him, but she wasn't. Curt was recovering, she'd gotten a job offer of sorts, and she was in love. *Actual real-holy-shit-love.* "Do you have any idea what I will be doing? I'm not sure I'm well-suited to being a spy."

Curt laughed and put his hands over his stomach while wincing in pain at the effort. "Jeez, honey, don't kill me. You'll probably be better at it than me. Hey Watson, has Dirkson's wrist healed yet?"

"Dirkson's an asshat. He'll be fine."

Lizbeth covered her mouth when she made the connection. "Oh god. Right. I feel so bad, but I had no idea he was CIA when I did that."

Curt was grinning, and it wasn't from his morphine drip. "Watson, did you bring *the thing?*"

"Oh, right. Yeah..." Watson patted his jacket and fished out something Lizbeth couldn't see before he passed it to Curt. "I'll see you two tomorrow." He was grinning when he left the two of them alone.

Lizbeth perched on the edge of the bed next to Curt. "What's in your hand? Show me."

He closed his fingers tightly around whatever it was and a serious expression crossed over his face.

Just as he was about to speak, their favorite doctor and her nurse swept in to do late-afternoon rounds.

"Well, Mr. Wu, you've made amazing progress. Let's talk about home-care for you. If you have enough support, I might be sending you home tomorrow."

"I can be with him full-time. And he's got a friend who's been coming in daily to check on him. I'm sure he'd help us out," Lizbeth said.

"Let's get a good look at things, shall we?"

Until now, Lizbeth had vacated the room, leaving Curt to his privacy when the nurses changed his dressing. Part of her was unwilling to look at the wound itself, afraid of the hole the gun had left in his stomach. If she was going to be taking care of him at home—hers or his—she needed to buck up and figure out how to help him.

The nurse lifted Curt's gown and cut away the bandage. The bullet had missed his tattoo completely. The small crater of the wound looked dangerously innocuous to her.

The doctor shone a light on it and pulled at it with her fingers. "Looks good. It's healing quickly. A good pink. No infection. You'll have a scar. You're walking and pooping?"

Curt glanced at Lizbeth. "Yes, to both. I'm not running yet. I can make it down the hallway without a walker."

The doctor called Lizbeth over to get a closer look at the wound. "You see this, here?" she asked, pointing at the wound with the tip of a pen without touching it. "You'll want to keep an eye on the color."

Lizbeth paid attention to the doctor, but her eyes kept wandering up to Curt's tattoo. She hadn't seen Malachi for several days, and she had missed him. But there was something different about it as well.

She forced herself to listen to the doctor's description of wound health and how to care for him, taking the pile of papers and directions when they were offered to her. She scanned every inch of Malachi, trying to figure it out what was different.

"Everything will be included in the discharge packet," the doctor said, tapping her clipboard. The nurse finished dressing his wound, and they finally left.

When the door closed, Curt took her hand in his. "Lizbeth, I know we've only known each other for a few days..."

"Two weeks, technically," she said. "Unfortunately, one of those weeks you've been mostly unconscious."

"Fine. Two weeks is still pretty short, but I was sure I've known since the moment I first laid eyes on you, you were *the one*."

Lizbeth's heart thumped hard in her chest, a steady, quickening beat. This was real. Curt was real. What they had was real.

"There's something I want to show you," he said, one hand playing with the edge of his hospital gown.

Lizbeth sucked in a deep breath of air as she figured out what had been different about Curt's tattoo. There was new ink. She tugged at the light blue fabric, pulling it up to make sure she hadn't been seeing things.

"Ow," he said. "Hey, slow down. You're gonna hurt this old man."

"Hold on," she said, and rubbed her finger over the dragon. Her heart racing, she followed the outline of it down to his heart. A delicate goat was tattooed into the scale next to Curt's rabbit.

An explosive joy rippled through her body. Even with all their ups and downs, she wasn't surprised. She had known he was the one for her, but her body reacted as if it was a revelation.

"Look at me."

She glanced up and into his eyes, dark brown and envcloping her.

"I am madly in love with you." He opened the box and took out a ring. "I want you to be my wife," he said as he slid the ring on her finger. "This was my grandmother's engagement ring. It's not big. It's not super shiny, but it's meaningful. Will you marry me?"

The ring had a tiny square diamond in the middle surrounded by classic Art Nouveau scrolls on the sides. She held out her hand for him, and he slid the ring over her finger. It fit perfectly.

She kissed him gently, wishing she could celebrate by giving him more than a chaste kiss. They would have to wait for him to heal before they could celebrate any further. She was content for now. A deep certainty that everything would sort itself out fell over her and filled her heart. The job would fall into place. They'd marry, move to China and have some adventures, and, eventually, start their own family.

"Yes, Curt," she said, circling his nose with hers. "I will marry you."

More by Juno Chase

The DC Knights series can be read in any order, but we hope you don't miss any of them!

New to the Game—D.C. Knights Book 1

Chloe's the new intern, but she jumps into the game both feet first.

Playing For Keeps—D.C. Knights Book 2

Katherine thinks she's got things figured out until a sexy scientist tangos his way into her heart.

All In—D.C. Knights Book 3

Madeline has no problem playing games until she meets Ewan a man who knows how to treat her like a woman.

Fair and Square—D.C. Knights Book 4

Lizbeth doesn't have time for games, but she ends up in the midst of a political game no one in Congressman Pierce's office saw coming.

Only Bluffing—D.C. Knights Book 5

Eleanor Winslow and Daniel Prado are from different worlds. Will their love overcome dark histories and ancient legacies?

Game On—D.C. Knights Book 6

Cheyenne LeFleur lives on the wild side. Will Alexander Moore be able to handle her history, or will he reject her like so many before him?

For the Win—D.C. Knights Book 7 The final chapter in this series. Congressman Lincoln Pierce deserves love, too. Can he find it while maintaining his principles?

Also by Juno Chase:

ARTIFACT of BETRAYAL: an exciting romantic suspense novel

If you had to choose between saving your life or the love of your life, *who would you choose?*

Claire Townsend has it all, a great job, her own shop in Brooklyn, until one night when she loses everything. With thirteen days to pay off a dangerous loan shark, she decides to partake in a black-market smuggling operation to save her own neck.

Bruno Canul is an archeologist who works as a consultant with the FBI. He chases a suspect to Belize only to find the ex-love-of-his-life as part of the crew. He can't tell if he should trust Claire or if she's joined forces with the smuggler.

Afraid her choices will get Bruno killed, Claire tries to resist falling back in love with him. If she goes through with the smuggling scheme, she can pay off her loan, but she'd lose Bruno's love and trust *forever*. If she stands up for their love, she's a dead woman.

This adventurous romantic suspense is sure to keep you on the edge of your seat as Claire and Bruno find love in the jungle and ancient Mayan ruins of Belize.

About Juno Chase

Who said chivalry is dead? They were totally wrong! We love, love, love hot guys who are modern day knights and heroes but also know how to heat things up between the sheets.

Juno Chase is the nom de plume of two married moms who love reading and writing happy stories. We wanted to see these modern day knights celebrated in romance, so here we are. We're not a big group of people writing—there is just the two of us. We both spend lots of time reading and writing in each story to bring you the most complete, hot, and exciting stories possible.

Thank you so much for reading *New to the Game*, we hope you enjoyed reading it as much as we did writing it. If you sign up for our newsletter, you will be the first to know whenever we have a new book available.

Follow Juno Chase on your favorite social Media. We'd love to hear from you!

www.Junochase.com
juno@junochase.com

Acknowledgments

We'd like to thank a few people who helped us get this book into your lovely hands, dear readers. We are part of an amazing writing group who has listened to our ideas, helped us with plotting, and given us some straight feedback. We couldn't have done this without your energy and help-—you ladies rock! Thank you for all your reading time and thoughtful suggestions to help make the D.C. Knights series a reality.

To our intrepid beta readers. Thank you for taking the time to read and give us honest criticism. Especially to Dawn who has faithfully read everything we've handed her and keeps asking for more!

And to our families—our fabulous husbands and children who have supported us in so many different ways and picked up the pieces as needed. We love you!